THE FAMILY LIES

ANGELA HENRY

Storm
PUBLISHING

Ebook ISBN: 978-1-80508-728-1
Paperback ISBN: 978-1-80508-729-8

Cover design: Lisa Horton
Cover images: Shutterstock

Published by Storm Publishing.
For further information, visit:
www.stormpublishing.co

For my father Larry Henry. Our relationship was never what it should have been. However, I will forever be grateful to you for sharing your love of books and reading with me. Thanks, Dad.

PROLOGUE

Harper's Ferry, Ohio

2018

The woman ran through the woods, oblivious to the branches that slapped her in the face and the roots she stumbled over. In the distance, she saw light through the trees from the road ahead. All she could hear was her own labored breathing. She was so close. All she had to do was get down the embankment to the road below and flag down a passing car. She briefly glanced behind her at the mansion, still visible through the trees. Why had she trusted him? She thought he was her safe place, with his shy, sweet smiles and tender kisses. But it had all been a lie. And now, she was running for her life.

She stopped to lean against a tree to catch her breath. The unmistakable snap of a twig made her body tense in alarm. She clamped her hands over her mouth and peeked around the tree. There, about thirty feet away, was a dark figure scanning the woods. Could she reach the road in time? There was no other choice. She had to try. The figure's gaze swung in her direction. She took off toward the embankment, aware of the footfall behind her. She'd just reached the edge, when a hard shove sent her tumbling over the side.

She rolled into the road—and into the path of an oncoming car.

Later, when police interviewed the driver of the car that struck her, he swore he'd seen a person standing at the top of the embankment. But the driver was arrested for drunk driving, and the identity of whoever he thought he saw remained a mystery. Until another woman died.

ONE

SABRINA

Harper's Ferry, Ohio
Present Day

The letter was waiting for me when I got home from the grocery store. Sitting atop a stack of other bills, it was just one in a long line of thanks-but-no-thanks letters I'd gotten in the past six months since I'd lost my job. To date, I had applied for over thirty library jobs in Harper's Ferry and nearby Cincinnati. Currently, I was working part time in a small indie bookstore. The owner couldn't afford to take me on full time. And while I loved any job that let me immerse myself in books and help other people discover books, I needed more money. I needed a job in the field that I had spent time, effort, and money getting a master's degree in.

"What's the big deal?" I could hear my sister's words echoing through my head. "Bookstore, library, what's the difference? It's all just books, right?"

My sister, Cami, wasn't a book person, a library person, or even a very nice person. Our fifteen-year age gap meant that I had grown up alone with books being my only friends. My mother spent long hours working as a custodian at Dorsey Snacks, and when she wasn't working, she was holding court in her favorite bar a few blocks from our house. She wasn't a cruel mother. She did the best she could, and I didn't want for anything other than her attention and affection. Getting pregnant with me at forty had to have been hard, especially when both Cami's father and mine were bums. My sister had joined the military right out of high school, and we hadn't seen much of her for years when she turned up back at home for our mom's funeral, with a husband I'd never met in tow. My sister and I kept a polite distance from each other afterwards with dutiful phone calls, usually initiated by me, once a month. They always ended up awkward AF because my sister and I had absolutely nothing in common.

Then my position at the Harper's Ferry Public Library was eliminated because of budget cuts. I had no money for rent on an apartment that I hadn't really been able to afford to begin with, and had to move into Mom's house where my sister and her husband Bruce were now living. She had no choice but to let me stay there because the house was half mine, the one and only thing of value our mom had to leave us.

I snatched up the envelope and ripped it open, already knowing what it was going to say, but I was a glutton for punishment.

Dear Miss Adams,

Thank you for your interest in the position of reference librarian at Harper's Ferry Community College Library. However, we regret to inform you...

I didn't bother to read the rest and just balled it up and tossed it into the trash can as I headed into the kitchen and started putting my groceries away. I hadn't really wanted the job, but I had to show the unemployment office that I was seeking and applying for jobs. In hindsight, I went back to the trash can and retrieved the letter, smoothing it out, folding it up, and shoving it into my back pocket to put in my folder of rejections. I didn't want anyone saying that I wasn't trying. I was constantly applying for jobs because I wanted out of this house. The reason for which was now standing in the doorway to the kitchen, leering at me.

Cami's husband, Bruce, has been hitting on me ever since I moved in. He only ever did it when my sister wasn't home, like this weekend. She was away on Army Reserve duty, leaving me at home alone with Bruce. I could usually find something to do to keep me occupied and out of the house. But I was currently broke and needed to save on gas, which meant I was stuck at the house. Should I have told my sister her husband was hitting on me? Absolutely. Did I already know how that conversation would go? Well, if the situation were reversed, I know how it would go. But I was honestly too afraid to tell my sister what her husband had been doing.

"You're home early. You get fired again?" asked Bruce, leaning inside the door to the kitchen in a way that meant I would have to touch him to get past. The thought made me nauseous. He lived in sweatpants and T-shirts, and his hygiene was questionable. This was a man who'd rather piss in an empty Gatorade bottle than get up and go to the bathroom when he was gaming.

Except for a brief attempt at running his own landscaping business, Bruce was on disability. But what exactly his disability was beyond being a lazy pervert, I'd yet to figure out. When I asked Cami about it, she just got mad and told me to mind my own business. But he received a monthly check, which he then signed over to my sister. So, she didn't care what was or wasn't wrong with him just as long as she got her money.

"I said you're home—" he began when I ignored him.

"I heard you," I snapped. "And, no, I haven't been fired again."

"Well, are you gonna cook something or what?"

"Cami left you a pot of chili and some chicken salad if you're hungry."

"And what if I don't want that shit?"

"Then I'd say you have a problem, don't you?" I grabbed a loaf of bread and some peanut butter and jelly from the fridge and made a hurried sandwich. There was no way I was going to touch the food that she had left for her husband. I had my own food.

"You look like you're losing weight, girl. I'd hate to see you lose that ass."

"My ass is none of your business."

"We could do something about that, couldn't we?"

Ignoring him, I wrapped my sandwich in a paper towel and went out the back door to sit on the back porch steps to eat in peace. When I finished my sandwich, I sat and stared out into the backyard, glancing over at the blackened spot where the garage used to be. A couple of months after I'd moved in, the garage had caught fire and burned to the ground. The fire marshal determined that the piles of mulch from Bruce's failed landscaping business, which Bruce had stored in the garage, had ignited. Who knew mulch could combust?

I looked at my watch and jumped up, realizing I had about twenty minutes to get to my afternoon shift at the bookstore. I headed back into the house; happy Bruce's attention was now occupied with 2D women. I quickly brushed my teeth and changed into a purple wrap dress and black sandals. I pulled my long braids into a thick coil at the back of my head and spritzed myself with some vanilla body spray. I surveyed the results; happy I didn't look like a barely employed former librarian living with her sister and horrible brother-in-law. I usually took the bus when I was low on gas money. But I didn't have time and hopped in my gray Camry and headed to work.

No sooner had I walked through the door of The Book Barn when Shelly, the only other employee besides me and the owner, pulled me aside and stage whispered, "Where have you been? Prince Charming is here."

"Where?" My eyes darted around the interior of the small store. No sooner had the words left my mouth when a man rounded the corner holding two books in his hand and made his way to the front counter.

Even though I hadn't technically clocked in yet, and still had five minutes until my shift started, I stepped in front of Shelly and smiled up at the man we'd been calling Prince Charming. If you googled tall, dark, and handsome, this man's picture should have popped up. He was about six feet tall and well-built, with broad shoulders that were filling out the blazer of the dark gray suit he was wearing. His white dress shirt was open at the neck, and I could see a burgundy tie peeking out of the pocket of his blazer. His dark hair was close cropped and his brown skin glowed. When he saw me standing at the register, he gave me a megawatt smile revealing deep dimples that made me weak in the knees, and as he got closer, I could smell the spicy tang of his cologne.

The entire time I'd been working at The Book Barn, Prince Charming had been coming in faithfully at least once a week. He was always very polite but distant and even though he wore no wedding band, I assumed a man this fine had to be taken. Although I had seen him looking in my direction on more than one of his store visits, he never approached me for any reason other than to ask about certain books. But Shelly told me I should ask him out. However, in my current state, I don't think my ego could stand a rejection from this man. I didn't want him to feel so uncomfortable that he didn't come back. Plus, I wanted to work here without feeling self-conscious if he still kept coming in after rejecting me.

"Did you find everything you were looking for, sir?"

"I did, thank you." He sat his books on the counter. One by James McBride and the other by Walter Mosley.

That this beautiful man was also a book lover, at least I assumed the books were for him, just made him even more perfect as far as I was concerned. Not sure what else to say to him, I rang up his order and put his books in a plastic bag.

"It's Theo," he said as he took the bag from me. It had been a while since he'd done more than nod and smile when I'd rung him up, and I'd forgotten just how deep his voice was.

"Excuse me?"

"My name is Theo. Not, sir." He said it with a smile, so I didn't take offense. But heat rushed to my face, anyway.

"Oh, I'm sorry. Force of habit."

"No worries. Have a good one." And then he was gone. Shelly and I watched him walk to his black Infinity, get in, and take off.

"He likes you." Shelly nudged my arm to get her point across. "I'm telling you, Sabrina. That guy likes you."

From her lips to God's ears, I thought to myself. I couldn't remember the last time I had a date, let alone got laid, and the last thing I needed to be thinking about was dating when I needed to find a full-time job.

TWO

SABRINA

It wasn't until after he'd left, and Shelly had gone home, that I realized I had forgotten to give Theo his credit card back. It was the first time he hadn't paid with cash. And I finally knew his full name, Theodore Dorsey. *Shit!* If I was right, this man was the son of the late Martin Dorsey, founder of Dorsey Snacks, the biggest employer in Harper's Ferry. No wonder he looked like a million bucks. He was literally worth a million bucks. Probably several million bucks. The Dorseys were one of the most prominent families in Harper's Ferry. And *Mr. Call Me Theo Dorsey* was one of the most eligible bachelors within one hundred miles. He probably had all kinds of women of every age, race, shape, and economic background after him, not only in real life but online as well. I shuddered just thinking how many women were sliding into his DMs every single day.

I knew little about the Dorsey family. Just Martin Dorsey because he owns the company that employed most of the town, including my late mother and now my sister. I knew the man had children, a son and a daughter. I even knew that his wife had died giving birth to Theodore. But the Dorsey kids didn't travel in the same circles as the rest of us. They had attended boarding schools and private colleges. After I had gone away to college, I stayed away until I got my job at the Harper's Ferry Public Library when my mom got sick. So, unless my mom talked about something that was going on at work, or I stopped at the gas station or the grocery store and saw bags of Dorsey Snacks in the snack aisle, I didn't give the Dorsey family much thought.

But now I had Theodore Dorsey's credit card, and I wondered how long it would be before he remembered I never gave it back because I had no way of contacting him to let him know his card was at the store. All I could do was wait. It wasn't until four hours later, as I was closing up the shop for the day, that a black Infinity pulled up to the curb and Theo Dorsey got out. He'd changed from his suit into faded jeans and a cream-colored sweater.

"I bet you're looking for your credit card, right?"

"Not until I just tried to get some gas and realized my card was gone." He gave me a sheepish grin.

"I understand," I told him teasingly. "Probably couldn't wait to get home and read those books you bought. And by the way, you have excellent taste in authors."

I unlocked the door and Theo followed me inside. I turned on the lights and headed over to the cash register where I unlocked the drawer I'd put his credit card in. "You have identification, right? I wouldn't want to give this credit card to the wrong person." I was just kidding, but he got such a serious look on his face as he pulled his wallet out of his back pocket and produced his driver's license that I had to laugh.

"I'm just kidding. Here you go." I handed him the card, and he gave me another killer smile.

"You can't be too careful these days, can you? I mean, I could've stolen this card, and you wouldn't have known, would you?"

"True. But I hardly think anyone who stole a credit card would use it in a bookstore, do you?"

"I guess that would depend on what books they are. I hear some of them can be quite expensive, especially first editions."

"Well, we're just a small bookstore. We don't have any first editions here."

"That reminds me of something I've been meaning to ask every time I come in here. But it just keeps slipping my mind." He gave me an appraising look, which made me blush. Was he hitting on me?

"And what's that?"

"How about I buy you a coffee? I'd love to pick your brain about something. I need some advice."

All I could do was nod in agreement and will my heart to stop beating so fast.

We headed across the street to the Riverside Coffee Bar. Theo ordered an iced Americano and bought me a mocha latte. We sat at a table by the large picture window. I was feeling so awkward, wondering why he'd wanted to talk to me outside of the bookstore. But I was pretty sure he wasn't about to ask me out on a date. I was also pretty sure that if he had been truly interested in me, he would've asked me out a long time ago. Men like him, who had everything in the world going for them, had a glut of opportunities when it came to women. I wasn't putting myself down, but I was hardly the kind of arm candy that the Theo Dorseys of the world dated.

"What was it you wanted to ask me?" I was half finished with my latte, and he still hadn't told me what he wanted. He was hardly chatty whenever he'd come into the store, but I expected him to be more straightforward.

"I was wondering if you knew anything about library restoration and appraising books."

I tried hard not to let the disappointment show on my face. Of course, this man hadn't been about to ask me out. Suddenly, my face burned with embarrassment that I quickly played off. "What kind of books are we talking?"

"A collection of rare first editions, mostly by African American authors."

The embarrassment I felt seconds ago quickly evaporated at the mention of rare book editions. "You mean a private collection?"

"That's right," he said, before taking a sip of his Americano. "My family's private library on our estate hasn't been in use for more than a decade. My dad had it specially built as a gift for my mom, but it hasn't been in use since she died, and I'd love to see it restored. Within the library is a small collection of first editions."

I sat back in my chair and let out a breath. "So, what you're really needing is a private librarian?"

"If you say that's what I need, then I believe you. I'm guessing you have way more experience than me with books and libraries and all that. I'm just a guy who likes to read."

"To be honest, Mr. Dorsey—" I began, before he cut me off.

"I thought I told you to call me Theo." He flashed that megawatt smile at me again, and it caught me off guard, making me flustered.

"To be honest, Theo, before I started working at The Book Barn, I was a librarian at the Harper's Ferry Public Library."

I'm not sure exactly what I was hoping to gain by mentioning this to him, but who was I kidding? I knew exactly what I was hoping to gain by mentioning this to him. He needed a librarian to restore, appraise, and most likely catalogue his private library. And I needed a damn full-time job.

"Why are you no longer a librarian? Why are you working at a bookstore?"

"Because this town doesn't value libraries. I got laid off from the public library along with a third of the staff because of budget cuts. The funding was diverted elsewhere."

"You mean building the new jail?"

"Exactly." I tried to keep the bitterness out of my voice but failed. Theo gave me a sympathetic look.

"Does that mean you're looking for work in another library?"

"Absolutely. Does that mean you're offering me a job? I can get you a résumé and I have excellent references," I threw in when he stared at me with a neutral expression. This man's poker face was impressive, and he continued to stare at me like he was sizing me up.

"Depends on if you'd enjoy working by yourself with little supervision. And this isn't a permanent position. We're talking twenty-four months. And you would be required to live at the estate for the duration of the job."

A short-term library job for a couple of years for the Dorsey family, living on their estate, or continuing to work part time for a little over minimum wage in a bookstore while still living with my sister and her pervert husband. Seemed like a simple decision to me. Plus, working for the Dorseys would open other doors for me in private librarianship. Rich people know and hang around with other rich people who have estates and private libraries. I had been wanting to expand my horizons and couldn't believe that this had just fallen into my lap.

"I love books, Mr. Dor... I mean Theo. Not just reading them, but being around them. Taking care of them and fostering the love of books and reading in others. So, it would be my pleasure to restore your library, and catalog and appraise your collection."

He looked taken aback and gave me a look of surprise. "Just like that? We haven't even discussed a salary. I don't know what librarians make."

He was right. Just rushing into this job without question

was a bad look. It was desperate and sent a message that he could lowball my salary and I'd just take it. I sat back in my chair, willing myself to calm down before I sold myself short. Then I grabbed a napkin and pulled a pen from my purse and jotted down the salary I made at my old job plus an extra fifteen grand and shoved it across the table at him.

He barely glanced at it before declaring with a smile, "You're hired, Miss Adams."

It took me a few seconds to realize that I was still wearing my work name tag that read S. Adams.

"Really? Just like that?"

"You seem more than capable of the job. So, yes, I'm hiring you."

"Thank you, Theo. And you can call me Sabrina," I told him, wishing I'd asked for more money.

"Well then, Sabrina," he said with a smile as he got up to go, suddenly making me feel deflated, "if you'll give me your number, I'll have my assistant call you with all the details."

Two minutes later, he was gone, leaving me elated and terrified. Elated at the thought that I'd found a job in my field that I was excited about doing. Who wouldn't want to live on an estate for the next two years working to restore the library of a wealthy family? However, I hadn't been totally honest with my new boss. Yes, I'd worked at Harper's Ferry Public Library. However, I had limited library experience. I'd been a reference librarian. I was the one who helped people find the books they were looking for, and helped people do research into whatever it was they needed to find, whether it be for a research paper, genealogy, or even the books to consult for a do-it-yourself divorce. But I had zero experience with cataloging books beyond the one class I took when I was in grad school.

And that was another thing. While I had attended grad school for library information science, I had left when my mom got sick and was two classes short of getting my master's. I'd lied about my credentials to get my old job too. And it had come back to bite me. You'd have thought I'd learned my lesson when I lost my library job, but apparently not. I knew nothing about appraising books, let alone the cataloging of a rare book collection. Nor had I ever restored anything in my life. Yet, I needed this job desperately.

I wasn't at all surprised that Theo Dorsey had similar views on librarianship as my sister. No clue at all what librarians actually do. Most people just think we sit around and read books all day. Was I disappointed that Theo seemed to be just as ignorant as everyone else about my chosen profession? Yes, especially when it seemed like he had so much else going for him. But why would he need to know details of my profession when he probably had people at his beck and call to do whatever he needed them to do? Why did I care when his ignorance just helped me land a job and a new place to live, even if it was temporary? In two years, I could add private librarian to my résumé and use that to get the hell out of this town.

THREE

JARED

Detective Jared Green watched as Dorsey left the coffee shop where he'd been having coffee with a pretty young woman. Was it a date? He didn't think so after he saw Dorsey leaving and the young woman still sitting in the coffee shop, lost in thought. He probably should've followed Dorsey, but something told him that following the young woman might be a better idea.

So, he sat and waited while she finished her coffee and then got into her Camry. Once she was half a block away, he finally started his car and followed her to an area of town that had seen better days. At least he assumed it had, since he wasn't from Harper's Ferry. He watched her park in front of a modest-looking brick Cape Cod with an overgrown lawn in need of cutting and a rusted-out Chevy Tahoe parked in front of an empty cement slab where a garage used to be.

Who was she? More importantly, what business did she have with Theo Dorsey? And the biggest question of all was, did she realize what happened to the people who got too close to the Dorseys? Well, if she didn't, it was time she found out. He sat in front of the house for a few more minutes before leaving.

FOUR

BELLE

The sound of breaking glass woke Belle abruptly. She attempted to sit up but couldn't seem to make her muscles work and gave up. The room was dark, though she could see tendrils of sunlight peeking through the curtains. She didn't know what time it was, just that it was daytime. And that's how most of her days went. She never knew what time it was, just that it was day or night, depending on whether there was sunlight or moonlight streaming through from the other side of the curtains. She heard swearing and figured someone must've dropped a glass somewhere in the house, but she couldn't tell where or what direction the noise had come from. She could smell food wafting up from the kitchen. It smelled like bacon, and her stomach growled. She couldn't remember the last time they'd fed her, or even bathed, or changed her clothes for that matter because not only could she smell the bacon, she could also smell her own body odor. She didn't know what she hated more, being so helpless that she had to be bathed by someone else or lying in her own filth.

The drugs they kept giving her kept her fuzzy-headed and drowsy most of the time. She spent a lot of time staring at the ceiling. Occasionally, one of them would take pity and put headphones on her so she could listen to music or an audiobook. Then, often they would forget, and the headphones remain on her head for hours at a time until they remembered to come and remove them. A doctor would show up a few times a month and try to get her to move her arms and legs. He'd poke and prod her and talk to her in a soft voice, like he was talking to a child. Then he'd declare that she was unchanged. He offered no solutions, just declarations of the obvious before patting her on the cheek and leaving.

Lots of people tended to her in the beginning, but as time went on, she felt like an overflowing trash can that people ignored and only paid attention to when it was too full to put anything else in, or too smelly. But the most disturbing thing of all were her dreams. Dreams of when her life had been different. Dreams of when she had a life outside of this bedroom and the bed that confined her. She was a prisoner of her own body. She should've welcomed sleep every night for a chance to escape her reality, but the hours she slept were wasted time she could have used to get stronger.

She'd realized something recently. There had been a couple of days when they were late in giving her her pills, and she felt more alert and awake than she had in months. She could even partially flex the fingers on her right hand and was wondering if it was her condition that was making her weak and bedbound, or the drugs.

"Good morning, miss," came the voice of her latest nurse.

She walked into the room, and she could see the woman's nose wrinkle at the smell. But to her credit, the look was gone in an instant and she pulled back the blinds and opened the window to let some fresh air in. Belle knew that as soon as somebody else saw the window was open, this young lady would get yelled at because they always kept the room in darkness, claiming that it hurt her eyes when it didn't.

Within the space of an hour, she was wheeled into the walk-in shower and thoroughly bathed, re-dressed and put back into her newly remade bed with fresh sheets. She made a note to count the days between now and the next time she got bathed, because she had a feeling that this nice young lady wouldn't be around for much longer. After she'd been fed a breakfast of oatmeal and scrambled eggs, the young nurse left. And Belle lay her head back down, fighting sleep. The next morning, there was a different nurse, and the curtains and window remained firmly closed.

FIVE
SABRINA

The Dorsey estate was in the Highland Hills area of Harper's Ferry. An affluent area that, true to its name, overlooked the city and the Ohio River. The Dorseys lived in a yellow brick Italianate style mansion with three floors and a two-story porch across the front. The house was surrounded by about five acres of lush, manicured lawns that gave way to a wooded area visible behind the house.

When I arrived at the estate a week after Theo's initial offer, an older black woman who looked to be in her early sixties answered the door. With her salt and pepper feathered pixie cut, light brown skin, black slacks and a wine-colored twin set, the woman looked me up and down and then beyond me to my Camry with its sagging muffler. Her expression called me poor without her having to say a word. Determined not to let this uppity woman ruin my joy over starting a new job, I sat down the box that I'd been holding on to when she opened the door next to my rolling suitcase and stuck out my hand.

"Hi, I'm Sabrina Adams. I'm the new librarian starting today," I added when she stared at me with disdain.

At the mention of my name, the sour expression immediately fell from her face and she looked mortified, as well she should.

"I am so sorry, Miss Adams. I was expecting you tomorrow and thought you might be a Jehovah's Witness or something. Occasionally, they get past security determined to save our souls."

She gave me a big smile, but I wasn't buying it. When I had arrived at the security gate, the guard had been expecting me and told me he'd call up to the house to let them know I was on my way. But I wasn't about to make a bad impression or rather even worse impression by calling out this woman on her crap.

"No worries. It's okay. Is this a bad time?"

"Sabrina," exclaimed Theo, walking past whoever this woman was to greet me. "Welcome." He stood aside so that I could enter, grabbing the box I had just sat down.

"Mrs. Manning, this is Sabrina Adams, our new librarian. Sabrina, this is Mrs. Anna Manning, who's been our housekeeper since before I was born."

"Nice meeting you, ma'am."

"Welcome, Sabrina. We're so glad you're here." She gave me another smile that didn't quite reach her eyes, and I instantly understood what this woman's problem was.

This was her turf, and she wasn't about to share it with me, not that I wanted to. I was here to do my job and only my job. But you couldn't have told her that. All she saw was another woman moving in on her territory. And by territory, I meant Theo, who she was looking at as lovingly as a mother would. I trailed into the house behind them, wondering if this had been a big mistake.

However, once I stepped inside, I had to pick my jaw up from the floor as my eyes were drawn up toward the vaulted ceiling of the foyer where a large crystal chandelier hung. The floor beneath my feet was dark, highly polished oak parquet, the center of which was inlaid with gray octagonal shaped marble tiles that led to a double staircase. Fresh flowers in crystal vases occupied recessed niches in the cream-colored walls on either side and filled the air with the scent of jasmine. But the double staircase was the star of the show. You could walk up either side to the floors above or up the short flight of stairs across the landing and down another set of steps into what looked like a family room where the whole back wall was floor-to-ceiling windows. To the left of the staircase was a large room with a fireplace that looked like a study.

I stopped gaping at my surroundings when I saw Theo's amused smile. I had seen places like this in magazines but never thought I'd be living in a house like this. Suddenly, I was so self-conscious in my thrifted jeans, Ohio University T-shirt, and my dingy white canvas high tops that I'd had since high school. I was in such a hurry to leave my sister's place it had never occurred to me that I should have dressed up a little. Just one of the crystal vases in this foyer probably cost more than everything I owned, including my car.

"If you'll follow me, Miss Adams. I'll show you to your room." Mrs. Manning seemed to have thawed out a little, and I quickly glanced at Theo for reassurance as he sat my box down on a table in the foyer.

"I have a meeting to get to, Sabrina, but Mrs. Manning will take care of you. I'll see you later at dinner."

He was gone before I could protest, but I couldn't help but notice the quirk of the housekeeper's eyebrow when Theo called me by my first name. I knew it would be useless telling this woman to call me Sabrina, just as I knew she would never invite me to call her Anna.

I picked up my box and followed Mrs. Manning, who grabbed my rolling suitcase, into the family room and through a light airy Tuscan style kitchen down a long narrow hallway. There were two rooms on either side of the hallway and a bathroom at the end.

"This is your room, Miss Adams. I really hope you'll be comfortable here, and I'm just across the hall." She gestured toward the closed door directly across from my room.

"Thank you so much, Mrs. Manning." She nodded, her expression unreadable, before heading back into the kitchen.

Once she was gone, I looked around where I'd be living for the next two years. The room was easily bigger than the living room and kitchen combined at my sister's place. The floor was in the same shiny dark oak as the rest of the house. There was a large picture window with a seat that overlooked the backyard, and a queen-sized mahogany sleigh bed sat along the far wall to the left of the door, with a bench seat upholstered in burgundy leather at the foot of the bed. A matching chest of drawers with a mirror was along the wall opposite the bed. Side tables were on either side of the bed, one with a large crystal lamp and the other with the same type of ceramic vase of fresh flowers that had been in the foyer.

I sat my box on the leather bench at the foot of the bed and took in my surroundings for a few minutes before taking a picture to send to Shelly and maybe even my sister when I stopped being mad at her. I thought back to her reaction when I'd told her I'd gotten this job and got angry all over again.

"I got a job. I'm moving out." I hadn't meant to be so blunt about it because I knew that my moving out was going to be a financial hardship for her. She hadn't wanted me to move in. But once I was there and helping with the expenses and the housework, she quickly became dependent on the money and the help I'd been providing for the past six months. The light went out of her eyes, and for a split second, I thought about telling Theo Dorsey that I could come work in his library, but I would live at home. I soon came to my senses when Bruce's snores from the living room pierced the momentary silence like gunfire. I had to get out of that house.

"When?"

"Wow. Not even congratulations or anything? Thanks, sis." I tried not to feel hurt that she hadn't asked about my new job, the details, or the location, let alone the salary.

"Sorry," she said, shocking me.

Sorry wasn't a big word in my sister's vocabulary when it came to me. I wondered if maybe, just maybe, it was me she was going to miss instead of the financial and household help I'd been giving her. Would she miss me?

"What's wrong?" I'd asked her.

"They've cut Bruce's disability and now with you leaving, that will leave me carrying the load all by myself."

So, this *was* about money. I'm not sure what she thought my response was going to be. No one told her to marry that useless sack of shit lying on the couch.

"Why are you here, sis? You don't have children you have to be worrying about and now the one and only thing that Bruce was bringing to the table is gone. Maybe it's time you figured out what your future holds for you." I didn't wait for her response and got up and went to my bedroom to pack when Cami's voice from my doorway startled me.

"You know why I'm still here. And you, of all people, know why I can't leave." We stared at each other for a few tense seconds with me looking away first, unable to meet her gaze. When I finally looked back, she was gone.

This afternoon, she'd watched me carry my stuff out to my car and never once offered to help or even tell me goodbye or good luck. I didn't want to acknowledge that she had been right when she said I knew why she couldn't leave and why she stayed with Bruce. I knew her reason because it was the same reason I desperately needed to leave. But in that moment, I didn't care. In that moment, I needed for her to be my big sister and be happy for me. Unfortunately, I also knew she didn't have it in her.

As I unpacked my few belongings, I spied the bundle of

mail that I'd grabbed on my way out the door as I was leaving my sister's house. I quickly flipped through the stack, noticing most were bills that I would finally be able to get caught up on. But one jumped out at me right away. It was a plain white business envelope with just a stamp and my name and address scrolled across the front in black ink. No return address. The handwriting was sloppy and nearly illegible. But I could make out my name, Miss S. Adams. Without thinking, I tore the envelope open to find there was only one thing inside. A newspaper article, or rather a photocopy of a newspaper article, from the *Cincinnati Inquirer*. The date on it was June 10, 2018. The headline read:

Man Arrested in DUI Death Claims Victim Was Pushed

Joseph Paul Sellers, 45, of Harper's Ferry, is facing charges of DUI and vehicular manslaughter. Sellers, who allegedly struck and killed Cherise A. Gamble, 24, of Cincinnati, late Tuesday afternoon in the 800 block of Denton Road, claims someone pushed Gamble down an embankment and into the path of his vehicle. However, there are no witnesses to his claim and Sellers' blood alcohol level was three times over the legal limit at the time of the incident.

The deceased woman's family and friends are uncertain about the circumstances that led her to Harper's Ferry. Gamble, a resident of Cincinnati, had no known connections to the area, and her presence in Harper's Ferry raises many questions. The authorities are currently investigating her whereabouts and activities leading up to the tragedy.

As the investigation continues, police are asking anyone with information about this case to call...

There was a phone number to call. But I was too busy staring at the message scrawled in black ink underneath the article that read: *Ask Theo Dorsey what happened to Cherise Gamble.* "What in the hell?" I whispered. Who had sent this to me and why?

I didn't recognize the handwriting, but someone could have disguised their handwriting. Then something else occurred to me. Denton Road was the road that ran behind the Dorsey estate on the other side of the woods at the back of the house. I'd had to cross that road on my way here. I glanced at the date on the article again: 2018. In 2018, I was in library school. But clearly whoever sent me this article thought Theo knew something about this woman's death and thought I should know. Apprehension crept up my spine as a knot formed in my stomach. This job had seemed too good to be true, and now I was worried I'd made a mistake in coming here.

I quickly googled Joseph Paul Sellers and found out the court had sentenced him to eight years in prison for vehicular manslaughter. I kept looking, but no other article mentioned Cherise Gamble being pushed. Let alone any connection linking her death to Theo Dorsey. That made me feel a lot better. Still, whoever had sent this to me clearly thought otherwise. Who else knew I'd taken this job besides Theo, my former coworkers at The Book Barn, my sister, and Theo's employees? Two of which I'd just met today, the man who let me onto the property and Mrs. Manning. Who'd be trying to warn me about Theo?

Before I fell down that rabbit hole, I spied another piece of mail. It was from the Ohio Department of Jobs and Family Services. I opened it as I lay back on my new bed. It was a letter informing me that my six months of unemployment benefits would come to an end in two weeks and gave the date I'd be receiving my last check. Even if Theo Dorsey was Jack the Ripper, I had signed a legally binding contract to work for him and now had no bookstore job to go back to. They had already replaced me, and I had exhausted my unemployment benefits. I had no choice but to stay. I yawned and tossed the letter onto the bed next to me. Minutes later, I was fast asleep.

I awakened to gentle raindrops hitting the window. I lay there listening to the sounds of the house and noticed the smell of food coming from down the hall. It smelled like garlic and my stomach rumbled. A quick peek at my phone told me it was almost six o'clock, and I figured it must be almost time for dinner. I changed into a black sleeveless top, retouched my lip gloss, and put on sandals and a red hairband to hold my braids back from my face. Then I left the room to head down the hall and into the kitchen, where Mrs. Manning was draining spaghetti at the sink. When she looked up and saw me, she gave me what appeared to be the first genuine smile I'd gotten from her.

"Did you have a nice nap?"

"I did, thank you." I gave her a smile, but suddenly wondered how she knew I'd been asleep. Had she knocked on the door, and when I didn't answer, peeked inside and saw me knocked out?

"Dinner will be ready in about thirty minutes. But I'm glad you're here. It gives me a chance to go over the rules with you before dinner."

"The rules?" I tried not to look as taken aback as I felt, but she looked so serious that I couldn't help it.

"Yes, dear. The rules." She set the colander with the steaming pasta in the sink, wiped her hands on her apron, and gestured for me to sit opposite her at the kitchen island, which I did. Why did I suddenly feel so apprehensive? "I'm assuming Mr. Dorsey hasn't spoken to you about the house rules?"

"No, ma'am. I've barely spoken to Mr. Dorsey since he

offered me the job. Today's the first time we've seen each other since last week."

It had taken a few days for Theo's personal assistant, a young man named Gabe, to contact me about my start date, end date, which was two years from today, and the address, along with specific instructions on how to get to the estate. Prior to my arriving, Gabe sent a contract with the salary that I had quoted to Theo and the benefits that I would receive working for the Dorsey family, including room and board.

"Well then, I'm glad I've got time to talk to you before dinner. I had a feeling he hadn't gone over any of this with you, but there are certain rules that we all abide by that just make the running of this household go much smoother." She stopped and glanced at me like she was making sure I was listening to what she was saying.

"Of course. I understand," I said, not sure what she was about to tell me, but wanting her to know that I would abide by whatever rules they gave me if I could stay and not have to go back to that house with my sister and Bruce.

"I am glad to hear that. We've had employees who we've had to let go for flagrant disregard to the rules of this household. I'd hate for you to be one of them." I merely nodded, and she continued. "First, breakfast, lunch and dinner are all served in the dining room. I am the only one allowed to cook in my kitchen. So, if you would like to eat, please be on time for meals. Breakfast is at 8:30 every morning, lunch is served at 12:30. And dinner at 6:30."

"Got it," I said.

"Do you have any food allergies, Miss Adams?"

"No. I—"

"Good," she said, cutting me off. "There's to be no eating in your room as this is an old house and we've had problems with insects and mice over the years from people eating meals in their bedroom and getting crumbs and food all over the floors. I don't mind if you have your own snacks, but I prefer if you would eat them here in the kitchen." She looked at me to make sure I was following along, and I nodded.

"And of course you're welcome to take your meals elsewhere outside of this house, as long as you let me know first. Next, the front gate to the estate is locked at midnight. If you leave the grounds and you're not back by midnight, you will not be allowed back onto the estate until 7 a.m. when our morning gatekeeper, Mr. Gaines, arrives for work. So, make sure you're back in this house by midnight if you don't want to be locked out. Also, we lock the door of this house at midnight. You will not be given a key to any room other than your bedroom. So, again, if you don't want to be locked out, make sure you're in this house by midnight. The most important rule of all is that there are certain areas of this house that you will not have access to, namely the third floor. And last, we ask that you do not bring your friends or family here as this is your place of employment and not your home. I know that sounds harsh, but we are a very private family and don't open our home to just anybody."

"I completely understand." And I did. Not that I had anyone to bring here. I've always been a loner with few good friends. The ones I had in high school and college I'd gradually lost touch with over the years. Bringing my sister here was out of the question when it was her and her husband I was trying to get away from.

"Glad to hear it." Mrs. Manning gave me a thin smile before continuing. "And I'll let you know about the rest as we go along."

The rest? How many more rules could there be? I quickly pushed that thought out of my mind when I was suddenly reminded I didn't even have the credentials even to be doing this job. But now that I was here, I would do my damnedest to see this job through.

"Is there anything I can help you with?" I asked Mrs. Manning as she went back to preparing the pasta.

The heavenly smell of the spaghetti sauce filled the air, and I realized I had eaten nothing since breakfast. Instead of turning to address me, I noticed the slight stiffening of her spine and realized I'd overstepped my bounds. This woman didn't need any help. She'd probably been running this household for decades, and now I'd probably made her feel incompetent when I was only offering to help out of politeness.

"Could you please go out to the study just off the foyer and let Mr. Dorsey know dinner will be on the table in twenty minutes? He gets caught up with work and doesn't notice the time."

"Of course." I quickly got up and hurried out of the kitchen and away from Mrs. Manning and her rules. A little of that woman went a long way.

I took my time walking through the family room I'd rushed through earlier when I'd arrived. The room was subdued in its elegance. Nothing over the top, yet you could tell everything in this room was expensive, from the buttery caramel-colored leather sofas to the contemporary art on the walls. This room screamed quiet luxury. Family photos lined the shelf hanging under the large flat screen TV mounted on the wall. I didn't have time to look at them all, but noticed they were all of Theo and a girl I assumed was his sister as kids, teens, and young adults.

One picture jumped out at me immediately. It was a photo of a beautiful, smiling black woman with glowing russet brown skin, a thick chin-length bob with bangs and huge dark brown eyes. She was tall and slender, wore a strapless floral sundress and held a chubby baby girl of about six months. This had to be Theo's mom, Lorraine Dorsey, holding his older sister, Belle. Aside from a single wedding photo of him gazing adoringly at his stunning bride as they stood on the steps of a cathedral as the wind caught Lorraine's lacy veil, other photos of Martin Dorsey were conspicuously missing. As was Belle Dorsey's smile. So prevalent as a child and teen, it seemed to vanish in the pictures of her as a young woman and I wondered why. There also didn't appear to be any recent photos of Belle.

I could hear soft laughter coming from the study and followed the sound. The quiet luxury extended to this room with the large mahogany desk occupying almost the entire right-hand side, in front of another large picture window that overlooked the front lawn. Bookshelves lined the back wall along the left side of the room and were filled with books that I doubt anyone in this house had read. Was I hired to restore this library? I certainly hoped not. As large as this room was, there would be nothing in this room that would warrant two years' worth of work.

Theo sat in a high-backed burgundy leather chair. I could tell he was on his cell phone. There was something about his laughter, and the way he was talking to whoever he was on the phone with, that told me this wasn't a work call and whoever he was talking to was most likely a woman. The stab of disappointment I felt shocked me. This man was now my boss, and his personal life was none of my business. Not to mention the possibility of his involvement in Cherise Gamble's tragic death.

I knocked softly on the door, hoping to get his attention, but he continued talking on the phone. I knocked louder this time, startling him as he abruptly looked up.

"Hey, let me call you back later," he said into his phone and didn't even give whoever he'd been talking to a chance to respond before clicking off the call and setting his phone down on his desk.

"Sorry to bother you. Mrs. Manning sent me to tell you dinner will be ready in twenty minutes."

He quickly glanced at the Rolex on his wrist before

standing up and giving me a big smile. "We have a little bit of time before dinner. Would you like a tour of the grounds?"

"Absolutely, lead the way," I told him, ready to see everything about the place I'd be calling home for the next two years.

I followed Theo out a set of French double doors off the dining room to a large stone patio. I was glad the rain had finally stopped as we ascended the steps leading down to an ornate garden. The garden was surrounded by eight-foot-high manicured hedges, and through the hedges tiled walkways led to recessed benches along the hedgerow. In the center sat a large pond with an ornate three-tiered fountain, each basin shaped like an upturned shell, with water cascading down into the pond below. What the garden lacked in actual flowers it more than made up for in decorative topiary bushes and small Greek style statues.

"This is beautiful, Theo." There was so much to see in the garden I hardly knew where to look.

"Thanks." Theo smiled and I could tell he was flattered, but he barely looked around the garden and I wondered if he spent much time here.

If this were my house, I'd be having garden parties every weekend in the summer. Or so I thought. You had to have friends to invite to a party, and I was never that girl. I could've spent all day in the garden sitting reading in one of the recessed nooks along the hedgerow. We left the garden by a wrought-iron gate and went down another path to a large tennis court.

"Do you play?" I could tell he was interested in my response and got the feeling he was looking for a tennis partner.

"I took lessons for a hot second when I was a kid. But I haven't played in years." It wasn't a lie. I'd taken exactly three tennis lessons when I was a teenager but gave it up when my mom showed up to one of my tennis lessons drunk and cussed out my coach because he was taking too long to turn me into the next Serena Williams.

"I'm happy to give you a refresher course?"

I don't know why but I suddenly remembered the article. Should I tell him about it? What would his reaction be? He should know someone suspected him of being linked to the death of the woman killed on the road behind his property. I might have told him if I had any idea who'd sent it to me. It could just be a joke, or something designed to cause problems for me on my new job. If that was the case, I wondered if Cami had sent it. She hated her job at Dorsey Snacks. Could that hate extend to Theo Dorsey? Then I remembered the date of the article, 2018. Cami was still in the military in 2018. How would she have known about what happened to Cherise Gamble?

"Sabrina?" Theo was looking at me with concern, and I realized I was staring off into space and hadn't answered his question.

"Sorry. That would be great."

Once we left the tennis courts, I spied a pavilion in the distance about a hundred feet away with a structure that looked like a mini version of the pantheon in Rome.

"What's that?" I didn't wait for Theo's response and headed off down the path ahead of him toward the structure. When I arrived at the steps leading up to the entrance, Theo caught up with me just as I was about to climb the steps.

"Uh... this is the Dorsey family mausoleum. You're welcome to look around. I'm happy to show you the crypt with my name on it. But I don't think it's very interesting."

I stopped my ascent to look at him, seeing his lips twitching, and my face flushed.

"Maybe another time. We should probably get back."

"Yeah, we don't want to keep Mrs. Manning waiting."

"I've only been here a few hours and I've already gotten that impression loud and clear."

We both laughed as we headed to the house and into the

dining room where place settings for three people were set on the dining table. Mrs. Manning glanced at us as we sat down. I could tell by her raised eyebrow she didn't like us looking so chummy together. What was this woman's problem? Did she think I'd come here to snag a rich husband? Not that the thought of getting close to Theo wasn't extremely appealing, but from what I'd just overheard from him on the phone, this man did not lack for female company.

"We serve all meals buffet style, Miss Adams. So, please help yourself." Mrs. Manning stepped back from the side-board laden with food. Not only was there the amazing marinara that I was smelling, but there were also two different kinds of pasta, meatballs, garlic sticks, a salad, and a terrine of soup.

Theo gestured to me to go before him, and I filled my plate as Mrs. Manning watched.

"This all looks amazing," I told the older woman.

"I've eaten at high-end restaurants all over the world, but nothing beats Mrs. Manning's home cooking," said Theo, earning him a beaming smile from the housekeeper.

At that moment, I got it. Mrs. Manning was very protective of Theo, which shouldn't have been a surprise since she'd probably known him since he was a baby. It was no wonder she was looking at me suspiciously. She didn't know me from a hole in the wall and was worried about what my motives were. If I was going to be here for two years, being on Mrs. Manning's good side would be in my best interest, and the only way to win this woman over was to keep my head down, do my job, and leave Theo Dorsey the hell alone.

We were halfway through the meal when I realized the extra place setting was still empty. Mrs. Manning was in the kitchen and hadn't come out since we'd started eating.

"Is Mrs. Manning going to join us?" I nodded toward the extra place setting.

"Oh, that place setting isn't for her. She prefers to eat in the kitchen."

"Then who is it for?"

Theo finished chewing his food and wiped his mouth before answering. "My big sister, Belle."

I'd completely forgotten about Belle Dorsey. I didn't know she was still in Harper's Ferry. "I didn't realize she still lived here."

"She does," he said with a heavy sigh. I waited for him to continue, but he didn't.

So, I assumed maybe there was bad blood between them, because why else would she not show up for dinner? And not getting along with your sister was something I could absolutely relate to.

"There's actually someone else I wanted to introduce you to today. But getting her to come out of her room at this time of day is damned near impossible and will have to wait until tomorrow."

"And who would that be?" I asked, wondering who else was living in this house.

"My goddaughter."

"Goddaughter? I didn't realize you had a goddaughter. How old is she?"

"Sixteen going on thirty, and that's all I'm going to tell you. I don't want to scare you away." The grim smile on his face made me apprehensive.

"That bad, huh?"

He finished chewing his food before replying. "Not really. She's a good kid. She's just had it rough, and she takes a while to warm up to people. Don't take it personally if she's not friendly at first."

"Got it." But the thought of dealing with a moody teenager didn't exactly fill me with excitement.

We finished our meal in relative silence, and Mrs. Manning

appeared to clear the table before bringing out dessert, which was tiramisu and just as delicious as the rest of the meal. I noticed Theo kept checking his watch and practically inhaled the tiramisu, clearly ready to be gone.

"I'm really sorry, Sabrina, but I've got somewhere I've got to be. I won't be able to show you the library until the morning."

"No problem." I wiped my mouth and sat my napkin next to my empty dessert plate.

"I'll see you at breakfast." And then he headed out of the dining room.

"Good night," I called out after him, to which he put up a hand to acknowledge he'd heard me. I stared after him, feeling somewhat deflated at being abandoned.

"He's probably got a date," Mrs. Manning said casually as she slid a second piece of tiramisu onto my plate, startling me.

Instead of replying, I gave her a smile and dug into my second helping of dessert, realizing she was letting me know I had no chance with this man.

By the time dinner was over and the plates cleared, it was after eight o'clock and I was exhausted despite my nap. I headed back down the hall to my room and the crunch of paper as I walked across the threshold. I looked down to see a sheet of paper and picked it up to see a list written on it. It was the additional rules that Mrs. Manning had referred to earlier.

Number one: I am not to use the washer or dryer in the laundry room. There would be a laundry basket with my name on it in the laundry room for the woman who came in twice a week to do the family's laundry. I could either have her do my laundry or I was welcome to take my laundry to a laundromat and do it myself.

Number two: I could take none of the books in the library out of the library. All work done to the collection was required to be done in the library.

Number three: I could not burn any candles, incense, or diffusers in my room.

Number four: I could only park my car in one of the estate garages behind the house. At no time could it be parked in front of the house for longer than half an hour.

Number five: If I wanted certain snacks or food, I was to write them down on the notepad hanging on the refrigerator door to be included in the weekly grocery order.

Number six: I was not to consume any alcohol, except for a glass of wine at dinner while I was working/living at the estate. If I wanted to consume alcohol, it had to be on my time away from the estate. And I was not to come in drunk ever.

Number seven: The family would cover my health coverage while I was working for them, but only if I saw their doctor. A man named Dr. Barrett Hill. Dr. Hill's number was supplied.

Number eight: I was to keep my room clean as the cleaners would only be changing the sheets, and the flowers, once a week. Cleaning supplies and a vacuum were located in a closet inside the pantry.

All of the rules seemed nitpicky and excessive. But the last one, number nine, was what really shocked me.

Number nine: I was to keep my bedroom door locked after midnight and only open my door for Mrs. Manning.

What the hell? Not only was I required to be in the house by midnight, but I also had to be locked inside my room as well? What in the world? After locking my bedroom door, I sat on the side of my bed and took a deep breath, wondering what the hell went on in this house after midnight?

I woke with a strangled scream and tears streaming from my eyes, coughing and choking on imaginary smoke. It took a minute to realize my bed wasn't engulfed in flames. After my breathing slowed down, I wiped my eyes and sat up in bed. It had been a nightmare, or rather another nightmare about being trapped in a fire. But it had felt so real, right down to the thick, acrid smoke and the flames burning my skin. I'd been having them for months and chalked them up to stress and anxiety. I needed to talk to someone about it but hadn't been able to afford a therapist and knew I still wouldn't go now that I could thanks to this job.

I couldn't get back to sleep and was thirsty. A quick glance at my phone on the bedside table showed it was after two in the morning. I threw back my covers and got up and headed out to the kitchen for a glass of water. The glass was halfway to my mouth when it hit me that I was already breaking rule number seven. I was supposed to be locked in my room at midnight. Yet here I was in the kitchen waiting to turn into a pumpkin when I heard a noise.

The soft laughter was coming from the foyer. I crept through the family room and out into the foyer. Theo's office door was slightly ajar. I crept closer until I could peek into the office. He was in his chair, but he wasn't alone. A woman was straddling him, her soft moans piercing the quiet of the house. His shirt was open, and she was naked from the waist up with her breasts pressed against his bare chest. A large tattoo of a blue butterfly nearly covered her left shoulder. I stood frozen to the spot for a few tortured seconds before I took a step backward and backed into a hallway table, nearly knocking a picture frame to the floor, which I caught. The sound in the office stopped, and I heard a woman's voice echo into the empty foyer, "Who's out there?"

I turned and fled to the safety of my room, wondering who that woman was, and feeling foolish for thinking Theo Dorsey had ever been interested in me.

SIX

JENNIFER

The Uber was long gone by the time Jennifer realized her back left tire was completely flat.

"No," she groaned as she kicked at the offending tire, wondering how the hell she was going to get back to Cincinnati.

She couldn't call her husband because then he'd know she'd lied about being out with her friends from work, and she couldn't go back to the hotel bar for help because it was closed. A quick glance at her phone showed multiple missed calls from Danny, causing her stomach to clench in knots. She should have known her extracurricular escapades would catch up to her eventually. It had been eight months since Danny's affair with his ex-girlfriend from college. He was doing everything she'd asked and more to repair their marriage. They were even in marital counseling. Yet she still couldn't get past it.

Instead, she'd embarked on her own form of therapy: revenge therapy. It involved picking up random guys in hotel bars for anonymous hookups, using a different name each time. Tonight, she'd been Amber, a graphic designer for a clothing company. She always picked out-of-town hotels to do her dirty work. It had been a while since she'd been to Harper's Ferry, a half an hour's drive from Cincinnati, where she lived with Danny and their two kids.

She'd already spent most of the evening at the Parkwood Hotel in downtown Harper's Ferry. An older businessman, in town for a conference, had bought her drinks. She might have gone back to his room with him if he hadn't gotten an emergency work call and hurriedly left. She was about to leave herself when she spotted Mr. Tall, Dark & Handsome himself sitting at the end of the bar.

Theo Dorsey.

She was a little stung that he didn't recognize her when she slid onto the barstool next to him, even after she gave him her real name. Her and Danny's company, J&D Catering, had catered many events at Dorsey Snacks in the last two years. She and Theo had even flirted a bit since Danny handled all the accounts and was never on-site. But snagging Theo Dorsey tonight would be the feather in her revenge cap, because Danny was jealous of Theo. Of course, he pretended otherwise, but he never had anything good to say about the man whose business their struggling catering company needed. Now her impulsiveness was about to blow up in her face.

Tall, dark, and handsome Theo had been a bust. When she struck up a conversation with him, he'd seemed charming if subdued. She hadn't realized he was drunk until he invited her back to his place but couldn't get his car door open. She knew better than to leave a hotel with a strange man, but Theo Dorsey, the CEO of Dorsey Snacks, seemed safe enough to her. And his car was a baby blue Porsche. Her dream car. Before she'd even thought it through, she'd shoved Theo into the passenger seat and slid into the buttery leather driver's seat.

A few seconds of fumbling around on the car's navigation system brought up the route map. She pressed *home* to bring up the directions on the screen and then she was off, expertly guiding a car that cost more than she'd earned in five years around the twisty back roads to Theo's house, or rather estate.

When she pulled up to the gate, Theo perked up long enough to wave at the guard, who merely nodded at them both before letting them through. The house was massive, but she barely had time to take it all in. Once she'd parked in front of the house, Theo had promptly gotten out and lurched up the front steps to the door. She'd had to take his house key from him to open the door when he couldn't unlock it.

"Thanks," he mumbled with a smile before clumsily punching a code into a security panel by the door. "You're beautiful. What's your name?"

"Jennifer." She sighed in annoyance because she'd already told him her name during the hour-long conversation they'd had at the hotel bar.

"You want a drink, Jennifer?" He didn't wait for her answer and walked into a large study just off the darkened foyer.

She followed him into the room and watched him take off his suit jacket and toss it on the back of a leather chair behind his desk. He sat in the chair and gestured her over to him with a smile, showing that maybe he wasn't as drunk as he seemed. She walked over to him, slowly reaching behind her to unzip her strapless black dress. She straddled him, reached between his legs and... nothing. She should have put her dress back on and left, especially when she thought she'd heard a noise in the foyer. But her mama didn't raise a quitter, so she got to work to remedy the problem.

Ten minutes later, the deed was done, and Theo Dorsey was fast asleep and snoring in his leather chair. Feeling sleazy and swearing that this was her last rodeo, Jennifer headed out of the house and did the walk of shame down the long drive to wait at the gate for her Uber. The guard was friendly, and let her wait inside his station, then walked her out and put her in the Uber when it arrived. But now she was back at the hotel parking lot with a flat tire. Danny had taught her how to change a tire when they were dating, but that had been a million years ago. She opened her trunk and saw the spare tire, wondering if she could change the tire herself when she spied something else, a can of Fix a Flat. Danny must have bought it for her, and her guilt only amplified. She didn't know how to use it. But she knew how to read and follow the instructions on the back. Once she was finished and the tire was inflated enough to drive home, she noticed something that made her heart drop into her stomach. She wasn't wearing her wedding ring.

Jennifer prided herself on always taking her ring off during her encounters. It didn't change the fact that she was cheating on her husband, but it made her feel a little less guilty about doing it. Thinking back, she thought she'd put her ring in her purse at the hotel bar, but it wasn't there. Could she have lost it at Theo Dorsey's house?

"Shit! Shit! Shit!" she screamed into the night.

It was now well after 2 a.m. But she had no choice. She had to go back to the Dorsey estate. She climbed into the driver's seat and turned on the ignition when a hard rap on her window made her almost jump out of her skin. She tried to see who was knocking, but they were shining a light through her window. Was it a cop? Because that's all she needed, to be arrested for drunk driving. She knew she was fine to drive, but she also knew she would fail a sobriety test. She pressed the button to roll her window down and someone tossed her wedding band through the open window into her lap.

"Oh my God! Thank you so much. I was on my way back to get this." She quickly put the ring back on and looked out her window at the figure standing by her car, but they continued to shine the flashlight into her eyes, blinding her.

"Theo? Hey, what's with the light?" She held up a hand to

shield her eyes and got a brief glimpse of someone dressed in all black. Alarm flooded her body.

Before she could step on the gas, the hand shot into her still open window, grabbed the back of her head, and slammed it hard against the steering wheel. Right before she lost consciousness, she felt herself being shoved into the passenger seat.

SEVEN

SABRINA

I woke up on my own around seven and quickly put on a robe and slippers, got my bath things, and headed out my bedroom door. The sound and smells of Mrs. Manning cooking breakfast greeted me as I headed into the bathroom. Forty-five minutes later, I was dressed and ready for work. Theo was already at the dining table, scrolling on an iPad. He looked up and smiled when he saw me. Once again, I noticed a third setting at the table.

"Good morning," I said to him and Mrs. Manning, who was setting up breakfast on the same sideboard where dinner had been last night.

"Morning. How'd you sleep?"

"Great," I said, barely able to look at him as I grabbed a plate and filled it with scrambled eggs, sausage, and toast and took it to the same spot I'd sat at the night before.

"Did you get my note?" Mrs. Manning looked at me, and I nodded.

"I did. Thank you." I slathered blackberry jam on my toast as the woman stared at me.

"Did you have questions?"

I hesitated only a moment before asking what I was dying to know. "Uh, yeah, why do I need to lock myself in my room at midnight?"

"Because that's when I go to bed, and I turn the security system on. All the rooms except the kitchen have motion sensor cameras. There's no reason for you to be wandering around the house after midnight, Miss Adams. You'll set off an alarm and wake up the entire house."

She said it like it made all the sense in the world, but I realized that's why the alarm hadn't gone off last night when I'd left the kitchen. Theo must have been in such a hurry to get laid he'd forgotten to reset it after he came home. I felt my face flush and pushed the image of that chick in his lap out of my mind, wondering if this was a rule for the entire household, or just me. Plus, I could understand why there would be cameras on the property monitoring the outside. But why were so many cameras needed inside? And were they on all day, or just after midnight? The idea that someone could be watching my every move in this house made me uneasy.

"Any other questions?"

"No. And thank you for clearing that up."

Satisfied by my answer, Mrs. Manning smiled and headed back into the kitchen. I immediately looked over at Theo, whose lips twitched with suppressed laughter.

"Here," he whispered as he handed me a folded slip of paper while watching the kitchen door Mrs. Manning had just disappeared through.

"What's this?" I whispered back.

"It's the code to the alarm system. Don't let her know you have it."

I nodded my agreement just as Mrs. Manning returned to the dining room with a pitcher of orange juice and topped up our glasses. I winked at him conspiratorially as I took a bite of toast.

. . .

After breakfast, during which Theo's sister still did not make an appearance, he showed me to the library where I would work for the next two years. I had expected to follow him up a flight of stairs to the second floor. Instead, I followed him down a narrow hallway just off the foyer and watched him press a panel that was flush against the hallway wall. It slid open, and he turned and gave me a devilish grin. Confused, I followed him through the opening in the panel, onto a landing overlooking a sunken library the likes of which I had never seen before. My eyes widened as my pulse quickened with excitement. Theo reached out and put a finger under my chin to close my mouth, which had fallen open. The warmth of his unexpected touch startled me back to reality.

I was looking at the culmination of every book nerd's dream. It was the kind of library that I dreamed of. When I was in library school, I had done a tour of some of the most famous libraries in the US, the Peabody Library, the Library of Congress, and the New York Public Library. They'd all been beautiful and unique in their own way, but this library was different because it belonged to someone. This had been Theo's mother's space. I would bet any amount of money it was her sanctuary. The place she went to shut out the world and escape into a new one with books.

"This is amazing," I breathed, pushing past Theo to walk down the winding wooden stairs into the library.

This was not a basement. The space spanned all three stories of the house to create a multilevel library encompassing all the windows of every floor so that sunlight shone through and illuminated the space. It was anything but dark and dreary. The lowest level was a reading room with comfy leather chairs and the same shiny hardwood oak inlaid with marble that was everywhere else in the house. The other two floors were floor-to-ceiling bookshelves that probably housed at least 10,000 books. And the books that were not actually sitting on the shelves horizontally were stacked in piles or piled up along the walkways that led to each floor. There were no ladders or staircases to get to each floor, just a walkway that wound its way up to each floor.

The bookshelves themselves were also in the same oak as the flooring but, unlike the rest of the house, if you looked close enough, especially with all the sunlight pouring in through the windows, you could see the neglect. There was dust everywhere and I could tell that this space hadn't been used in a very long time. Thick dust also coated the tops of the books that were piled on the floors and on the tables in the room. The only thing that I could tell had been regularly cleaned were the windows, probably because they could be seen from outside the house. I still spun around slowly to take in the space, which was probably about the equivalent of a small branch library. It wasn't so much wide as it was tall. Each level probably comprised about 500 feet, but whoever had designed this had made good use of every inch.

"I'm told my mom called this her Beauty and the Beast library." Theo let out a soft chuckle, but I couldn't help notice the sadness in his eyes which made me remember he had never known his mother because she'd died giving birth to him.

"Your dad must've loved her very much."

"Probably about as much as he could love anyone. One thing is for sure," he said, staring off into space.

"What's that?"

"He could definitely be a beast. I mean, I'm not criticizing him because everything I currently have is because of him and all his hard work, but there's a certain personality that you have to have to be as successful as my father was."

"Meaning?" I prodded.

"Let's just say he wasn't always very nice."

How was I supposed to respond to that? Fortunately, Theo broke the silence when he gestured to a pile of boxes against the wall at the bottom of the steps.

"Looks like your supplies are already here and waiting for you. I hope everything you asked for is here. If it isn't, let me know and I'll get right on it and make sure it's delivered."

"Thanks, Theo. This should be everything I need to get started."

"Great. I'll leave you to it."

When he was gone, I glanced over at the boxes of supplies and a knot of apprehension formed in my stomach. What the hell was I doing? I was not qualified to do this job, but I was going to make a damn good show of it. Theo had his assistant ask me to make a list of all the equipment I would need. I requested a MacBook Pro, a barcode scanner, cleaning supplies, and invisible barcodes, not like the ones used in public libraries, but the kind that could be placed in the book discreetly and scanned if anyone like a corporation or another organization wanted to borrow from the collection. I'd emailed Theo a few days before I'd started that he should give the library an official name, and he decided on the Lorraine Dorsey Memorial Collection.

It was my job to restore, inventory, appraise, and catalog this entire collection in two years. So, I decided it was time I got busy but quickly realized there were some packages I couldn't open because they'd been sealed too tightly. I headed back up the stairs to get a knife or some scissors, pressing the panel by the door so that it slid open, and stepped out into the hallway. I stopped when I heard raised voices coming from the direction of the kitchen. I could've gone back into the library and waited, but I was frozen to the spot.

"Why do you keep putting a place setting out for her? You know she's never going to sit at that table again." Theo sounded highly annoyed.

"It's just my way of keeping her with us in spirit. What harm is there in remembering how things used to be?"

"Because it keeps us from moving on, that's why? And now Sabrina is asking questions."

"She's not here to ask questions about our private lives. She's here to work in the library, and that's all she needs to be concerned about. The next time she asks, just tell her to mind her own business."

I heard an exasperated sigh and footsteps rapidly coming my way, at which point I slipped back behind the panel and pressed it, so it slid closed, concealing the fact I had been standing there listening to a private conversation. But what I really wanted to know was what the hell had happened to Belle Dorsey?

I was happy Theo had a desk brought in for me so I could get to work immediately. I had decisions to make. I wouldn't even worry about appraising or cataloging the collection until after I saw exactly what the collection included. Plus, the entire library, including all the books, needed to be cleaned, which would buy me much needed time to research how to do the parts of my job I had no experience in. After everything was all set up and organized on my desk and I'd broken down all the boxes, I started at the very first level of shelving and filled my cart with books, then took them back to my desk and began wiping them down with a dry cloth to get all the dust off. I flipped through each one, noting any torn pages or damage and the title and publication date, which I noted on a notepad. I knew there was probably a much easier and more efficient way of doing this, but I was stalling for time. It would probably be at least a few months before I could even think about doing the more complicated things that I'd been hired to do. But then again, this was not a public library, and the public would not be in here checking these books out.

I'm sure I could probably come up with a cataloging system that would work for this collection. Until then, I was happy to be doing something relatively mindless while exploring the collection. At first, I felt disappointed. Most of the books were generic classics that every high school and college student had to read. The complete works of Shakespeare, Charles Dickens, Mark Twain, and Jane Austen, but it didn't take long for other books to pique my interest. The complete works of Zora Neale Hurston, and a pristine first edition of *The Conjure Man Dies* by Rudolph Fisher. I googled it to get an idea of its worth and all the listings for it online were for low five figures. I made a note to contact some local book dealers to see if their prices matched what was online. Next, I took a quick peek in the boxes of books that lined the walkways. A quick assessment showed them to be of no value and had yet to be added to the already packed shelves. It looked like the more valuable books in the Lorraine Dorsey Memorial Collection would have to be found by me while doing my inventory.

Hours later, a quick glance at my watch showed it was almost noon. I quickly headed to my room to freshen up for lunch. I stepped inside and froze. There was a stranger leaning against the side of my bed, looking under it, and my sudden entrance made her jump up. To say she was a woman was generous. This kid looked about sixteen. She was slightly overweight and had very light skin, with a smattering of freckles across the bridge of her nose and acne dotting her cheeks. Her oversized black sweatshirt read *Chaos* in a gothic script across the front, and her pink and black leopard print leggings matched her black flip-flops and short pink afro. From the *o* of surprise that popped up on her lips, I could see she had a mouthful of braces. I was so shocked to find someone else in my room, and she appeared equally shocked to have been caught, so we both stared at each other in silence for a few seconds.

"Hi," I said, taking a step toward her. "Can I help you with something?" The girl, who I deduced was the infamous Luca, looked like she wasn't sure I was talking to her, and her face flushed bright red.

"Uh... I'm Luca. And you are...?" She narrowed her eyes at me. Her attitude had gone from flustered to annoyed in thirty seconds flat.

"I'm Sabrina, the new librarian."

Luca opened her mouth to say something when Mrs. Manning finally made an appearance and looked from me to Luca.

"I see you've finally come back to the land of the living. Miss Adams, this is Luca Harris. She's Mr. Dorsey's goddaughter. Luca, this is our new librarian, Miss Adams."

"I didn't know there was someone staying in this room," Luca replied sulkily as she chewed on her thumbnail.

"Well, I was going to introduce you to her when you finally emerged from that black hole you call a room."

"Whatever." Luca sighed, rolled her eyes, and pushed between Mrs. Manning and me to get out of the room. I distinctly remembered being extremely moody, self-conscious, and easily embarrassed when I was her age and felt for the kid.

"Sorry." Mrs. Manning stared after the girl and shook her head. "Luca's awkward and a bit rough around the edges. But she's a sweet kid once you get to know her."

"How long has she lived here?" And what had she been doing in my room I'd wanted to ask but didn't.

"She's been with us for six years, ever since she was ten. Her mother is a good friend of Mr. Dorsey's from high school who had drug problems. Luca came to stay when her mother, Heather, went into rehab and remained with us even after she cleaned herself up. She's a singer on Amnesty Cruise Lines and is away most of the time."

"That's got to be rough on her with her mother always gone."

"It was at first. But we've all adjusted, and she's happy here. Mr. Dorsey won't be home until dinner, so I've set up lunch for us in the kitchen if you're ready to eat."

I nodded and gave her a phony smile because eating lunch alone with this woman was the last thing I wanted. I'd have been happy with a peanut butter and jelly sandwich washed down with a Diet Coke. But rules were rules. I was required to take meals with the family, and I had nothing else to eat. I followed Mrs. Manning into the kitchen, hoping she didn't notice I hadn't had a chance to freshen up first.

Five minutes later, I had a heaped helping of spaghetti and meatballs on my plate, leftovers from last night's dinner, which had been delicious. Mrs. Manning sat across from me with a plate about half the size of what she'd fixed for me. I was surprised to realize that I *was* hungry. I'd worked up an appetite in the library and hoped it would work a similar miracle at dinnertime, because I knew Mrs. Manning wouldn't appreciate me wasting their food.

"Is Luca not joining us?"

Mrs. Manning sighed. "Before Luca came to live with us, her mother raised her on junk food, and after her first three years of living here, and eating my cooking, became a vegan. I don't do vegan food," she replied dryly with a quirk of her eyebrow. "Mr. Dorsey pays for a vegan food delivery service for her. She eats in her room ninety-five percent of the time. She has a microwave up there," she concluded. When she saw the look of shock on my face that Luca was allowed to eat in her room, she added, "I have her room cleaned once a week since she refuses to join us for meals. I've learned with teenagers it's best to pick your battles."

I merely nodded, suddenly realizing food was probably Mrs. Manning's love language and how much it must have stung the older woman that Luca didn't want her food. We dug in. It was quiet before she finally broke the silence.

"And how are you finding the library? Do you have everything you need?"

"Yes, thank you. Mr. Dorsey has supplied everything that I required on the list I gave him before I started. So, I could get right to work. Can I ask you something?"

"Of course," she said, looking up from her plate, eyes slightly narrowed.

"When was the last time the library was used? Everything is so dusty. And it's such a beautiful space that I just assumed it would be used."

"Well, it was before my time. But from what I've heard, that library was Mrs. Dorsey's private sanctuary. And no one else was allowed in there except her. She took care of it alone. Dusted, cleaned, and shelved. She would go on trips across the country and overseas to purchase books for it. Then when she had Belle, she spent less time in there because Belle was a sickly child and needed a lot of her mother's attention. Mr. Dorsey Sr. was a workaholic and rarely home."

"And no one's been in there since her death?"

"Mr. Dorsey Sr. was so distraught after his wife's death that he closed it up. Then, when Belle was in her teens, she asked about her mother's library. She started using it for her private space but then she went away to boarding school and then college and it was locked up again."

I had wanted to ask about Belle Dorsey but noticed how Mrs. Manning's lips tightened when she mentioned Belle's name. Instead, I asked, "Would you know if there was any kind of inventory list that Mrs. Dorsey kept that might help me identify some of her more expensive purchases? You said she traveled all over to purchase books for the library. I know Mr.

Dorsey said there were rare books in the collection, but since there seem to be several thousand books in there, I just want to know what to be on the lookout for."

Mrs. Manning eyed me suspiciously, and I realized instantly that she probably thought I wanted to cherry-pick the books just to find the ones that were worth something, and that they might leave the house in my bag or something. She was silent for a moment before answering.

"I'm afraid I wouldn't know. And even if she had receipts, I'm not sure where they would be. But I can look up in the attic for you if you tell me what I should look for."

I almost offered to help her but then remembered rule number four. I wasn't allowed past the second floor. I felt my face flame as I realized this woman thought that there was a possibility I might steal from them. That must be a horrible way to live, to always suspect everyone because of money.

"Receipts possibly. Maybe a logbook or a ledger logging the purchases."

"And are you sure there's no ledger with those purchases somewhere in the library?"

I felt a little embarrassed. It hadn't even occurred to me that there might be a ledger listing all the books, or at least the valuable ones, already in the library.

"I've just barely scratched the surface. It could be in there, but I was just wondering if you knew. It would save me the trouble of trying to find it if it existed outside of the library."

"I do not." She turned her attention back to her food. I shoveled a big forkful of spaghetti into my mouth, ready for this lunch to be over. But Mrs. Manning had some questions of her own for me, and I almost choked.

"Tell me about yourself, Sabrina." Her voice sounded casual, but her eyes were boring into me so intently I almost flinched.

"Not much to tell. I was born and raised here in Harper's

Ferry. I have an older sister named Camille. I never knew my father and my mom died a year ago."

"And what about school? Where did you train to be a librarian?"

"Kent State University. I did my undergraduate degree at Ohio University." It was true. I had attended library school at Kent State. I just hadn't graduated.

"What was your undergrad degree in?"

"English Lit."

"And why did you want to become a librarian? Was your mother a librarian?"

"My mom was a custodian for almost thirty years at Dorsey Snacks."

Mrs. Manning's eyes widened in surprise, but she didn't comment. I wondered what the hell she was thinking. If she thought I might steal the valuable books that were in the library I'd been hired to work in, what would she be thinking about my mom having worked for so long at Dorsey Snacks? Saying that out loud made me feel like I was carrying on some kind of legacy by working for this family. But while my mom was happy to work for Dorsey Snacks her entire life, my working for them was much more mercenary. To me, the Dorseys were a means to an end, a stepping stone to someplace better, not a path to a pension.

"And to answer your other question, I've always loved libraries. I was a work-study student in Alden library all four years at OU, and it made me feel like a detective helping people find what they needed, and just being around books energizes me. Libraries are sacred spaces to me."

Mrs. Manning gave me a smile. "You sound just like Rainey," she said and then froze like she'd said something she hadn't meant to.

Rainey? Was Rainey short for Lorraine, Theo and Belle's mother? Had she known Lorraine Dorsey? But the smile that had graced the older woman's face when mentioning Rainey was gone and her face was now blank and expressionless as she pushed food around her plate. I knew better than to ask.

"What about you, Mrs. Manning? How long have you worked here?"

"I started working here when Mr. Dorsey Jr. was a baby and Belle was ten," she said, perking up a little.

"So, you were their nanny?"

"That's right. I was planning on leaving once Mr. Dorsey Jr. went off to boarding school at twelve, but Mr. Dorsey Sr. offered me the job of housekeeper. And that's what I've been ever since."

I highly doubted this woman was a mere housekeeper to this family. With Lorraine Dorsey having died so young, I'm betting Mrs. Manning was more like a mother to Theo and his sister. Speaking of which. "I was hoping to meet Mr. Dorsey's sister. Will she be joining us for dinner tonight?"

The look on her face coupled with what I'd overheard her telling Theo earlier should have kept me from asking. She was right. It was none of my business. But was I supposed to pretend Theo Dorsey didn't have a sister? Was I not supposed to wonder why there was an empty place setting at the dining table for every meal?

"No. She will not. Are you finished eating?" She got up and took my half-finished plate and began angrily scraping my uneaten spaghetti into a trash can under the sink.

I wiped my mouth and got up from the kitchen island, regretting asking what should have been an innocent question, but clearly the topic of Belle Dorsey was taboo, and I made a mental note never to ask again. Even so, I was more curious than ever about the woman, and when I thought about it, I had seen nothing in the papers about her since her father died. Not that I was looking for information about her. I'm not even sure I knew what she looked like and the only pics of her in the house were of her as a little girl and a young woman of about twenty-five. She would be in her forties now.

"I guess I'll get back to work then." Mrs. Manning said nothing, and as I left the kitchen, I looked back to see her staring out of the window above the sink.

Instead of cleaning more books, I googled Belle Dorsey. There were multiple women named Belle Dorsey, but the one I was looking for didn't seem to have a presence on social media. I clicked the news tab and found a reference to her in her mother's and father's obits, and a mention of her being a volleyball standout at Kenyon College, but nothing else. No obit or death notice. She was still alive, at least. Why did I care, anyway? My phone rang. It was my sister.

I stared at my sister across the table at the café that I'd met her in later that evening, once again marveling at how much she looked like our mother. Cami was petite, chesty, and light-skinned, just like our mother had been. She still wore her hair in the same short natural style she'd worn the entire time she'd been in the army. A no-nonsense style that suited her no-nonsense personality. My sister didn't suffer fools, except the one she married. She was blunt and bossy, and everything had to be her way. She was our mother's clone, and sometimes I forgot she was my older sister and not my mom. But today she looked tired with dark circles beneath her eyes, and she looked like she'd lost weight.

"What's going on, Cami? Why was it so important that you talk to me in person?"

"Bruce is cheating on me." Her face reddened and her eyes filled with tears that she quickly wiped away with the back of her hand. She hadn't been this upset at our mom's funeral, and I realized she truly did love that idiot.

"What? With who?" I tried to muster up some outrage for my sister's benefit, but instead wondered why she was so surprised when Bruce didn't work and had all the time in the world to be shady. If he could hit on me, his wife's sister, he was capable of anything.

"Some chick he was gaming with online and invited to come for a visit."

"And she just showed up at the house?"

"Yep." She let out a shaky sigh, which told me she was worried about this woman. "She said she was supposed to have been here on Saturday morning, but her flight from Atlanta got delayed. He'd been planning on hooking up with her at her hotel when I was away on my reserves weekend. She even had the nerve to ask me if I was his sister because, apparently, he told her he lived with his sister."

"What did you tell her?"

"I told her I was his wife and to go kick rocks. That's what I told her. She ran back to her car like her tail was on fire."

We both laughed. But it wasn't funny. Not in the least. And when did Bruce find the time to cheat? What kind of game did this man have that he snagged my sister, this woman from Atlanta, and Lord only knows how many others? He had nothing of value to offer any woman. He had no money, no job, and no home. The only thing he owned was the rusted Chevy Tahoe currently sitting in the driveway. I also knew how desperate some women were to be coupled up. I'd figured out a while ago that my sister had been one of them.

"And what does he have to say for himself?"

"He said they're just gaming buddies and he's not responsible for her turning up on our doorstep."

"You need to kick him out, Cami."

"How? Because you know he ain't leaving willingly. It's his legal place of residence. I can't kick him out."

I had no answers for her, because she was well and truly in a bind. I took a sip of my latte and looked away from her.

"Well, when you figure out what the hell I'm supposed to do and how I'm supposed to do it, call me."

"Cami, wait!" But I may as well have been talking to the wall because she kept right on walking, and I watched her disappear around the corner, probably headed to the bar.

EIGHT
BELLE

They forgot her medicine that morning, and she quickly realized she wasn't crazy. She was feeling much more alert than she had in a very long time and now she knew it was the pills that were making her so groggy all the time. She laid in the dark listening to the sound of rain against the windowpanes behind the curtains. She closed her eyes and concentrated, and with supreme effort, was able to flex her toes. Next, she tried her hands but only managed to partially curl the fingers on her right hand. Then the door abruptly opened, and she quickly shut her eyes and slowed her breathing. Whoever had entered the room had stopped by her bedside. She vaguely wondered who it was. Was it him? Then she felt fingers stroking her hair and it took everything in her not to flinch or react in any way. The person gently pulled the covers up to her chin. Instinctively, she knew she had to remain silent and unchanged. Everything in her was telling her that nothing good would come of them knowing that she knew it was the drugs they were giving her that were keeping her incapacitated, and the sporadic feeding was keeping her weak. When the footsteps retreated from her bed, and she heard the soft click of her bedroom door close, she opened her eyes. Hope flooded her heart and her brain. All she had to do was bide her time. All she had to do was get stronger and then she could finally, finally leave this house for good.

NINE

SABRINA

I sat lost in thought for a few minutes after my sister left and then finally looked at my watch. I had twenty minutes to get back before dinner was served, then realized I couldn't take another dinner in that house. Even though I'd been living there less than forty-eight hours, I needed to be out amongst people just like me and not breathing the same rarefied air as the rich Dorseys.

Instead, I grabbed a burger and fries at a nearby diner, then went to a movie that I'd been wanting to see. When the movie was over, it was after ten o'clock, and I was glad that I had enough time to grab a chocolate milkshake before heading back to the estate. The ice cream parlor was crowded, or I would've sat inside and taken my time drinking my dark chocolate mint shake. Instead, I drank it in my car. I would have headed to the Riverwalk, but at this time of night it was usually filled with couples, and I didn't need to be reminded that I was alone.

I wondered if Theo was home. And then got mad at myself for wondering, since he apparently was involved with someone; and he was so far out of my league he may as well be in another area code. Even uptight Mrs. Manning knew that. I don't think she was being mean when she let me know that he'd had a date the other night. I think she was just being very matter of fact.

By the time I slurped up the last dregs of my milkshake and glanced at my phone, it was twenty to twelve. Where had the time gone? I couldn't believe I'd sat here lost in thought for over an hour. I started my car and headed back to the Dorsey estate up the winding roads to the elite neighborhood, hoping no one spotted my out-of-place Camry and called the police. Mrs. Manning would probably die of embarrassment if the police brought me home, and lock me out to sleep in my car, midnight or not. Luckily, I got back with eight minutes to spare and parked my car in the garage—and met Mrs. Manning, who was in her pajamas and a robe, on her way to lock the door just as I stepped inside.

Her eyes were hard and unfriendly. "We missed you at dinner."

I was an almost thirty-year-old woman and really didn't appreciate being treated like a sixteen-year-old sneaking back into the house after going to a party I was told I couldn't go to.

"I'm sorry about that. I met up with my sister in town and time got away from me." I brushed past her, figuring that my explanation would be good enough. But apparently it wasn't.

"Please let me know next time you won't be joining us for dinner. That way, I can plan my meals out better."

Heaven forbid Mrs. Manning waste any food on my behalf. What was the big deal? I'm sure I'd be served the plate I didn't eat tonight at lunchtime tomorrow. But I didn't want to aggravate this woman because if she wanted, she could make the next two years of my life hell. So, I gritted my teeth and apologized again.

"I'm very sorry. I had every intention of being back by dinner. But I haven't seen my sister in a while, and we had a lot to discuss." I wasn't about to tell this woman that I met with my sister for all of ten minutes before she walked away from me.

"I would appreciate being told beforehand." She didn't even give me a chance to respond before locking the door and turning on her heel to head toward her bedroom. I figured she had to be pretty mad because she'd failed to set the alarm on the panel next to the front door.

I let out a frustrated sigh and stood rooted to the spot, giving the housekeeper a chance to get into her room so I wouldn't have to run into her again in the hall. The house was eerily silent, the only sound coming from an ornate grandfather clock in Theo's study. The study door was open, but it was dark and empty. I knew he wasn't home because I hadn't seen his Infinity when I'd parked my car in the garage. I finally headed toward my room when I heard it. I stopped dead in my tracks. Was that crying? I walked back out to the foyer and stopped to listen, and I was right. I could hear someone crying. It sounded like it was coming from somewhere upstairs. Even though I wasn't banned from going to the second floor, I hesitated all the same, quickly looking around until I determined I was alone, then crept up the steps to the second-floor landing.

It was mostly dark, and all the doors on either side of the hallway were closed. I listened and realized I could no longer hear the crying. Feeling stupid, I turned to head back down to the first floor when I heard it again. It sounded like a woman. I walked in the direction the crying sound was coming from, stopped and then turned the opposite way before realizing the crying was coming from a vent in the ceiling, from the third floor. I was so busy staring at the ceiling vent and trying to hear more that I missed the shadowy figure approaching me until it was right in front of me. I yelped and nearly jumped out of my skin. The figure reached out a hand and put it on my shoulder.

"Sabrina?" It was Theo. "Are you okay? What are you doing up here?"

"Where did you come from? You scared the shit out of me." I put my hands over my chest to still my wildly beating heart.

"Sorry." He took a step back. "I just got home and was on my way to my room. Everything okay?"

I listened but could no longer hear the crying.

"I thought I heard someone crying up here, and I came to check it out."

He listened, but of course, the crying had stopped, making me feel like the biggest idiot. "I don't hear anything. Are you sure that's what you heard?"

"Well..." I hesitated. Because what had I really heard? "I could've sworn I did. But I guess I was wrong." I was suddenly self-conscious and embarrassed. Was I hearing things?

"Luca's room is down the hall." He gestured toward the hallway to the right. "She loves scary movies. I bet that's what you heard." Theo wore a black tux, and between his killer smile and spicy cologne, I was extremely aware of him as he stood so close to me in the dark.

"Yeah, that's probably it." But I could have sworn what I'd heard was coming from the third floor and felt instantly stupid. "I'm sorry. I need to get to bed. I have a lot of work to do tomorrow." I quickly headed past him down the stairs.

"Hey, Sabrina, wait."

I stopped at the top of the steps and looked back at him.

"How about a nightcap in my study? I had to attend a charity event tonight and those things always drain my energy. I'd love some company."

I just wanted to go to bed, but I found myself unable to resist his offer when he was giving me such a friendly, hopeful smile.

"Sure, why not? You're the boss." I gave him a teasing smile, and we headed down to the foyer and into his study.

When I'd arrived, I'd poked my head into this room briefly, but I hadn't noticed there was a bar cart in the corner next to his desk. He shrugged out of his tux jacket and tossed it over the back of his leather office chair, the same chair he'd been getting busy in the other night. With supreme effort, I pushed the image of the two of them out of my mind and watched as he headed straight to the cart.

"What can I get you, Miss Adams?" he asked with a mock formality that made me smile. I didn't live a nightcap type of lifestyle. In fact, I rarely drank at all, having grown up with a functioning alcoholic for a mother. Both my mom and my sister never missed a day of work and were reliable to a fault but couldn't go a day without drinking to excess. Although I drank occasionally, my feelings for alcohol were complicated.

"I'm not much of a drinker. You got any Diet Coke over there?"

Theo gave me an exaggerated look of horror before holding up a finger. "In that case," he said, heading for the study door, "hold tight and I'll be right back."

I sat in the plush leather chair opposite his desk and watched him leave, wondering where he was going. I took the chance to get a better look at the room. It was heavy on dark wood and leather. It was a lovely room, and I could tell it had been professionally decorated. But it didn't seem like Theo's style other than the bookshelves. I didn't bother getting up and looking around further because I didn't feel like I'd get to know him any better by looking around this room and figured this was a room he'd inherited from his father. A minute later, he was back with a small bottle of red liquid.

"What's that?"

"You'll see." He gave me a wicked grin and got busy mixing the liquid with some seltzer water and splashed some red syrup into the glass before plopping a cherry into it and handing it to me. I took a tentative sip. It was both tart and sweet and heavenly.

"Delicious," I breathed, closing my eyes and taking another sip. "What is it?"

"It's a tart cherry spritzer. It's something my sister used to have every night to help her sleep."

I was surprised he'd mentioned his sister when she seemed to be such a taboo subject. I took another sip of my drink while Theo poured himself a cognac and settled himself behind his desk. He took a sip and sighed, returning his attention back to me. I figured since he had already brought her up, now would be a good time to find out what happened to Belle Dorsey.

"When I heard the crying, I wondered if it might be your sister." I eyed him over the rim of my glass and his right eyebrow lifted in surprise.

"I wondered when the subject of Belle was going to come up."

"I'm sorry." I set the spritzer glass on his desk to give him my full attention. "It's none of my business. I shouldn't have brought it up."

"No worries. I'm the one who brought her up. And if you're going to be working here, you may as well know about what's going on with my sister." He was silent for several seconds, like he was trying to figure out exactly what to say. What was the big secret? "It couldn't have been my sister that you heard crying because Belle hasn't spoken a word or made much of a sound for years."

This was not what I'd expected him to tell me. "What happened to her?"

"Belle suffered a traumatic brain injury ten years ago and has been in a vegetative state ever since. The reason Mrs. Manning doesn't want you on the third floor is because that's Belle's space. She tends to her needs during the day, and we have a night nurse that takes care of her in the evenings."

"I am so sorry, Theo. I didn't know."

"Few people do, and we'd really like to keep it that way." He gave me a pointed look, and I quickly shook my head.

"Of course. I won't tell anyone. Your secret's safe with me. But how were you guys able to keep this out of the press? I had heard nothing about her injury. Something like that would have made national news. And if I hadn't read about it in the paper, my mom would have told me about it."

"That was my father's doing. This happened not long before he died. And I'm not sure who he had in his pocket on the police force, the media, and at the hospital, but he kept it out of the news."

I picked my drink back up and took a sip. I didn't say another word, but I'm sure he sensed my disapproval. Not that I had a right to judge, but from what I knew about the man, it screamed of Martin Dorsey being ashamed of his daughter.

"I know it sounds harsh, but my father was an extremely private man and a shrewd businessman. He didn't want his enemies on the board using my sister's condition and his own cancer diagnosis as an excuse to force him out."

"That must have been so hard for your family, Theo." Now I understood why Mrs. Manning still set a place setting for Belle at every meal. It was her way of coping with a hopeless situation.

"I know this sounds horrible, but I've barely seen my sister since her injury." He stared into his cognac, unable to look me in the eye. "We weren't exactly close, but I can't stand to see her like that. I'm rarely on the third floor myself." He finally looked up, and I could see the pain in his eyes. He quickly got up to pour himself another drink.

"I have no right to judge you when I'm not sure what I would have done in your shoes." Though I knew exactly what I'd do if I were in his shoes. I couldn't imagine not spending time with my sister if she were in Belle Dorsey's condition, even though I wasn't close to my sister either. But men were completely different animals, and as hard as I tried not to judge Theo, I couldn't help myself.

"I'm a coward. I know I am," he said absently, more to himself than to me. "Mrs. Manning has tried many times to get me to come up there more often to sit with her. To read to her since we both love books. Engage her in some kind of regular stimulus. She's still hoping that my sister is going to wake up one day like sleeping beauty, and sometimes I go up there and sit with her in the dark."

"You shouldn't be so hard on yourself. I'm sure your sister appreciates the times you come to see her," I offered. But I wasn't sure I believed it myself. Was Belle Dorsey even aware of anyone's visits, let alone the brother who couldn't bear to look at her anymore?

"I hope you're right, and I know I need to do better. It's just so hard to see her that way when I remember how she used to be. Sometimes, I wonder if it would just be better if..." His voice trailed off, and he didn't need to finish his thought because I knew exactly what he was going to say.

"If she were dead?" I asked. Theo nodded. "Better for who? Better for her or better for you?" I instantly regretted my words when his head snapped up and his eyes hardened. As quickly as the anger flashed in his eyes, it was gone. He sat back in his chair and looked at the ceiling.

"I don't know. Maybe better for all of us because, right now, we're all stuck in a state of limbo. Mrs. Manning is still hoping that she's going to snap out of it."

"And you don't?"

"No. To be honest, I think my sister is long gone and that we need to accept that and move on. Make her as comfortable as possible until the end."

I didn't know what to say to that, so I said nothing and finished my drink.

"Sorry, Sabrina. That got dark really quick. I just wanted a simple chat to unwind and here I am boring you with my family tragedy."

"Not at all," I assured him. "Besides, I'm the one who asked, and it's time I got to bed." I glanced at the crystal and brass clock on his desk. It was after one o'clock. "Seven o'clock comes mighty early, and I wouldn't want to make Mrs. Manning mad again."

"Again?"

I quickly explained about having dinner in town and neglecting to let Mrs. Manning know.

"Just a friendly piece of advice about Mrs. Manning. She loves routine, and she doesn't do well with change. Having someone new here has totally thrown her off, but just give her time and she'll come around. She really is a sweetheart once you get to know her."

I'd just have to take his word for it. But then another question occurred to me. "When was the last time anyone worked in the library? Am I the first librarian you've hired?"

"I vaguely remember someone my dad hired years ago, but I never met this person because I was in boarding school."

"So, no idea what they did in the library?"

"None. Sorry. Why are you asking? Is there a problem?" He looked concerned. And I felt stupid for asking.

"No, not at all. I was just wondering." I got up. "Good night, and thanks for the nightcap."

"Good night, Sabrina. See you in the morning. Or rather, later today."

After I brushed my teeth and put on my pajamas, I went to close my bedroom curtains, briefly glancing out into the backyard and into the woods, and froze. I took a step closer, practically pressing my face against the glass to get a better look at what seemed like a dark shadowy figure standing just beyond the tree line and staring at the house. My heart hammered hard in my chest. I went to turn my light off to get a better look since the inside of my room was mostly reflected in the glass, but by the time I got back to the window, whoever or whatever I thought I'd seen was gone.

TEN

BELLE

From the sliver of moonlight shining through the gap in the curtain, she knew it was nighttime. Once the night nurse had come and gone and she'd dutifully taken her meds, she spat the pills out onto her blanket just as soon as the door had shut behind the nurse. Next would be the excruciating slow and painful attempt to grab the pills, but she'd been practicing and was getting stronger. It was a process that usually took a long time. Even when her fingers could graze the pills, it took more strength and flexibility to grab them, and when she had, she was exhausted and covered in sweat.

She never gave up if for no other reason than she didn't want the morning, and daylight, to come with the pills still lying on her cover. So, she tried with all her might until she could curl her stiff fingers around the pills. Then she took a rest and ended up falling asleep only to be awakened by the sounds of the household stirring early the next morning. The pills were still in her hand, but slowly and painfully she retracted her hand, sweeping the pills underneath the covers before the creepy housekeeper who now took care of her during the day arrived. Later, when she was alone again, she would try to lift her foot.

Yesterday she did it. She lifted her left foot a few millimeters off the bed, but the effort had left her completely exhausted.

But this time when the housekeeper gave her the pills, she lingered in the room and Belle had no choice but to swallow the pills. She soon began to succumb to the stupor that she knew the pills would bring. She was almost asleep when she heard it —the unmistakable sound of a baby crying.

ELEVEN

SABRINA

The next morning there was someone sitting at the third place setting at the table for breakfast. It was an elderly white man with sparse gray hair combed over a pink scalp and dressed in a brown suit, the jacket of which was draped over the back of his chair. He had a plate laden with bacon and eggs and a smaller plate piled with buttery toast. He was so engrossed in his food that he didn't even look up when I walked in until I said good morning to him. Theo sat at his usual place at the head of the table drinking coffee, and looked up when I walked in.

"Good morning, Sabrina. This is Dr. Barrett Hill. He's our family doctor and an old family friend."

"Good to meet you, Sabrina," he said around a mouthful of toast, causing crumbs to spray from his mouth. He covered his mouth in embarrassment, and we all laughed. He put his fork down and held out a hand, which I shook.

"Nice to meet you, Dr. Hill." I gave him a smile and went to the sideboard and got a plate, wondering if there was ever anything different for breakfast besides bacon, eggs, toast, fruit, and oatmeal.

Then I remembered what Theo had told me about Mrs.

Manning not being a big fan of change. Not in the mood for anything too heavy, I opted for fruit and some toast, then poured myself a cup of coffee and sat down opposite Dr. Hill.

Mrs. Manning came out with the pitcher of orange juice, and when she spotted me, she gave me a small smile and nodded in my direction, giving me the impression she'd forgiven me for last night's transgression.

"Theo tells me you're working in Lorraine's library. How's that going?"

"It's going very well so far. And it's such a beautiful library. I'm so excited about bringing it back to life."

"And I'm very glad to hear that, young lady. That library has sat empty for so long it's a crime. I'm glad you finally took my advice and hired someone to restore it," he said to Theo, who nodded absently. I wasn't even sure he'd heard what the older man had said. "Have you given any more thought to opening it to the public?"

That got Theo's attention, and he vigorously shook his head. "Not a chance. I'm willing to loan to places who might want to borrow books like libraries or private corporations or museums. But Mrs. Manning would lose her mind if we let strangers traipse through the house, and you know it."

Dr. Hill burst out laughing and that's when I realized he'd been joking.

"What's so funny?" Mrs. Manning had come back from the kitchen, this time with a tray of jams and jellies which she set on the table in front of the doctor.

"Nothing," said Theo, quickly shooting a glare at Dr. Hill. "Doc Hill's got jokes, that's all."

"Jokes? Barry Hill must be the least funny man on the planet." She gave Dr. Hill a wry smile.

"I'd just like to state for the record, Miss Adams," Dr. Hill said, looking at me. "That I hope you last longer than the last librarian. He sure didn't last long, did he?" He directed his question at Mrs. Manning, who gave him a warning look, which he completely ignored and continued. "But he was doing a lot more than shelving books, wasn't he?"

Theo and Mrs. Manning exchanged looks, and I wondered why Dr. Hill was still chuckling and had failed to read the room. As for me, my curiosity about my predecessor had ramped up into overdrive when I realized Theo must have known more about this person than he'd claimed to last night. I opened my mouth to ask the doctor what he'd meant when Mrs. Manning cleared her throat and spoke.

"Dr. Hill, why don't I take you on up to see Belle if you're finished eating." Mrs. Manning picked up the man's plate, which still had food on it, and gave him a look that told him he was dangerously close to wearing out his welcome.

He must've got the hint, because he cleared his throat and gave Mrs. Manning a sheepish grin before wiping his mouth and rising to his feet.

"That sounds like an excellent idea, Anna, my dear. Lead the way."

Mrs. Manning steered the elderly man away from the table by his elbow, guiding him out of the room toward the foyer. Though I couldn't tell when I sat down at the table, I realized now that Dr. Barrett Hill must be nearly blind.

"Is he...?"

"Legally blind. Yeah, he is."

"And he's your family doctor? How?"

"He has macular degeneration and can barely see two feet in front of him and he no longer drives. He had to give up his practice several years ago. But he was my dad's best friend, and we keep him on out of respect. Mrs. Manning will escort him upstairs, where he'll take Belle's blood pressure, listen to her heartbeat, test her reflexes, and make sure all her prescriptions are updated. She has another doctor that comes to see her once a month, but we're just trying to help Doc Hill feel useful."

"That's nice of you. I'm sure it must've been very hard for him to lose his vision and have to give up his practice. But what was he talking about? What happened with the other librarian?"

"Like I said last night," he said with a sigh, "I wasn't here. And no one really wanted to talk to me about it when I got home. Let's just say your predecessor had his eye on more than books when he was working here. He romanced my sister and then ran off and broke her heart. She was never the same afterwards."

"That's horrible."

It suddenly occurred to me how much it had to suck having money and always being worried about someone being after it. I can only imagine how Belle Dorsey must've felt knowing that the man she fell in love with was only after her father's money.

There were so many things that I wanted to ask that were completely none of my business. I might've even asked them if Mrs. Manning hadn't come back into the dining room. I could tell by the stern look on her face she wasn't open to answering questions about something that happened in the past, least of all from me. I quickly finished my toast and fruit so I could escape to the quiet sanity of the library.

"Hey," I said as what I'd seen the night before suddenly popped back into my head. How could I have forgotten that?

"What's up?" Theo noticed the troubled look on my face, and I saw real concern in his eyes.

"I could be mistaken. But I could've sworn I saw someone in the woods last night."

"Seriously?" He looked alarmed and instantly got up to look out the dining-room window toward the woods. "Could you see what they looked like? Was it a man or a woman?"

"They were too far away for me to see their face. But maybe I was tired and imagining things because by the time I tried to get a closer look, they were gone."

"It was probably Mr. Pearson, our gatekeeper." Mrs. Manning came in to clear away the breakfast dishes and must've overheard what I'd said to Theo.

"But it was after one in the morning," I pointed out. "Does he work that late?"

"Mr. Pearson is our nighttime gatekeeper. Mr. Gaines works days."

"And what does a gatekeeper do at night when the estate is locked down at midnight?" I asked, earning myself an annoyed look from Mrs. Manning and causing Theo to speak up.

"He also does light security work. We've had quite a few poachers in the woods. We have a fence on the other side of the woods that leads to the road. There are *No Trespassing* signs back there, but people still managed to find their way onto the property hunting for deer and groundhogs and such. We've had to call the police several times," said Theo as he started packing his briefcase.

"So, it could've been a poacher I saw last night?" That made me feel slightly better, but not much. And why would a poacher have been staring at the house?

"Possibly," said Mrs. Manning. "I'll talk to Mr. Pearson and have him check the woods to see if he can find any footprints or anything."

"Thanks. That makes me feel a lot better. I was really freaked out when I saw that person out there." It also made me think about the article I was sent about Cherise Gamble's death.

I was so caught up in wondering who would send me the article that I didn't think about the logistics of her death. Why was she on the road behind the estate? Was it because she'd been on the property? In the woods? Theo had just said there was a fence separating the woods from the road. When had that been installed? Was it before or after Cherise's death? And why was I dredging all this up in my head when I knew I wasn't leaving this job. Cherise had been killed in a tragic accident and her killer was in prison. End of story. I pushed the questions out of my head and got up from the table, only to see a look pass between Theo and Mrs. Manning before he told us all to have a nice day and left the house for the office.

I spent the rest of the morning cleaning books, but I didn't want to spend the next two years merely cleaning. So, I devised a system to inventory them as I went along. Soon I was flying through the books, happy to know that by the time I finished, I would also have an inventory of everything on the shelves in this library. I noticed that many of the books had cataloging marks, which I figured must've come from the librarian before me. I wondered what his name was and whether I should try and contact him to find out exactly what had been done in the library, so I didn't duplicate efforts. He could've had the whole thing inventoried, and I just didn't know where to find the file. But I figured I needed to wait a little while before I brought up the subject of how to contact this man to Theo. Even though Theo claimed not to know anything, I got the impression that he knew plenty, and I didn't dare ask Mrs. Manning. Another thought occurred to me. If this guy had been after Belle Dorsey's money, why did he leave? Did she find out and break up with him or did he move on to greener pastures? So many questions, but I figured I had two years in this place to find out.

I loaded my cart with another fifty books when a file folder slipped out from between two of them. It was dusty, and the dust tickled my nose and made me sneeze. I took the file over to the desk and wiped off the dust. Inside were twenty-five pages with book titles handwritten on both the front and the back. Some titles I recognized because I'd recently cleaned them, and then I realized this was an inventory. Probably not a complete one, but definitely an inventory. And I wondered who had compiled it, Lorraine Dorsey or whoever this mysterious previous librarian had been? I flipped through the pages and quickly deduced that about a thousand books had been inventoried. I also noticed red asterisks by certain titles, one of them being the first edition of *The Conjure Man Dies* that I'd found. I opened my laptop and typed in the other asterisked titles, quickly discovering that they were all rare first editions worth several thousand dollars on the low end.

Then I found something else. On the very last page were the initials MP. Obviously not Lorraine Dorsey's initials. These had to be the initials of the librarian who was unable to finish their job because they'd been too busy seducing Belle Dorsey. What had the man hoped to accomplish by messing around with his boss's daughter? Did he think they were going to open their arms wide and welcome him into the family? Did he have to follow all the same rules that I did? Or were the rules I was being forced to follow the result of what he had done? Clearly, Mrs. Manning didn't want me getting too close to Theo. Was she afraid history would repeat itself with the youngest Dorsey and the new librarian? I'd only been working here for two days and was already wondering if I'd made a big mistake. Because who the hell needed all this drama?

Later, after lunch, which predictably comprised my uneaten dinner from the night before, chicken cordon bleu, mashed potatoes, and peas, I logged all the books from the inventory into my inventory sheet on my laptop. When I was done, I filled my laundry bag full of all the clothes I didn't have time to wash when I left my sister's place. I didn't want whoever did the Dorseys' laundry pawing through my underwear, so I headed into town to a laundromat. I drove past The Book Barn and looked through the large picture window into the store to see someone unfamiliar manning the cash register. I was glad they'd been able to replace me so quickly. I hadn't given them the two weeks' notice they deserved and could tell that Jill, the owner, hadn't exactly been thrilled. But she wouldn't hold me back from an incredible opportunity. Still, I felt guilty and promised myself I'd go in with cookies or donuts to say hi next time I was in town.

After putting in a load of laundry, I headed across the street to the CVS to pick up some personal items. That's when I noticed the guy at the end of the block. He was a black man who looked to be in his early thirties, brown skin, bald, with a goatee. Attractive, but probably not anyone I'd look at twice if I passed him on the street. He was watching me intently. First when I walked back into the laundromat and then again when I left and loaded my clean laundry bag full of clothes into my backseat. He started walking toward me, his step quickening as I got behind the wheel and started my car. He started waving his arms, clearly trying to get my attention and even though all my windows were rolled up, I saw his mouth moving and could make out the words *excuse me*. I was in no mood to get hit on by some strange guy. I pulled off and left him in my rearview, standing on the curb looking frustrated with his hands on his hips.

As I was folding and putting away my clothes, my sister called. I thought about not answering but felt petty and childish. Even though I knew she wouldn't apologize, I answered anyway.

"Hey, Brina." My sister rarely called me Brina anymore. She did when I was a little kid. But by the time I was four, she was in the military. After that, we rarely saw her.

"Hey," was all I got out. Cami was moody as hell. I never knew which Cami was going to show up. These days it was mostly mean, annoyed, and irritated Cami. And I also noticed that, much like our mother, she was drinking more and more. But I guess you'd have to stay drunk to be married to Bruce.

"I know I was a bitch last night, but there's something I've wanted to tell you ever since you got your new job. I didn't know how because I know you won't appreciate it."

"What?" I was suddenly apprehensive because Cami wasn't the type to mince words. If she was warning me about something, it had to be serious. I wasn't sure I wanted to hear it.

"Did Mom ever tell you why she was blind in one eye?"

"You know she didn't." My mom had been blind in her right eye since before I was born. She never talked about it, and when I tried to ask her when I was a teenager, she told me to shut up. I should've known better than to ask, especially when she was drunk.

"It happened at Dorsey Snacks. She was at work and a piece of equipment exploded. A bunch of people got hurt and one guy died. Mom got some metal debris in her eye and that's why she was blind."

"How did that happen?"

"It happened because the safety manager was faking safety reports on the machines. It was big news in all the papers at the time and Martin Dorsey had to pay out a bunch of money to everyone who'd got hurt and a big settlement to the widow of the man who was killed. Mom used her settlement to buy our house."

"But what does that have to do with me now? Martin Dorsey's been dead for years. I work for his son, not at Dorsey Snacks." Those were the words that came out of my mouth because I didn't want my sister to worry. But my insides were churning. This was the second accident connected to the Dorseys I was hearing about in twenty-four hours.

"I'm telling you this because I don't trust those damned Dorseys. And even though I know you won't pay any attention to what I just told you, I just want you to watch your back, sis. That's all. Just be careful."

I'd wanted to ask my sister why she was working for Dorsey

Snacks if she didn't trust the Dorseys. But I knew why. She hadn't been able to find a job anywhere else. Plus, Cami's drinking meant getting up early every morning to go to a job was out of the question. Working second shift as a custodian meant she'd be sober by the time her shift rolled around.

"Wait," I blurted before she hung up, "are you the one that sent me that article?"

"What article?" she snapped.

"Never mind."

"*What* article, Sabrina?"

That I'd gone from Brina back to Sabrina told me how annoyed my sister was, and I regretted asking. Of course, Cami hadn't sent me that article. Being non-confrontational wasn't her style. She'd have just told me instead of mailing me the article when I was living in the same house with her.

"Someone mailed me an article and I thought it might have been you."

"I have no idea what you're talking about," she said with a weary sigh. "Why would I mail you anything when I don't even know the address up there? And who the hell mails shit these days, anyway?"

I started to tell her the article had been mailed to me at her house, but she'd hung up before I could.

I'd heard nothing from Mrs. Manning about whether she'd checked with the nighttime gatekeeper about having seen or found any evidence of the person I saw in the woods last night. Had I really seen someone? Was it a trick of the light or was my overtired brain seeing things that weren't there? I was more than happy to forget about it, but made sure to keep the curtains in my room closed. I ended up eating the roast chicken dinner Mrs. Manning left me alone that night in the kitchen as she was out and, predictably, Theo wasn't at home either; probably out with his lady friend. Luca also never made an appearance. After dinner, I settled in my room with a book that I'd smuggled up from the library. *The Conjure Man Dies* by Rudolph Fisher. I probably should've been wearing gloves while handling it, but I didn't have any. I just told myself that I'd have to be extra careful when I read it. As much as I loved books, I wasn't much into the classics, but I was interested in African American authors and Fisher was an author I hadn't read.

Thump! I jerked awake, unsure of what had happened until I realized that not only had I fallen asleep, but the five-figure book I was reading had fallen to the floor with a thud. I quickly scrambled out of bed to retrieve it from the floor, carefully checking it to make sure it wasn't damaged and none of the pages had ripped. Thankfully, it looked just the same as it had before I'd started reading it. As I was kneeling by the side of my bed examining the book for damage, something flashed in the corner of my eye. Something shiny was lying under my bed. I picked it up and realized it was a charm. A gold turtle charm with the shell inlaid with mother-of-pearl. It was about half an inch in diameter and looked expensive. I wondered who it belonged to because it certainly wasn't mine. Then I remembered Luca had been looking under the bed my second day here. Was it hers? I hadn't noticed if she was wearing any jewelry. I stood up and laid the charm on my bedside table and put *The Conjure Man Dies* into my work bag.

I decided to get some water. I was at the kitchen sink drinking a glass of water and realized the window looked out onto the woods that ran behind the house. This time, when I looked out and scanned the tree line, there was no one there.

TWELVE
JARED

He stood just inside the tree line of the woods behind the Dorsey estate, staring up at the house. He'd just seen a light go out and wondered if it was her window. He had to talk to her. He had to warn her. But he also needed her help. He knew he shouldn't be there. It was dangerous. It was risky, and he'd already almost been caught once. He knew that spying on the house from the woods wouldn't just get him arrested for trespassing. They'd probably pin a stalker charge on him as well. But he was so close, and she was his last shot. Had she seen him last night? He'd watched from the safety of the woods as she stared out the window. He'd taken a risk coming back because if she had seen him, she probably told someone, and they'd be on the lookout for him. But as he stared at the house and the grounds, he could see no movement and realized no one was looking for him. He stood there for five more minutes before turning and slowly making his way back through the woods.

THIRTEEN

SABRINA

I looked around the library the next morning surveying my work of the past few days. I had so much to do. It was slow going for so many reasons, and the dust coating the books was just the tip of the iceberg, because the same dust also coated the shelves, which I would need to clean before re-shelving. I'd also set aside three carts, one for the books that needed minor repairs, another for books that were beyond repair that I'd need to find replacements for, and the third for the rare editions. I wondered if two years would be long enough for me to get everything I needed to do done, but I was feeling a bit more confident I could create my own catalog system for the books. I wasn't even sure why I'd been hired when the entire time I'd been here, except for the first day, neither Theo nor Mrs. Manning had set foot inside the library. Did it hold that many bad memories? I knew Theo was an avid reader, yet he had an entire library of books outside of his study at his disposal and never came in here. Why?

I was still pondering this question when, an hour into my morning, the man himself showed up. Theo arrived carrying two lattes from Riverside Coffee Bar where we first had coffee.

Had that really been almost two weeks ago? It felt like I'd been here forever, and I couldn't figure out if that was good or not.

"Good morning." He handed me a latte, and I tried to push the image of that woman moaning and grinding in his lap out of my head and failed. Blood rushed to my face.

"Looks like you're off to a good start." He gestured toward the section of shelving that I was working on, then looked around the rest of the library, his gaze coming to rest on the carts of books lined up next to my desk.

"Yeah, but I've got a lot of work ahead of me. These books are so dirty, I can't really get anything else done until the place is cleaned."

"Do you need some help?"

"Don't you have to get to your office?"

He let out a snort of laughter, almost choking on his coffee. "I wasn't talking about me. I was talking about hiring some help. Mrs. Manning employs a cleaning service, and I bet they could spare a couple of people to come in here and help you clean the shelving and the books, even if it's only a couple of days a week."

"Really?" It would be great to have some help, but that would just get me to the point in my job that I had lied about, before I'd figured out what I was going to do about appraising and cataloging the collection. I knew I could do it. I just needed a little time to figure out how. But I also didn't want to look suspicious and make this man think that I didn't know what I was doing. So, I compromised.

"Can you give me a week to get a little more organized and then I'd absolutely love some help, even if it's just for one or two days a week, like you said?"

"Sounds like a plan. Just let me know when you're ready."

"Thanks, Theo."

"Not a problem. And please ask me for anything else that

you need. I know this is a big job, Sabrina. Don't feel like you have to do everything all by yourself."

I nodded, and he took a step closer to me, which caused me to take a step back. He leaned toward me, and I stood still as a statue as he reached out and plucked something off my shoulder. It was a large clump of dust. I was relieved he hadn't been about to kiss me so soon after witnessing him with that other chick.

"Hazard of the job." I let out a nervous laugh, and he smiled and left.

I emerged from the library half an hour before lunch so I could wash up, to find an older white woman in a gray jumpsuit with the words *Flemings Florals* embroidered across the back in lavender stitching. She was switching out all the flowers in the foyer. I couldn't help thinking what a waste it was since the flowers still looked so fresh and were still so fragrant. Maybe I'd feel differently if I'd grown up wealthy.

"Good morning, ma'am," she said with a smile upon spotting me.

"Good morning." I started to walk past, but I just had to know. "Can I ask what happens to the flowers you're taking out of here? It seems like such a waste when they're still so fresh."

"Yes," she said, nodding toward the bouquet in her hands that she had just removed from one of the crystal vases. "They are still very fresh. But the ones I'm taking out of here today will be donated to nearby hospitals. And a few of these bouquets are headed to the family's mausoleum."

"That makes me feel a lot better. I was afraid all of these beautiful flowers were going into the trash." Not that it was any of my business how the Dorseys spent their money.

"No, ma'am!" The older woman looked slightly offended.

"Even the ones that aren't donated are put to good use by our floristry students. Nothing gets wasted. I promise."

I let her get back to work and headed to the bathroom, glancing through the double doors of the garden on my way to see Mrs. Manning walking through the garden with a large bouquet of flowers. She must've been on her way to the mausoleum. I'm not sure why I followed her, but I did. I hung back and followed at a distance watching her mount the steps to the mausoleum and open the door, disappearing inside. I waited a minute before ascending the stairs myself and slipping inside. I instantly noticed how much cooler and quieter it was inside the mausoleum, and I could hear the older woman's footfalls echoing through the small space.

The inside was floor-to-ceiling white and gold marble with two rows of wooden bench seating on either side of a narrow aisle leading to a small altar with a cross mounted on the front and a large freestanding golden candelabra behind it. Light flooded the small chapel from an ornate stained-glass dome in the ceiling. The scent of flowers and candle wax were heavy in the air. To the right of the altar was a wall housing the Dorsey family's crypts. I counted four with room along the wall for more. Mrs. Manning was standing in front of one crypt in particular pulling the dead flowers out of a wall-mounted marble vase next to it and refreshing them with the ones she had brought from the house.

I'm not sure why I hid behind a pillar to keep her from seeing me. Maybe it was because I felt like I was intruding on something sacred. She pulled a small plastic trash bag from her pocket to dump the dead flowers into. Next, she used a handkerchief from her other pocket to wipe off the front of the crypt she was standing in front of. I was too far away to see whose it was. She pressed her fingers of her right hand to her lips and then pressed it against the front of the crypt before turning to leave. I waited behind the pillar until I heard the soft click of the mausoleum door shutting. Then I headed over to the crypt she'd been standing in front of. It read:

Lorraine Marie Dorsey beloved wife and mother June 8, 1962 – September 16, 1994

Why was Mrs. Manning faithfully tending Lorraine Dorsey's crypt when she claimed not to have known her?

The one directly next to it was Martin Dorsey's.

Martin Edward Dorsey Senior. March 10, 1950 – May 18, 2015

There was no epitaph on his crypt just his name and the dates of his birth and death. I couldn't help but notice the dead flowers still in his vase as well as a large cobweb beginning to form at one corner. Clearly, Mrs. Manning's loyalty had been to her former employer's wife and not him. Again, I wondered why she was pretending not to have been close to Lorraine Dorsey.

I turned to go when something on the front of Lorraine Dorsey's crypt caught my eye. At first, I thought it was a design underneath her name, but when I took a closer look, saw that it was a name: Martin Edward Dorsey Junior. A tiny angel blowing on a trumpet was next to the name, but there was no date of birth or death. Theo and Belle had another brother whose crypt was inside their mother's. I'd never heard anything about Martin Dorsey having more than two children. It must have been a very painful loss if no one in the family had publicly acknowledged it. And what had Martin Dorsey done to make Mrs. Manning neglect his crypt?

After lunch, I'd located three of the books the mysterious MP had starred in red on the inventory. The first edition of W.E.B.

Du Bois' book *Dark Water: Voices from Within*, and two other first editions by Zora Neale Hurston, *Mules and Men* and *Jonah's Gourd Vine*. I looked them up and saw all three were similar prices to the Rudolph Fisher book. So far, nothing I'd found was worth more than several thousand dollars. Not exactly chump change, but I'd been expecting books of greater value. At least, that's what I'd thought until I found a first edition signed copy of Ezra Jack Keats' *The Snowy Day*, which online was listed for a whopping $35,000. It was the only first edition I'd found thus far not by an African American author. The next was a copy of *Cane* by Harlem Renaissance author Jean Toomer, also listed online for $35,000. But the next book was the most expensive by far. It was a first edition copy of *The New Negro* by W.E.B. Du Bois and signed by him and two other men, James Weldon Johnson and Walter White. Online, it was listed for a whopping $85,000.

Now these were the kind of prices that I was expecting for a rare collection of books. The Dorseys had a small fortune in rare books in their home and probably didn't even realize it. Plus, the inventory I had was only for about a third of the collection. Who knew how many other rare editions this library held? I searched for the care and handling of rare editions but stopped when I realized Theo could probably access my search history through the house Wi-Fi server. I don't know why he would, but he could if he wanted to. If he saw I was looking up how to handle rare books, he would know I didn't know what I was doing and would probably fire me. Well, maybe, but I didn't want to take that chance because I needed this job. I would live in a cardboard box on the side of the road before I went back to my sister's house again.

Around four, I told Mrs. Manning that I needed to go into town for some supplies and headed for the public library. I could've gone to the Harper's Ferry Community College's library to avoid my former coworkers, but I wanted to get in and out as quickly as possible. I'd never been to the community college library and didn't know where anything was. I could've also gone to one of the smaller branch libraries, but with the budget cuts, they were only open on certain days and today wasn't one of them. When I arrived at the public library, I was happy that the staff were too busy helping patrons to notice my arrival. I hadn't been back here since my last day over six months ago and nothing much had changed except the level of staffing.

I quickly headed to the back where they had computers for public access and used my library card to log on to a terminal. I looked up articles and books on everything that I was going to need for the job, how to handle rare books, the supplies I would need, as well as the names and addresses of some book appraisers in nearby Cincinnati. I may not have had the experience that I'd lied to Theo Dorsey about, but I was still a librarian, if not in degree, then in experience. I knew that if I didn't know something, I could always find someone who did. After a few hours of research, I figured I had a pretty good handle on how to do exactly what Theo Dorsey had hired me to do, as well as having found quotes for cataloging software. I was feeling a lot more confident and made a bunch of printouts and put them in my tote before heading out. But I couldn't make the clean getaway I'd hoped for.

"Sabrina?" An older white woman in her sixties with short brown hair and glasses stopped me as I was leaving.

Joanne Campbell had been my supervisor for the three years I'd worked for the Harper's Ferry Public Library. She was the one who'd hired me and, ironically, she was the one who had fired me. Budget cuts had eliminated a lot of positions at the public library, but I'd been fired for a very specific reason that had nothing to do with budget cuts. I had lied to the public library about my credentials, just like I'd done with Theo. They were already short-staffed even then and turnover in the HR department was high. So, the lack of documentation of my MLIS in my employment file went unnoticed for two years. I kept telling myself that by the time it came to light, I would have my MLIS. I finished one class. But as Mom got sicker, I never got around to taking the other class I needed to get my MLIS. I was one of two other people who didn't have the credentials to do the job I was doing. Jo had tears in her eyes when she told me she had to let me go. She said her hands were tied and told me that if I had just explained my situation from the beginning, she might've been able to help me out with HR. Instead, I'd lied and ended up losing a job I had grown to love.

"Hi, Jo. How have you been?" I gave her a warm smile to let her know there were no hard feelings. I had taken total responsibility for my situation from the beginning and knew that she'd had no choice.

Instead of responding, she pulled me into a big hug and held me tight. That made me want to cry. I gently pushed her away.

"Sabrina, I was so sorry to hear about..."

"Thanks, Jo." I cut her off abruptly because I wasn't in the mood for any more condolences. She looked a bit taken aback but seemed to understand and changed the subject.

"It's so good to see you. Are you still here in town? Were you able to find another position?" I could tell she wanted to ask if I'd finally got my MLIS, but thought it might be a sore subject, which it kind of was. I appreciated her not asking.

"Yes, still here, and I was just hired for a wonderful new position."

"A library position? I saw the community college was looking for a reference librarian and I hoped you'd applied."

"I applied for that. Didn't get it. But my new job more than makes up for it."

"I was just headed out for a smoke." She patted her sweater

pocket where I knew her pack of Virginia Slims were. "Come out with me for a little chat?"

"Sure." I really wanted to get back to work and order the software I would need, but I didn't want to be rude and followed Jo outside to the designated smoking area.

Once we were settled on the bench, she lit a cigarette. After taking a long drag and blowing the smoke away from me, she turned to me with a smile.

"Tell me about this new job of yours. Is it here in town?"

"Yes, I'm working as a private librarian for the Dorsey family."

At the mention of the Dorsey name, Jo's eyes narrowed slightly, and slowly turned in my direction. "The Dorseys? Seriously?"

"Yeah, the Dorseys. The late Mrs. Dorsey had a beautiful private library that hadn't been touched in a decade. They hired me to inventory, catalog, and appraise the collection." I would've gone on, but the look on Jo's face stopped me.

"What's wrong?"

"Nothing. Sounds like a great job. Also sounds like a lot of work. I hope they're paying you well." She took another drag on her cigarette.

I hadn't worked for Jo for three years not to know when the woman wasn't being honest. Whenever she lied about something, she would rub the side of her nose with her index finger. She'd done that the day she fired me, after telling me that if I got my MLIS, she would consider me for the next available position.

"Out with it, Jo. Is there something I need to know about the Dorseys?" First my sister and now Jo. Did I really want to know what this woman was about to tell me when I had absolutely no intention of leaving this job?

She stubbed out her barely smoked cigarette and tossed it into a nearby trash can. "Look, I'm sure it's nothing, it's just that..." Her voice was off, and she looked away from me, staring off into the distance. And that's when I realized.

"You knew their previous librarian, didn't you?"

She finally turned her attention back to me. "His name was Myles. Myles Patterson. He worked here for about a year before he was offered a position working in the Dorseys' private library. Doing the same things that you say you are doing for them, but I don't think he was there for long, and I haven't seen him in over a decade."

"I heard working in the library wasn't the only thing he was working on. Apparently, he had some kind of romance going with Martin Dorsey's daughter, Belle, that didn't end well."

"That doesn't surprise me. Myles was a sweet young man and very good at his job, but he was also very opportunistic and ambitious. Doesn't surprise me at all that he tried to worm his way into the family through Martin Dorsey's daughter."

"You have no idea what happened to him?"

"I hadn't heard the whole Belle Dorsey angle, but the rumor going around the library here at the time was that he got caught stealing and was fired."

"Stealing? What did he steal?"

"Supposedly a valuable first edition. He got caught selling it online, is what I heard."

"Was he arrested?"

"I doubt it. If there's one thing most people in this town know about the Dorseys, it's that they are all allergic to scandal. Ever since that accident at Dorsey Snacks years ago, the Dorsey family maintain a low profile."

I wanted to get away from the topic of the accident at Dorsey Snacks because I didn't want Jo to know that my mom was a victim. I was still trying to wrap my head around it.

"Is Myles from here? Does he have family in the area that might know where he is?"

Jo looked concerned. "Are you going to contact him?"

"I found an old inventory he did and thought it might be nice to touch base with him about any other info he may have about the collection." But considering what Jo had just told me and what I'd found out from the Dorseys about my predecessor, maybe trying to get in touch with the illustrious Myles Patterson wasn't a good idea.

Jo gave me a skeptical look. "To answer your question, yes, he's from here. Moved back here after he graduated from library school. He was an only child, and I know both his parents are gone now. I remember reading their obits in a paper. They died a year apart and he must still be out there somewhere because he wasn't listed as pre-deceasing them in their obits."

We were silent for a few seconds. I realized that since we were no longer sharing the day-to-day grind of working together, there wasn't much more to say. "I need to be getting back." I gave her a smile and got up to go when she stopped me again.

"Did you ever finish your degree?" Jo got up from the bench to walk with me back to the parking lot.

"I've still got one more class," I told her honestly. There was no reason to lie anymore.

"Well, I hope the Dorseys appreciate you. I'm sure you'll do an amazing job for them. Take care, Sabrina." She gave my arm a squeeze and made to head back into the library before turning and stopping me again. "Sabrina."

I turned and gave her an inquiring look.

"Say hi to Annie B for me."

"Annie B?" Who was she talking about? Then I remembered Theo introducing Mrs. Manning to me as Anna Manning. The B Jo was referring to must have been her maiden name. "You mean Mrs. Manning?"

"Yeah," Jo replied with a laugh. "We went to high school together and no one could believe it when she went to work for Martin Dorsey. I haven't seen her in years, but she used to be the life of the party. I bet she must be fun to work with."

"Loads," I replied sarcastically before tossing Jo a wave. I headed to my car with more questions than I had before I talked to her. Mrs. Manning, the life of the party? And why were people so surprised she'd gone to work for Martin Dorsey? I probably should have asked, but I just didn't care. I had zero intention of telling Mrs. Manning her old high school buddy Jo said hi. I couldn't risk Manning reaching out to Jo for old times' sake and finding out why I got fired from my old job, let alone what else I'd been lying about.

FOURTEEN
SABRINA

I got back to the estate at 5:30 and discovered I was the only one home. A note on the fridge from Mrs. Manning said she and Theo were out for the evening, Luca was spending the night with a friend, and my dinner was in the fridge. I wasn't hungry for a meal right then. But the idea of flouting Mrs. Manning's strict 6:30 dinner rule was too much to resist, and I pulled my plate of short ribs, mashed sweet potatoes, and garlic green beans from the fridge and heated it up in the microwave. Then I leaned against the countertop and devoured it along with not just one, but three glasses of red wine. Not because I wanted it, but because I was being petty.

When I was done, I washed my dinner plate, and then turned my attention to the pantry in search of dessert and found a three-layered carrot cake. I cut myself a big slice and ate it with my hands, dropping crumbs all over the place, realizing how pathetic it was that this was giving me so much pleasure. Being a librarian, there are a lot of rules that you must follow. Normally, rules didn't bother me, but the Dorseys' rules got under my skin like a rash, making me want to do everything in my power to take back some of my autonomy. Granted, I was living in someone else's house, but the rules just seemed excessive and unnecessary.

When I'd finished my big ass piece of cake, I looked around at the chaos I'd created and started panicking. It would be just my luck for Mrs. Manning to walk in and see the mess and give me that hard stare she gave me when she was less than pleased. I quickly cleaned up and noticed it was only five forty-five. I had the whole evening stretched out ahead of me in this big empty house. Not sure what to do with myself, I took a long, hot bubble bath and then changed into the silk pajama set my sister gave me for Christmas a few years ago. Then I settled in the family room in front of the massive flat screen on the wall. I found old reruns of *Laverne and Shirley*, a sitcom I used to watch with my mom after she got sick. She couldn't hang out at the bar anymore and began binge-watching classic TV shows. I had barely made it through a few episodes when I fell asleep on the couch. I woke with a start to the sound of a door slamming and figured my employers were back from wherever they'd been. A quick check of my phone showed it was a little after eight o'clock.

I waited. Yet five minutes passed, and no one came in. Confused, I got up and headed out into the foyer and opened the front door in time to see a van driving away from the house down the lane toward the security gate. There was a logo and name on the back of the van, but I only glimpsed it. It was a medical supply company. A black woman wearing navy blue scrubs, and a black head scarf was standing in the drive watching the van go before quickly heading into the house through the side service entrance. Theo told me his sister had a night nurse. She must've been accepting a delivery from the medical supply company.

I washed my wine glass, then put it away and made an early night of it. But I laid in bed wide awake staring at the ceiling for half an hour and regretting the nap I'd taken in the family room.

I knew what I could do to help me relax, and that was work. I went back to the library to clean some more books. I was about to flip on the lights when I saw something that made me freeze. Standing just outside the first row of windows that ran the length of the three-story library was a figure dressed in black. Their hands were cupped and their face was pressed against the glass staring in. I was still as a statue, unable to move.

This had to be the same person I'd seen near the woods the other night, and I could see it was a man. I don't know what was wrong with me, probably the wine, but I charged down the library steps and across the room until I was inches away from the man. Our eyes met and his widened in surprise as I held out my phone.

"I've called the police! Get the hell out of here!"

He instantly jerked back from the window, but he didn't leave right away. He was still staring at me and then mouthed something I couldn't catch.

"What do you want?" I shouted. I could see he was a tall, brown-skinned black man with a goatee. He looked familiar. Where had I seen him before? He gave me one last frustrated look and sprinted off back toward the woods and was gone, swallowed up by the trees and the darkness.

Theo and Mrs. Manning arrived back home half an hour later to the sight of flashing lights from a police car parked in front of the house. The two officers were taking a statement about the intruder I'd seen on the property looking through the window. I gave them the best description I could, given the brief time I'd seen his face. Plus, I'd had three glasses of wine, not because I'd really wanted it, but to spite Mrs. Manning, which I was now seriously regretting. Theo was instantly concerned upon seeing me talking to the police officers. But inexplicably, Mrs. Manning looked irritated. After giving my statement to the police and watching Theo walk them out to their car, Mrs. Manning exploded at me.

"What the hell were you thinking?" she said through clenched teeth. "Why didn't you call Mr. Dorsey or me?" I stared at her open-mouthed not understanding what the hell her problem was.

"Excuse me? Someone tried to break into this house while I was here alone with Mr. Dorsey's incapacitated sister, and you didn't want me to call the police?"

A vein throbbed in the older woman's temple, and I took a step back, just as Theo arrived to de-escalate the situation.

"I am so sorry, Sabrina. What Mrs. Manning meant to say," he said, giving his housekeeper a look that could've frozen water, "is that it would've been nice if you would've called one of us to tell us what was going on after you'd called the police. You didn't do anything wrong."

"The police arrived so quickly when I gave them this address that I didn't even have time to call either one of you. I'm sorry. But a man was trying to get into the house through the library windows. I was scared and felt extremely unsafe, so of course my reaction would be to call the police, and if calling the police was the wrong thing to do," I said, directing my statement to Mrs. Manning, "maybe this isn't where I should work. I refuse to be any place where I don't feel safe."

I walked away, leaving the two of them staring after me. I went back to my room and locked the door behind me. I closed the curtains over the windows and climbed into bed. Five minutes later, there was a soft knock on my door.

"Sabrina?" It was Theo. "Can I come in? We need to talk."

Reluctantly, I got up and let him in. He stepped inside looking around uncertainly before holding out a rectangular package wrapped in purple wrapping paper and tied with gold twine.

"What's this?" I asked, unable to keep the surprise out of

my voice. I already had my birthday this year, not that he would know that. So, why was he giving me a gift?

"Just open it," he said, looking down at the ground and then back up at me with a shy smile.

I did as I was told. Sitting on the side of my bed, I quickly unwrapped the package to reveal a copy of Nalo Hopkinson's novel *Brown Girl in the Ring*. I could tell this was an older edition, and when I flipped open the cover, was pleasantly surprised to see the author's signature. This book had been on my TBR list for quite a while, but I'd yet to get around to buying it.

"Why are you giving this to me? Is this a donation to the library?"

Instead of answering right away, he sat down on the bed next to me and I got the impression it was because he couldn't face me directly. "It's an apology and a confession."

"An apology for what happened tonight?"

"Yep," he said, staring at the rug.

"And what kind of a confession?"

He let out a sigh before answering. "This is really embarrassing, but I really needed for you to know..."

"Know what?" Why was he looking so embarrassed and nervous?

"I always knew you were a librarian, even before I approached you that day asking for advice."

"You did? How?"

"I used to see you sitting by the Riverwalk reading every single day. You were always so engrossed in whatever you were reading, like you had disappeared inside the pages and were living your best life there. I went for a walk on my lunch hour and would go to see you every day. I always wondered who the pretty girl with the braids and a book was. So one day I followed you back to the library and saw that you were one of the reference librarians, but I didn't know how to approach you.

Another day I saw you reading *Kindred* by Octavia Butler and wondered if you'd read Hopkinson. *Brown Girl in the Ring* is one of my favorites and I wanted to talk to you about it, to see if you'd read it."

"I... I had no idea," I stammered. But he wasn't finished.

"Then I didn't see you anymore and thought I'd missed my opportunity, until one day a couple months later I walked into The Book Barn, and you were at the register. I still couldn't get up the nerve to talk to you because, despite what everyone thinks about me, I'm kind of shy. I meant to give this to you on your first day working here as a welcome gift but chickened out. I didn't want you to think I was trying to hit on you. I hired you for very real reasons, and I just wanted you to know how glad I am that you're here and I'm so sorry about what happened tonight, and even sorrier that you don't feel safe."

To say I was stunned would be inadequate. I was, quite frankly, in shock. Theo Dorsey, wealthy, handsome Theo Dorsey who had dimples I could swim in, and could probably have any woman he wanted, had been too shy to talk to... me? How could this man who'd just made this sweet confession be the same man I saw getting busy in his office chair? If the saying, two things can be true at once, were a person, then I was looking at him.

"Theo... I."

But he quickly stood up. "I just thought you should know and please don't think I'm expecting anything from you. I just needed to get this off my chest and let you know how appreciated you are. Good night."

"Wait." I'm not sure why I did it, but I threw my arms around his neck and kissed him on the cheek. "Thank you for the book. I can't wait to read it." Theo flinched, and I quickly stepped back. "Are you okay?"

"I'm fine," he said, rubbing the back of his neck. I moved

behind him and looked up to see a long thin scratch on the back of his neck.

"What happened?" I reached out to touch it but thought better of it.

"Stupid accident at work. I was bending down to get a drink from the water fountain, and when I stood up, my work lanyard got caught on the fountain head and the cord cut into the back of my neck."

"You should probably put something on that before it gets infected."

"I will and you should probably get some sleep. Good night, Sabrina."

He reached out and squeezed my shoulder and was gone before I could say anything else. I'm not sure how long I stood staring at my bedroom door before finally turning in for the night.

I took my time getting ready the next morning, not sure what I'd be walking into at breakfast, only to find Theo seated in his usual spot. This time he didn't have his face buried in his iPad and appeared to be waiting for me. I looked around cautiously.

"Don't worry," he said, reading my mind, and gestured for me to have a seat. "She had a doctor's appointment this morning and then a hair appointment. She won't be back until early afternoon."

I let out a sigh of relief and grabbed a bagel with cream cheese before taking my usual seat at the dining table. I gave Theo a smile, still thinking about his confession and trying not to think it meant anything other than he wanted a friend to talk about books with.

"And, again, I am so sorry about last night. You had every right to call the police. Mrs. Manning was way out of line."

I took a bite of my bagel, nodded and swallowed before

asking him the $64,000 question. "What is her problem? Why did she get so freaked out because I called the police? I only did what any normal person would do in that situation."

Indecision flitted across his face before finally settling into a grim smile. "I shouldn't be telling you this because it's Mrs. Manning's private business and under any other circumstances I wouldn't betray a confidence, but I think it's important for you to know so you can understand her a little bit better. I know she can be a lot." He paused and I wanted to reach out and pull the words out of his mouth.

"What is it?" I sounded more impatient than I had meant to, but Theo snapped out of whatever trance he'd lapsed into.

"Mrs. Manning's husband was abusive. She ran away from him and ended up working for us. That was thirty years ago, but she still lives in fear of him finding her and I think she was probably afraid if this got into the news, he'd be able to track her down here."

I was speechless. I'd never been with anyone who'd abused me and had no idea of the fear that had to induce. No wonder the poor woman panicked when she saw police cars. The Dorseys are a prominent family in Harper's Ferry, hell, they were *the* prominent family in Harper's Ferry with Dorsey Snacks being the biggest employer not just here in the town but the entire region.

"After all these years she's still afraid he's going to find her?"

The man I saw last night certainly didn't look old enough to be her husband, he was in his early thirties.

"I didn't say it was rational. I just said that's what had her so freaked out last night. Several years ago, there was an accident on the road behind our house. A young woman was struck and killed by a car. It was all over the papers and Mrs. Manning wouldn't leave the house for weeks when the paper said that she had made a statement to the police."

I was suddenly lightheaded and the bagel in my mouth

tasted like sawdust. "Why would she have given a statement to the police? Did she know the girl?" I asked, trying to keep my tone as casual as possible.

"No," he said quickly. "The police thought this girl might have been on our property that night. None of us had ever seen her before and had no idea why she would've been on our property."

"Did your father or you try and track down Mrs. Manning's husband? It may have given her some peace of mind if she found out he'd moved on or away."

"My dad hired a private investigator, but he could never find a trace of him. As a matter of fact, Mrs. Manning started seeing a therapist for a short time. My father insisted because he thought she was being paranoid. You can't have a nanny taking care of your children who is too afraid to leave the house."

"That is so messed up." But what exactly was I referring to? Messed up that Martin Dorsey made his nanny/housekeeper feel like she was crazy for being worried her abusive husband would find her? Or messed up because Mrs. Manning is still so emotionally scarred over what a man had done to her thirty years ago? Honestly, it was all pretty messed up, which led to my next question.

"Does the groundskeeper know how this man keeps getting on your property? I thought you said something about a fence. Is it electric?"

"No. We do have a fence that separates our property from the road behind it. But it's barbed and not electric. Even though we have every right to protect our property, my father was afraid of getting sued by an unfortunate poacher. The fence is fifteen feet high and barbed on the top. And to answer your question, I have no idea how this guy keeps getting on the property. There's a good chance he could've crawled under it or cut a hole in it. I'm going to have the company that installed it come inspect it and repair it if it's been damaged."

"Is there any other way he could be getting onto the property? And why don't you guys have security cameras monitoring those woods?"

Theo opened his mouth to reply but was saved when his cell phone rang. He glanced at it before standing up. "Sorry, Sabrina, we'll have to finish this conversation later. I've got to take this."

He answered his phone and put it between his ear and shoulder as he shoved his iPad into his briefcase and left in a hurry, leaving me feeling like it was just the reprieve he'd needed to avoid answering a very valid question. I planned on asking him again, and he'd better have a good answer. But who was I kidding? Even if he gave me no answer, I couldn't leave. I had no place else to go. I'd thought all I had to do was get away from Bruce, but I'd managed to land in another situation where I didn't feel safe. First that article and now a shadowy figure trying to get into the house. I didn't want to think about what could be next.

FIFTEEN
JARED

Stupid! Stupid! Stupid! What had he been thinking going back to that house last night? This time he knew beyond a shadow of a doubt that she had seen his face. Now the one and only person who could help him was afraid of him, and it was his own dumb ass fault. He had to make this right, and he had to do it now, which meant he was going to have to approach her in the day and plead his case. He drained the dregs of the warm beer he'd been nursing in a dark corner of the bar and left, trying to figure out how he was going to initiate a meeting with Sabrina Adams and realizing he'd have to lie to get her to trust him. By the time he left the bar and was back in his car, he had a plan.

SIXTEEN

SABRINA

I was out running errands and had left Riverside Coffee Bar. I'd just unlocked my car door when the hairs stood up on the back of my neck as the reflection of someone standing behind me filled my driver's side window. It was a man. A man I'd seen recently. I whirled around, almost dropping my mocha latte. The man and I stood staring at each other for several long seconds before I finally found my voice.

"I'm calling the police! Who the hell are you? And what do you want?" I asked the man I instantly recognized from two nights ago. The man who'd been looking into the library. And now here he was waiting by my car as I'd come out of the coffee shop.

"Please, I just want to talk to you," he said, taking a step back. "I really need your help. I swear I won't hurt you." He was standing ten feet from me now with his hands up, trying to show that he meant no harm. But what kind of peeping Tom freak would be peeking into windows at night?

"I'm calling the police." I rummaged around in my purse until I found my cell phone and pulled it out, noticing the alarm on his face as I did so. Good! I wanted him to be scared. I wanted him to feel the way I felt when I saw him peering through the windows that night. He'd scared the shit out of me.

"If I could please have five minutes of your time, ma'am. I know I shouldn't have done what I did the other night, but I've been trying to catch you here in town. I am so sorry. But I need to speak to you. It's very important, please." He took a tentative step forward. "Just five minutes to explain myself and then I'll never bother you again. I swear."

Now that he'd mentioned it, I did remember him trying to flag me down the first time I'd come to town to do my laundry, and me driving away. That still didn't make what he'd done the other night okay. I quickly looked around and realized we were the only two people on the street and the only weapon I had in my hand besides my cell phone was my latte. Was he serious? Was this man seriously thinking I was going to have a conversation with him? I didn't know what to do and he could sense my apprehension.

"Please, I need to talk to you about Theo Dorsey. I think he killed my sister."

Against my better judgment. I found myself sitting on a bench in the nearby town square with the mystery trespasser. We happened to be in front of the Harper's Ferry police station, at his suggestion. His name was Elijah Gamble and according to him, Cherise Gamble, the woman killed in the road that ran behind the Dorsey estate, was his sister.

"You're the one who sent me that article, aren't you?"

He nodded but wouldn't look at me. I was about to ask him how he even knew my name let alone where I lived, but I didn't. It was pretty clear this man had been following me.

"All right," I told him. "You have my attention, and you've got five minutes."

"Like I told you, my name is Elijah Gamble. I'm thirty-two years old and I'm a freelance journalist working on my sister's case. My sister, Cherise, was twenty-four years old when she was struck and killed five years ago in the road that runs behind the Dorseys' estate. The man that hit her had enough alcohol in his system to put him over the legal limit, and for that he was arrested and charged with vehicular manslaughter while under the influence."

"But if he hit your sister, why do you think Theo Dorsey killed her?"

"Because in his statement the driver swears that there was another person there that night who pushed my sister down the embankment and into the path of his car. But since he was under the influence and already had another DUI on his record, the police just figured he was making excuses for it not being his fault. My sister's friends said she was dating a rich guy that none of them had ever met, and two months later she's found dead in the road behind the Dorsey estate. What would you think?"

Having a sister myself, I knew it would be a knee-jerk reaction to think something sinister had happened to her, but what motive would Theo Dorsey have to kill this man's sister?

"I have a sister, Mr. Gamble, so I completely understand how you must feel." That's all I got out before his head whipped around and he glared at me.

"You don't know a damn thing about how I feel! I'm assuming your sister is still alive?"

A lump formed in my throat, and I was instantly ashamed of myself for trivializing his grief.

"I've been telling this story for five years and no one wants to listen. You were my last hope and now I see that this has been a big mistake."

He got up to go and I felt horrible. This was a man who was grieving and grief was making him do stupid, reckless things.

Maybe all he needed was a friend. Someone to listen to him and acknowledge his pain.

"Mr. Gamble!" I called out after him. "Wait." He turned slowly and gave me a weary look, like it had cost him something to tell me what he had and now he had nothing left. "I am so sorry. Please come back and let's talk some more about why you think Theo Dorsey killed your sister."

Not surprisingly he was reluctant to return but eventually sat back down. "Thanks. And I'm sorry. I shouldn't have yelled at you like that after you were gracious enough to talk to me after I scared you the other night."

"Tell me about your sister. You said her name was Cherise? You must've been close, right?"

I'm not sure what I said to make his shoulders slump the way they did, and tears to fill his eyes, but I was immediately worried that I had somehow offended him further.

"I wasn't the brother I should've been. Too busy with my own shit. You think you have all the time in the world to make things right and then you don't, and it eats you up inside. Cherise was a sweetheart. Kind, beautiful and smart. And I'm not just saying that because she was my little sister. I'm saying it because it was the absolute truth. She was on a full ride scholarship at Indiana University. She wanted to be a librarian, with an emphasis on archives management."

The word librarian instantly made my stomach knot up. Another librarian, or rather an aspiring librarian, with a link to the Dorseys. What was going on? Elijah was quiet for a minute as he looked down at the ground.

"Go on," I prodded gently.

"She was about to graduate library school from Indiana University and was really looking forward to starting her career. She told me she got an internship at a private library, but I had no idea it was for the Dorsey family until after she had died."

Theo hadn't told me a single thing about this young woman

other than she'd died on the road behind the estate. Had he been afraid he'd scare me off? But why even bring it up at all if he wasn't going to tell me the truth. Unless he had no idea who Cherise Gamble was. Could Mrs. Manning have hired her?

"And how did you find out she'd gotten an internship working in the Dorseys' private library?"

"I was the one who went through her things after she died. My mom and dad couldn't bear to do it. She was the light of their lives and they've never been the same since her death. I found an appointment in her planner scheduled for the day she died with the initials TD and hearts inked around it. Given where she was found, what else was I supposed to think?" He pulled a picture up on his phone and handed it to me.

I glanced down into the smiling face of a beautiful young woman, her hair pulled into a messy top knot with long tendrils framing her face and highlighting her wide, deep dimpled smile. Her brown skin glowed. It wasn't a posed shot. It had been captured at a party and it didn't look like she knew she was being photographed. She was a lovely young woman, and my heart ached for the stranger sitting next to me who was pleading for my help to find out what had happened to her and why her life had been cut short. Did I believe that Theo Dorsey had anything to do with this woman's death? I didn't know. But I did know that this man would not stop looking for answers and desperately needed closure. Was it because of my own relationship with my sister and the regrets that I had over it, or was I just a sucker? Either way I gave the phone back to him and nodded slowly.

"I'm not sure how I can help you, but I'll do what I can." When he gave me a grateful smile and let out a sigh of relief, I wondered what I'd just gotten myself into.

Although I had agreed to help Elijah Gamble find out what had happened to his sister Cherise, I was at a loss as to how to start. Elijah texted me the pictures he'd taken of her planner, which I pulled up on my phone when I got back to my room. It read: *Internship meeting with TD*. There were hearts and smiley faces on this entry. Elijah seemed to think that the day she died was the day she was supposed to start her internship. If that was true, why had Theo lied to me? And what had caused Cherise to flee the house through the woods to her death? Who was the person the man who hit her saw? Had he really seen anyone or was it like the police thought and he was just drunk and trying to make excuses for what he'd done while under the influence? And then there was Theo.

Did I dare approach him about this? Accusing my boss of contributing to the death of a woman wouldn't do much for our relationship, and might even get me fired, and I was determined to see this job through. Though, I had agreed to help Elijah, and I was going to keep my word. If for no other reason than I didn't want him stalking me again. I got that he was desperate, but that was not cool. Before going back to the estate, I headed back to the public library and pulled up Cherise Gamble's obituary. It was accompanied by a different picture to the one Elijah had showed me. This looked like a professional headshot that would've been on a site like LinkedIn.

She wore a red suit with a cream-colored camisole underneath. Her hair was loose around her shoulders and although she was still smiling, it wasn't the carefree smile from the picture Elijah showed me. She looked professional, and capable. The obit listed her as being survived by her loving parents Russell and Marilyn Gamble and her brother Elijah. She received a BA in museum and archival studies from Xavier University and had been attending graduate school at Indiana University. From the comments left under the obit, she had been very loved and popular with dozens of people saying how much they would miss her. Despite myself, I felt tears coming on. What had happened to this beautiful young woman? More importantly, how could I find out?

. . .

Back at the estate, I'd been working feverishly in the library for two hours, my mind racing with all kinds of possibilities and fears, when there was a soft knock at the door.

"Come in," I called out, and was surprised to see Luca standing in the doorway looking hesitant and shy.

"Hi, it's Luca, right?" The girl nodded and I could feel myself getting a little irritated because I didn't have time to pull words out of her about what she wanted.

Turns out I didn't have to. Mrs. Manning quickly appeared behind her. It was the first time I'd seen her since the night I'd called the police, and she looked uncomfortable as well.

"Mr. Dorsey said that you needed some help cleaning books? I've sent Luca to help you if you don't mind?" I got the impression that it wouldn't matter if I did mind. Luca had been sent to help me and that was exactly what she was going to do even though I had expressly told Theo to give me a week. But, she was here now and to be honest I really did need help, especially since I was about to go poking my nose in matters that didn't involve me.

Why I felt obligated to give a stranger closure was beyond me, but I'd given him my word and now I had no choice but to help Elijah Gamble find out what had happened to his sister. The sound of someone clearing their voice snapped me out of my thoughts and I realized that I'd been staring off into space. Mrs. Manning was gone, and Luca was now staring at me expectedly.

"Welcome to the library, Luca. I'm so happy you're here because, as you can see," I said, gesturing to the three levels of shelving that made up the library, "I really need the help."

But I may as well have been talking to the wall because, with Mrs. Manning gone, Luca's curiosity had taken over and she was now wandering amongst the stacks, looking around like she'd just walked into Aladdin's treasure cave. I instantly knew a fellow reader when I saw one.

"Wow. This is amazing," she said softly as she perused the shelves with me trailing behind her. I'd assumed she was one of those teens that probably thought the library was boring and nerdy and had no interest in books or reading. I was happy to be wrong. She gave me a grin that transformed her. She was a pretty girl, but shy and awkward, and I suddenly felt a kinship with her because I could see so much of myself as a teen in her.

"Most of these books are pretty dirty and I'm going to need you to help me clean them as well as the shelves. And trust me, I know how tempting it's going to be to hide in a corner and read, but I really need to get these books cleaned before I can do anything else with them. Got it?"

"Got it," she said absently as she traveled a finger along one of the shelves and pulled back a dirty digit. She looked at me with a frown.

"How'd this place get so dirty? Mrs. Manning has cleaners come in and clean twice a week."

"This was Theo's mom's private space, and it hasn't been touched in years. You've never been in here?"

"Are you kidding? I've lived here six years, and I didn't even know this existed." She looked a bit sad, like a juicy secret had been kept from her and she was wondering why.

I wondered too, but the last thing I needed was another mystery on my plate. I gestured her to one of the empty carts by my desk. "I need you to take this cart to the end of the first range where I left off and fill it up with as many books as you can, and then I'll tell you what to do next. With both of us working together, we should be able to get through the books by the end of the summer."

"Cool," she replied and headed off with the cart.

· · ·

With the two of us working steadily, two hours flew by and before I knew it was almost time for dinner.

"Thanks, Luca. You were a big help today. Will I see you at dinner tonight?"

"Nope," she said absently as she climbed the stairs.

"So, I guess I'll see you when? Mrs. Manning didn't say how often you were allowed to help me."

"Manning said I can come every day because you really needed help, so I'll see you tomorrow...?" She paused, and I gave her a curious look.

"I don't even know what to call you, Miss Adams or Sabrina."

"You can call me Sabrina."

She turned to go when I remembered something. "Hey, Luca." She turned. "I think I found something of yours in my room."

"Huh?" She looked confused.

"When you were in my room the day we met, remember? I found a turtle charm under my bed, and I thought it might be yours. It's in my room. I can go get it."

Luca frantically shook her head. "It's not mine. I don't wear jewelry. Never have."

"Oh, I just thought it might be yours because I saw you looking under my bed and thought maybe it had come off of a charm bracelet or something."

Something behind her eyes closed, but it only lasted an instant before she gave me a big smile. "I thought I saw a mouse run into your room and went in to look. Sorry, that charm isn't mine." She headed up the steps and out the door before I could ask her anything else.

Dinner was awkward since the buffer between me and Mrs. Manning, aka Theo, was out for the evening once again. I wondered if he was with the woman I'd seen him having sex with in his study, and then I thought about Cherise Gamble. I doubted she'd lacked for male attention. But judging by the woman I'd seen Theo with the other night, he had a different type than sweet pretty Cherise. From the brief glimpse I'd gotten of the woman, she looked high maintenance. I'd caught sight of expensive-looking diamond hoop earrings and remembered the smell of her expensive perfume and the large butterfly tattoo covering her left shoulder. Her shoes had been kicked onto the floor and from their red bottoms I could tell they were Louboutin's; not a cheap chick by any standard. Once a man had a type, they usually stuck to it, either that or some place-holder to fill the slot until they could find what they were looking for.

In understanding this about Theo, I also realized I was not his type. I guessed she could've just been a one-night stand but why bring her here? I was so wrapped up in thinking about all of this that I managed to make it through half of my dinner without saying a single word to Mrs. Manning. She cleared her throat, and I jumped.

"I didn't mean to startle you, Sabrina." I think it was the first time she'd actually called me by my first name and not Miss Adams.

"No problem. I just have a lot on my mind."

"I hope one of those things isn't quitting. I know this is over-due, but I really am sorry about the other night. Of course, you had every right to call the police if there was a trespasser on the premises. I really hope you'll stay on. It's very important that Mrs. Dorsey's library be preserved and restored. After all, it was her legacy to this family."

"Thank you. I appreciate that. I was just so startled and calling 911 was just a knee-jerk reaction. But you're right," I admitted, "I should have called you or Mr. Dorsey after I'd called the police." I wasn't as angry as I had been, especially after what Theo had told me about Mrs. Manning's past. It was true what they said about everyone fighting a battle you can't see.

I noticed the older woman looked a lot more relaxed. It was on the tip of my tongue to ask her about Cherise Gamble, but she spoke up before I could.

"How do you think Luca is going to work out for you? She seemed really excited when I asked her if she was interested in helping you."

"She did a great job today and is looking forward to coming back tomorrow. Thank you for sending her because she's going to be a big help." I could tell what I said pleased her because she smiled and nodded and turned her attention back to her food.

Tonight's dinner was braised pork chops with mushroom gravy over garlicky polenta. Mushrooms weren't my favorite. But I didn't dare waste it. I dug in determined to finish it all and was surprised at how good it was.

"It's nice to see young people excited about reading, don't you think?" she asked before putting a forkful of polenta into her mouth.

"Absolutely. Books saved my life when I was growing up." That admission had just fallen out of my mouth, and I noticed Mrs. Manning's eyebrows raise. Why had I said that? It just opened space for her to ask questions I didn't really want to answer.

"How so?"

"Well, my sister and I are fifteen years apart in age and didn't grow up together. By the time I was four, she was in the military. I was a lonely kid, and books were my friends."

"That sounds a bit like Mr. Dorsey and his sister. There's a ten-year age gap there. But by all accounts, they were very close. Well, at least they were before her accident."

"If you don't mind me asking, what happened?"

Mrs. Manning's lips tightened, making me regret that I'd asked her something so personal.

"Sorry, that's none of my business."

"No, it's not that. It's just what happened still makes me so angry."

I stopped eating and waited for her to continue. It was almost a minute before she was able to go on.

"Belle was always very sweet and naïve. Always had her head in a book and didn't really know the ways of the world. She was the perfect victim for a man who did nothing but use her. He seduced her and talked her into running away with him, but they needed money to finance their new life, and he talked her into selling some valuable books that her mother had left her. Her father got wind of what was going on and paid him to go away and he took the money. After he'd spent it all, he came back a few years later and wormed his way back into Belle's life and convinced her to elope. It was foggy the night he'd come to get her, and they got into an accident. When the police arrived, the only person they could find in the car was Belle. The man who claimed to love her was nowhere to be found. He'd left her there to die."

"And she's been disabled ever since?"

"Disabled is a nice way of putting it, Miss Adams. She is in a vegetative state. I know she's still in there. She responds to the sound of her name but little else."

"I am so sorry. How could he just leave her like that?"

"Because he was a greedy, gold-digging social climber who thought he could use Belle to better his way of life." The bitterness in her voice was understandable. "Belle hasn't had an easy life. I know people think that, because she comes from a wealthy family, her life was easy, but Martin kept a tight rein on her and she didn't have the freedom many young women her age did. I've often wondered what would've happened if she'd been allowed to travel and do all the things she'd wanted to do before that bastard got a hold of her." Mrs. Manning's eyes filled with tears, and she quickly dabbed them away with her napkin before suddenly looking embarrassed. I could tell she'd realized she'd revealed too much and locked her feelings away behind her steely gaze. "Are you ready for dessert? Apple pie and ice cream tonight."

"Sounds great." She picked up our plates, then after rinsing and putting them in the dishwasher, disappeared into the pantry.

As I was getting ready for bed, I saw that I had a text from Elijah and was instantly annoyed. It had been less than twenty-four hours since I'd offered to help him and I'm not sure what he thought I'd find out in that short amount of time.

> Anything yet?

> This is going to take time. I'll be in contact as soon as I find out anything that might be important.

> Sorry, just feeling a little anxious. I know you're going out on a limb and risking your job to help me. I'll wait until I hear from you. Good night.

> Thank you for understanding and good night to you too.

That night I had another nightmare. I was in the passenger side of a car speeding down a twisty road. At least I thought it was a road because it was foggy, and I could barely see two feet beyond the car's front bumper. But when I looked over at the driver, I was surprised to see it was Theo.

"Slow down," I screamed. "We're going to crash!"

I looked out the windshield to see that the fog had turned into thick black smoke. It seeped into the car, and I began to cough and choke. When I looked at Theo, it was no longer him behind the wheel, it was my sister, Cami, and her hair was on fire. I woke up with a start. It was 3:30 in the morning and my heart was racing. Once my heart rate returned to normal, I pulled the covers over my head, too afraid to move for the rest of the night.

SEVENTEEN

BELLE

She didn't like the new night nurse at all. The previous nurse had been nice and talked to her like she was a human being and not a heap of bedbound flesh. Of course, she was imitating a heap of bedbound flesh so no one would know she was getting better. The previous nurse would open the curtains and windows, let in fresh air, and sit and talk to her about her day and even read to her. This new nurse didn't do any of those things, probably because she thought no one was home behind the staring eyes of the woman she was taking care of. The only good thing about the new nurse was that she didn't spend much time in her room which meant Belle didn't have to pretend for as long as she had to with the previous nurse.

As nice as the young woman had been, she was always glad to see her go now that she was recovering, and as much as she didn't like this new woman, she was glad the woman didn't seem to take any interest in her beyond what she'd been hired to do. She wondered what they would do, especially him, if they knew that she could now move her arms and legs and had even sat up on her own for almost a minute. She was surprised at how quickly she was regaining the strength in her limbs. When you had nothing to do but lie and look at the ceiling twenty-four seven you had nothing but time to exercise. The housekeeper had always wondered why she was covered with sweat when she came in every morning, not realizing how obsessively Belle had been clenching and unclenching her fists and toes and lifting her limbs. She could now bend her knees and arms. It wouldn't be long now before she could get out of this bed and this house forever.

EIGHTEEN
SABRINA

"Sabrina Adams? Is that you?"

I turned at the sound of my name. I'd just left the laundromat and was about to put the basket with my folded laundry into my trunk. I didn't have many clothes and needed to do laundry every few days. I didn't mind wearing the same stuff more than once, but since I'd started working at the Dorseys, my clothes were always dust covered. This was the second time in a week I'd had to do laundry. Next time I'd just buy some more clothes.

The person calling out my name wasn't instantly recognizable, but as she walked toward me and looked me up and down, followed by a smile that revealed an abundance of perfectly straight white teeth like a predator, I remembered who she was. I hadn't seen Kylie Mills since high school and that hadn't bothered me a bit since she'd bullied me, making high school torture.

"Kylie?" I gave her a tight smile that didn't reach my eyes and hoped that she'd notice I was less than thrilled to see her.

It had been eleven years since we graduated from high school, and I hadn't been to either of the two reunions because high school was a time I wanted to forget.

"Yeah, it's me, girl. Come here and give me a hug." She didn't even wait for my reply and pulled me into a stiff, awkward embrace that I didn't return.

It would never occur to this girl, or rather woman, as I guess we both were now, that people weren't exactly happy to see her. Kylie was queen of the backhanded compliments, and the flat-out insults disguised as jokes.

"Been a long time. How have you been?" I gently extricated myself from her grasp and took in her tight jeans, high-heeled sandals, and black T-shirt with the word babe emblazoned across her chest in tiny red rhinestones. Her shoulder-length hair was wavy and platinum blonde, accentuating her green eyes and tan. They enhanced her already sharp features and made her look like a fox, and not the cute furry kind that frolicked through the woods in cartoons. More like the ones that killed chickens.

"Did you hear? I got engaged." She held out her left hand where a three-carat pear-shaped solitaire glinted up at me.

The ring didn't shine half as brightly as Kylie's smile. It was probably one of the only genuine smiles I'd seen on her face until it morphed into a sneer accompanied by a glance at my empty ring finger. I quickly turned and put the basket into my trunk and closed it. I didn't have to wonder what she thought about seeing me at the laundromat. I knew she was taking in my cheap clothes, my car that had seen better days, and my ringless finger, and instantly knew that I wasn't winning.

"Congratulations." I made sure to sound extra enthusiastic and happy for her because the last thing I needed was her trying to set me up with some loser because she thought I was sad and lonely.

I could already see the gears in her brain working overtime trying to figure out who she knew that she could fix me up with.

"So, who's the lucky guy?" I asked to distract her from whatever evil she was plotting. "Do I know him?" I added when she didn't answer right away.

"You don't know him. I met him when I bought my house. His name is Jack Preston and he's a realtor here in town."

"Wow. A new house and a fiancé? You are so lucky. I'm so happy for you, Kylie."

"Yeah," she said, giving me another once-over. "I am very lucky. But enough about me, girl. What is going on with you? I was so sorry to hear about your..."

"Thanks," I said, quickly cutting her off much like I had Jo. I wasn't in the mood to deal with this chick's performative grief.

Because she obviously hadn't been sorry enough to have reached out to me or attended the viewing or even sent flowers. But whatever. Like I said, it's not like we'd been friends.

"I am doing just fine. I just started a new job recently and I'm really enjoying it."

"Where?" She was looking at me skeptically like I was Tommy from that old nineties sitcom *Martin*. The friend who no one knew what he did for a living, or if he even had a job at all.

"I'm working for the Dorsey family. I'm restoring their private library." Kylie looked momentarily impressed, but it didn't last long.

"That is amazing, Sabrina. I heard you got a master's, right? Something about the science of books, wasn't it?"

"Library science. I'm a professional librarian."

"Oh wow, I didn't realize you needed a master's degree to work in a library. I thought all you guys did was read books all day." She threw her head back and laughed.

I had walked right into that one and it had taken the last bit of energy I had after working all day to even talk to this chick. It was time to shut this down. "It was so wonderful to see you, Kylie," I said as I opened my car door. "Good luck with the wedding. And tell your fiancé I said good luck too."

Kylie looked slightly confused by my dig, and I could tell it had gone right over her head. Undaunted by my attempt to leave, she followed me as she dug into her big leather purse, standing in the way of my clean getaway as I got behind the wheel of my car. I purposefully ignored her, but she tapped on my window with a stiletto-nailed finger. I reluctantly lowered my window.

"Here." She thrust a cream-colored envelope at me.

"What's this?" I just stared at it already knowing what it was. The last time Kylie had invited me to a party was on her sixteenth birthday. I'd been so excited that popular Kylie Mills had invited me to her party. But the wrong address had been purposefully put on the invitation. I'd shown up in my party dress at the house across the street owned by the neighborhood crazy lady who turned her garden hose on me to get me off her property while Kylie and her guests were on her front porch screaming with laughter.

"It's an invitation to my engagement party this weekend. It's in Cincinnati. We rented a riverboat and we're having a band and everything. You need to come, Sabrina. Promise me you'll come."

"Uh... I." She'd caught me off guard and I couldn't think of an excuse quick enough.

"Great! I'll see you Saturday!" And then she was gone.

"Shit."

I didn't feel like going back to the estate, so I called Mrs. Manning and left a message on the house phone that I would be dining in town. Only, I didn't go to eat. I went straight to the Cat's Eye Bar, which had been my mother's old stomping ground and was now my sister's. Sure enough she was sitting at the end of the bar with a beer. When she saw me walking toward her, she did a double take.

"Is everything okay, Brina? What the hell are you doing in here?"

For a split second seeing my sister sitting in the exact same spot my mom used to sit at in this bar made me think that it was her and tears started to fill my eyes before I blinked them away. My mother and I hadn't been close like that. But she was still my mother, the only one I'll ever have, and I missed her, warts and all. Now it seemed my sister was determined to follow in her footsteps as the local barfly. But I guess it was better than the alternative of going home to Bruce.

"Nothing's wrong. I just wanted to see a friendly face." Friendly wasn't exactly how I would describe my sister. Wary, yes. Suspicious, yes. Grumpy, absolutely. But she was my sister, and after what I'd been through at the Dorseys, and then Elijah Gamble, followed by that idiot Kylie, I needed my own people and Cami was all I had.

The bartender came down and gave me an inquiring look, but since I'd probably be driving home within the next half an hour after my sister said something to piss me off, I simply said, "Sprite with a cherry, please." My sister rolled her eyes, but I didn't care. It may not bother her if she got a DUI, but I doubted Theo would let me continue to work for him if I got one.

I filled her in on my encounter with Kylie and was expecting sympathy. Instead, she laughed, and I realized she was already well on her way to being drunk off her ass. Still, it felt good to tell someone because in the retelling I realized how funny it had been, and I laughed with her.

"She belong to that Mills family with ten kids?" Cami asked with a slight frown.

"Yeah, that's her."

"I went to high school with her oldest brother Donnie. Sounds like they're both variations on the same theme, popular, not too bright, and peaked in high school." She took a long sip of her beer and then wiped her mouth with the back of her hand.

It occurred to me that Kylie had never told me, as she was

cracking jokes about my profession, what *she* was doing for a living, but I didn't recall her having much ambition in high school beyond being popular.

"You going to go to her engagement party?"

"Hell no. I don't go looking for ways to be humiliated. I'll pass."

"You should go." I gave my sister a hard look and she pressed on. "No, I'm serious, Brina. You should really go. How often do you get a chance to hang with people your own age. It will do you good after being up at that mansion working with those uppity assholes."

It was on the tip of my tongue to defend the Dorseys, but I didn't. Despite Elijah's theory, Theo was very down to earth and had been nothing but kind to me so far. Mrs. Manning, on the other hand, was uppity as hell with absolutely no reason to be when she was the hired help just like me.

"No, thanks. I'm good."

"Okay then. What are your plans for the weekend?"

"I don't know." I hadn't meant to snap at her, but my tone amused her, and a smirk lifted one side of her mouth that irritated me even more.

She took another sip of her beer. I wondered if I should offer to drive her home, but I knew she'd just refuse.

"All right, forget that you probably went to high school with most of the people who'll be there, and they treated you like shit. That was years ago, and they could've changed. Plus, you never know who might be able to point you in the direction of your next job. You aren't going to be working for the Dorseys forever, right? You need to be thinking ahead. Didn't you say Kylie's fiancé was a realtor?"

"Yeah, why?" But I knew why she was asking, and she had an excellent point.

Kylie's fiancé might be able to point me in the direction of other wealthy families with private libraries that needed restoring like the Dorseys. If I went and made the rounds and chatted about what I was doing, other opportunities could present themselves.

"I guess that makes sense," I agreed reluctantly.

"Damn straight. Use those fuckers! I'm not saying you should go to try and make friends. I'm saying, go there to rub elbows and make connections with people who might be able to help you."

"Are you okay, sis?" Cami still looked tired, and I wondered if there was something else going on with Bruce.

"Same old shit. Different day." She wouldn't look at me.

"Did that woman come back? I thought you shut that down."

"No. She hasn't been back. And if she did come back, I'd tell her she could have his ass, because he's sure no good to me anymore without that check he gets every month."

I opened my mouth to suggest that she leave again when she held up a hand to stop me.

"And enough with the asking me why I don't leave because, again, you know why."

I did know why and I'm not even sure why I brought this up because what she was telling me was the truth. At least for the time being she was trapped in that house with Bruce.

"Will you at least think about going to the party?" I knew she was just trying to change the subject because she didn't want to talk about Bruce anymore, so I didn't push.

Besides, she did have a point. I used to pride myself on only making friends that I had common interests with, whose company I enjoyed. But in my current situation with a temporary job, I needed to get out there and align myself with people who could offer me some new opportunities.

"I'll think about it." I drained my Sprite and got up to go when my sister grabbed me by my sleeve.

"Promise me, Brina. You need this, you really do."

"I promise," I assured her, and then headed out of the bar to the feel of her eyes on my back.

I grabbed some fast food before heading back to the estate and sat and ate it in my car. As I was driving past the public library, I noticed it was still open for at least another half an hour. I went inside and signed up for some computer time and could tell the librarian working the media center desk was not happy to see me, probably afraid I was going to be there past closing time.

"We close in twenty-five minutes," she said instead of a greeting.

"I just need to print something out. I'll just be ten minutes," I assured her, which caused her to relax and give me a smile.

I went to one of the computers and printed out Cherise Gamble's obit. Then as an afterthought, pulled up social media accounts for her parents who had a joint Facebook page they hadn't posted on since 2019. Their page was private, but their profile had a picture of their daughter's funeral program. There were at least fifty comments under it leaving condolences. I perused them but didn't see anything that jumped out at me, and I certainly didn't see a condolence left by Theo. I scrolled all the way to the end of the comments and saw one that merely said: *I love you and I will miss you for the rest of my life. Love J.*

I wondered who this person was and if they were male or female. If it was a man, did he know about her and Theo Dorsey? Next, I searched for any social media accounts belonging to her brother Elijah Gamble. The only thing I found was an abandoned Facebook account that hadn't been updated since 2018. It showed that Elijah Gamble was teaching English in South Korea. When had he left Korea? It was also a private page, and I couldn't access any of the pictures. His profile image was a tree with cherry blossoms.

Cherise Gamble's social media pages had been untouched, her last post being two days before her death. Again, lots of comments saying how much they would miss her and how unfair life was. I got everything I wanted printed out with five minutes to spare and sailed out of the media room to the librarian's grateful smile, and heard her lock the door behind me even though there were still a few minutes left until closing. I wasn't mad at her. I'd been there a million times myself when I'd worked here.

I got back to the estate around eleven and found Theo and Mrs. Manning in the TV room, and from the tension in the air, I could tell that I'd walked in on a disagreement. Mrs. Manning's face was hard and closed off, her lips were in a tight thin line. Theo looked exasperated, like he was at his wits' end with his intense gaze locked onto Mrs. Manning. What had I just walked into? They both looked at me when I walked into the living room, instantly stuffing their emotions behind phony smiles, but I could tell they were not happy to see me.

"Sabrina, we missed you at dinner." Mrs. Manning got up from the couch to greet me, purposefully ignoring Theo.

"I left a message on the landline. Didn't you get it?" I was instantly on the defensive after the last time I'd missed dinner.

"Yes, of course. Did you have a nice dinner out?" She couldn't have cared less about what I ate for dinner. She was just making small talk to fill the uncomfortable silence that had cropped up between her and Theo. What in the world could they have been arguing about? Was it about Belle again?

"I just grabbed some fast food while I was out and stopped by to see my sister. I'm sorry to have missed dinner because I know it was excellent."

"Don't worry," Theo said, getting up from the couch. "You'll be having it for lunch tomorrow. Waste not, want not."

He walked out of the room and Mrs. Manning's eyes instantly filled with tears. She quickly turned away from me to head back to her room, and then stopped and turned back to me with her eyes still glistening.

"I made a peach pie. It's in the pantry and there's vanilla ice cream in the freezer if you haven't had dessert. Help yourself. I'm going to bed."

She was gone before I even had a chance to say thank you and good night. I had to resist the impulse to follow Theo into his study, especially since every time I looked at his study, I thought about what I saw him doing with that woman. Who was she? And more importantly, why did I care? Instead, I went into the pantry and cut myself a wedge of pie, topping it with a big scoop of vanilla bean ice cream that looked homemade. I was half finished with my pie when Theo came into the kitchen and sat down at the island opposite me after getting his own slice of pie.

"Everything okay? That looked kind of intense back there."

"Don't get me wrong, I love Mrs. Manning to death, but sometimes she oversteps."

"Is this about Belle again?"

"What?" Theo's fork stopped halfway to his mouth, his eyes narrowed, and I realized I'd just revealed that I'd been eavesdropping on their conversation the morning after I'd arrived.

"You told me she still has high hopes that Belle will make a full recovery, remember?" I said casually, easily covering my tracks and feeling relieved as Theo's face relaxed. He took a big bite of pie and nodded.

"I want a specialist to evaluate her. I don't think she's getting the care that she needs, and Mrs. Manning thinks that being at home around familiar surroundings is going to cure her. I honestly don't know what she's thinking sometimes. Not when we have the money to get her the best care possible."

"She might just be afraid of what the specialist has to say.

Sounds like right now she's still holding on to hope and sometimes when hope is all people have, they hold on to it with both hands."

Theo was quiet for a moment before slowly nodding his head. "Yeah, you're right. I certainly don't want to take Belle away from her, but I just don't think it's fair to Belle when she could be in a facility that could offer her more stimulation and therapy than what she's getting here."

"She has a doctor, right? What does her doctor think?"

"I haven't talked to her doctor in a while. Mrs. Manning takes care of all Belle's appointments. I'm going to have to make a point to schedule some time to speak with her doctor because I have some very real concerns."

"Such as?"

"I'm sure you don't want to hear about our boring family drama, Sabrina. And I apologize for bothering you with it."

He'd just politely told me to mind my own business, but it was too late for that after he'd already confided in me what the problem was. He couldn't put the genie back in the bottle now that it was out.

"Seriously. You can talk to me. It's not like I have anyone to tell." At least not anyone that would get it. I was pretty sure my sister would enjoy hearing about the Dorseys' family problems.

"My biggest concern is that even if my sister does regain consciousness, she's going to need therapy, and I just don't think this house is the place for her to make a full recovery. She needs to be in a facility with round the clock care with professionals that can help her make a full recovery if that is even possible. Not a housekeeper and a nurse who's just there to tend to her basic needs and be there in case something happens."

"Completely understandable. I know Mrs. Manning means well and that she cares and she's holding out hope, but, in the end, this is about Belle, right? I think you need to do what you think is right for your sister."

Theo stopped eating for a minute before giving me a smile. "Thanks, I do feel a lot better now, and I do plan to do what's right for my sister despite what Mrs. Manning thinks. I've been trying to encourage her to retire."

"Really? Do you think part of her reluctance in letting Belle go is that she thinks she'll no longer have a purpose here? Do you think she's afraid of losing her job?"

He thought about it for several long seconds before responding. "Can I let you in on a little secret?"

"Sure. What's up?"

"I'm thinking about selling the estate. It's one of the reasons I hired you to restore the library, because it will add value to the house."

"What?" My eyes widened in shock. "Why? This estate has been in your family for years."

I'd grown up poor with a mother who raised me and Cami alone, and worked double shifts to pay the bills. My clothes came from thrift stores and outdated hand-me-downs from my sister. I'd lost count of how many times our utilities were shut off growing up or how we lived off boxed mac n cheese, canned soup, and bologna sandwiches paired with the free chips and cookies my mom got from work. If I'd grown up on this beautiful estate surrounded by luxury, you'd need to use dynamite to get me out of here. But I guess if you grew up with all of this, it would be easy to take it for granted.

"Like I said, I'm just thinking about it. If I do sell, it wouldn't be for a few years at least. Not until after Luca graduates from high school."

"And Mrs. Manning?"

"It would be nice to see her enjoy herself and maybe do some traveling. Her whole life has been this family and that was fine with my father, but it's not okay with me."

"What was your father like?" I had a pretty good idea what Martin Dorsey was like. The words that I'd heard in reference to him were always the same: a ruthless, cold-hearted, cut-throat businessman and, according to my sister, a cheap ass.

"Let's just say my dad was an experience, an experience that could be hard for some people to deal with."

He didn't explain further and didn't need to. I could only imagine what being one of Martin Dorsey's children must've been like. I looked at Theo's plate and realized he'd inhaled his pie in a few bites. Then he wiped his mouth and gave me another killer smile.

"I've got a busy day of back-to-back budget and investor meetings tomorrow, so I probably won't see you, but thanks for listening. I appreciate you. He reached out and stroked my cheek, then walked out of the room, leaving behind the warm imprint of his fingers. Once he was gone, I finally let out the breath I was holding. What had just happened? I was glad he was gone because I'm sure my face was flaming, though it wasn't like I hadn't been touched by men before.

"Get a grip, Sabrina," I whispered to myself as I finished my pie and half-melted ice cream.

NINETEEN
SABRINA

Kylie and her fiancé Jack's engagement party was being hosted on a boat called the *River Queen* that was docked at Newport Landing. I was lined up with the other guests to board on Saturday night at around six, wondering what I was doing there. I regretted having let my sister talk me into this. I wore a dress that I'd only worn once before Mom had gotten really sick and needed around-the-clock care. It was a purple strapless dress with a thigh-high slit at the front. I had on strappy gold sandals and carried a gold metallic clutch. My braids were loose around my shoulders, and I was already starting to sweat in the humid August heat. So far, I hadn't recognized anyone from high school and if anyone had noticed me, which was doubtful, they'd kept it to themselves.

Finally, we were allowed to board, and I made a beeline straight for the bar, telling myself that I would just have one drink to calm my nerves. Armed with a white wine spritzer, I headed over to the railing and watched the dock disappear from sight as the music started to play. Nothing too wild, mostly pop songs mixed with a little R&B by the DJ, a tatted up white guy whose muscles couldn't possibly have been built by spinning tunes. I wondered where the live band Kylie claimed they were having was, and wondered if they'd run out of money.

The guests were a mix of couples, predominantly white and affluent-looking. I was one of maybe three black people in attendance along with a few Asians and several Hispanics. The fact that there were any non-white guests at all surprised me. I figured they must be Jack's friends since Kylie hadn't been big on diversity back when I'd known her. She'd tormented me in high school until finally one day I couldn't take it anymore and accused her of being a racist bitch. She'd replied that she wasn't picking on me because I was black, she was picking on me because I was a freak who didn't talk to anyone and always had my nose in a book. She did at least leave me alone after that and found other people to torment.

About an hour into the party, Jack and Kylie thanked everyone for coming and for all the gifts, gesturing to a long table laden with gifts. Not knowing what to get for a chick I knew probably had everything already, I'd purchased a $50 gift card from The Book Barn out of spite and put the pink envelope on the table on my way to the buffet. I had to admit, at least they knew how to put on a spread. I hadn't eaten since breakfast and loaded my plate with beef medallions, asparagus, and roasted potatoes, then found a quiet corner to eat. I was half finished eating when I felt a hand on my back and jumped.

"Sabrina, I'm so glad you came."

Kylie looked like a million bucks in a form-fitting pink halter dress that amplified her big chest and fell to her ankles. Her platform ankle strap pumps were covered in gold glitter. She even smelled like money. Was she truly happy I was there? Of course she was. I was just another witness to her fab life, but I could play the game just like she could because I wanted something too.

"Thanks for inviting me. You look amazing, but then again you always do."

"And I love your dress, Sabrina. You need to dress like this more often. Seriously. Because if you did, I'd be going to your engagement party."

Good old Kylie, she'd always been the queen of the backhanded compliment, but with my stomach full and the slight buzz I'd gotten from the white wine spritzer, I didn't care as long as she introduced me to her realtor fiancé. I hoped it was soon because I wanted to leave just as soon as we docked.

"So, where's that handsome fiancé of yours?"

At the mention of the word fiancé, Kylie quickly turned and called out to a man a few feet away. He cut his conversation short to rush over to her side.

"Babe, this is my friend from high school, Sabrina Adams. Sabrina, this is my fiancé, Jack Preston."

"So nice to meet you, Sabrina." Jack held out his hand and gave mine a firm shake. It shouldn't have surprised me that, although he had the body of a younger man, Jack looked a good twenty years older than Kylie and was Botoxed to the gills. But he seemed kind and was clearly crazy about her. I just hated to think what would happen if he ever ran out of money.

"Nice meeting you too, Jack. Kylie tells me you're in real estate?"

"That's right." He wrapped his arm around Kylie's waist and pulled her close, kissing her on the cheek.

"Sabrina's a private librarian. She's working on the Dorsey family's library," said Kylie, grabbing a glass of pink champagne from a passing server.

At the mention of the Dorsey name, Jack's eyes widened and his politeness, which had been perfunctory, turned warmer as he looked at me with renewed interest.

"Is that so? Then I need to be getting your contact details, Sabrina. A lot of my clients buy houses with libraries they don't know what the hell to do with. I could pass along your name if you'd like."

"Yeah, that would be great. Thank you," I said, trying to keep my cool. "I'm contracted with the Dorseys for the next two years, but I could do some consulting if they'd like." I handed him one of the light gray business cards that I had thrown together and printed at Office Max before I came. It read: *Adams Library Consulting, LLC, cataloging, inventory, appraisal, and renovation. Sabrina Adams MLIS, proprietor,* along with my contact info. Did I have an LLC? No. Did I have an MLIS? No. Did I own my own business? I did now.

"Awesome." Jack took my card and barely gave it a glance before tucking it into the inside pocket of his rose-colored suit jacket.

I had a sinking feeling that he probably wouldn't find the card again until he got the suit dry-cleaned, if ever, but I couldn't do any more than what I'd already done. Jack and Kylie excused themselves to mingle with the rest of the guests, and I realized I had at least another two hours before we docked, when the party would move to a local bar near the docks, which I would not be attending. Per my usual party MO, I sat in a corner nursing another white wine spritzer and people-watched, expertly dodging conversation and invitations to dance from random drunk men. When the party came to an end, and we docked, I sat back and watched, not wanting to get caught up in the mass exodus, and spotted a familiar figure coming down from the upper deck of the boat. It was a bald black man with a goatee. It was Elijah Gamble.

What was he doing here? Had he followed me? I could feel my anger rising, then I realized I'd had more to drink than I normally did and maybe I was mistaken. After everyone left, I walked up and said to Kylie, "Hey, thanks again for inviting me. Do you know the black guy that I just saw coming from the upper deck? Bald, brown skin, goatee? I think his name is Elijah. Elijah Gamble?"

"Elijah? I don't know any Elijah. But a lot of these people

are Jack's friends," she replied with a shrug. Jack overheard our conversation and my description of Elijah.

"You must be referring to my buddy Jared. Jared Green. We met at the gym. He's a homicide detective with Cincinnati PD."

Jared Green? I thanked Kylie and Jack again for inviting me and left, planning to walk around for a while until my buzz wore off. I was walking down the path of the Riverwalk when it finally hit me. He was the J who had left the broken heart emoji on Cherise Gamble's parents' Facebook post, which meant he was not her brother.

After I'd somewhat calmed down, I went and sat in my car. Feeling much more sober, I realized I must've made a mistake and the man I saw on the boat was not the man who had introduced himself to me as Elijah Gamble. There was only one way to find out. I pulled out my phone from my bag and brought up the name Jared Green. The only social media profile was on Facebook, and it hadn't been updated in over a year. It wasn't a private page and there were plenty of pictures verifying that the man who was passing himself off as the brother of a dead woman was in fact Jared Green.

How could I have been so stupid? Obviously, no member of the family had been driving the car that had killed Cherise. But who had she been running from that night and why had she been on the Dorsey property? I should've checked out Elijah or whatever the hell his real name was before I had agreed to help him. I didn't want to think about what would happen if Theo or Mrs. Manning found out I'd agreed to help this man.

As I sat in my car lost in thought, my phone pinged with a text. Inevitably it was fake Elijah.

Anything?

We need to talk tomorrow morning at nine.
Coffee shop downtown.

You found something, didn't you?

Yes, I did.

It never occurred to me to be worried about how he might respond to the fact that I never wanted to see his ass again. All I knew was that I wanted out of this deal with the devil.

"I can explain." Jared Green looked around the crowded coffee shop and then lowered his voice. "Please, Sabrina, just let me explain."

"Explain what? It's pretty self-explanatory to me, Detective Green. So, was Cherise Gamble your fiancée, friend with benefits, or someone you were stalking? Because she sure as hell wasn't your sister."

"No, Cherise was not my sister. I am so sorry that I lied, but I thought if you knew that she was my ex-fiancée, you would think I was just obsessed and couldn't accept the fact that I'd been dumped for a rich guy."

"I guess we'll never find out now, will we? You made that decision for me without even giving me the benefit of the doubt." Of course, he was right, I wouldn't have given him the time of the day if I'd found out who he really was, but that was beside the point. The man had lied to me.

"I'm sorry. I really am. But I still need your help."

"I could have risked my job trying to help you. And you have no idea how badly I need this job."

"Can you at least tell me if you found out anything at all about Cherise?" I ignored the desperation in his voice and the sorrow in his eyes. That was how he'd fooled me from the beginning. I wasn't falling for it again.

"No, Mr. Green. I haven't found out a single thing about Cherise. And now that I think about it, how do I know it wasn't you who chased her into the road that night? How do I know you weren't jealous and followed her to the Dorsey estate, then chased her through the woods and into the road?" He looked like I'd just slapped him and was speechless as he stared at me in shock.

I got up and slung my purse over my shoulder. "I'm sorry about your ex-fiancée. Maybe you should see a therapist to help you get over your grief. Because I can't help you."

I expected him to stop me, but I got to my car and looked back to see him sitting at the table with his face buried in his hands. Dammit. I forced myself to look away, get into my car and start it. Feeling sorry for this lying asshole could have gotten me fired. It was time I got back to work.

Baldwin and Murray book appraisers was located on a quiet side street in downtown Cincinnati just a few blocks from the Duke Energy Center. I couldn't take any of the books out of the house to be appraised, but after what I'd just been through with Jared Green, I needed a field trip. Mrs. Manning sounded slightly annoyed when I called and told her I'd be gone all day and wouldn't be home until after dinner. But I didn't have time to worry about what her problem was, or what rule I may have broken this time.

As it turned out, Sarah Murray, daughter of one of the original owners of the business, ran it solely as her father, George Murray, and his business partner, Thomas Baldwin, were both long dead.

"You don't actually have the books with you?" Sarah Murray looked a bit surprised.

"No. Sorry, ma'am. I'm working for a private collection and my contract stipulates that I not take the books off the property.

But I have pictures." I pulled up the pictures of the books in question on my phone and handed it to her.

Sarah Murray was a big woman, not fat, but tall and stocky with graying brown hair pulled into a ponytail that hung down her back with sparse bangs and a large mole on her cheek.

"Well, I can tell you right off the bat that any library markings, barcodes, or stamps, as well as there being no dust covers greatly reduces the value of these books."

"Really?" I'd been so excited about getting these books appraised and now I felt like someone had stuck a pin in me.

"Now, mind you, they aren't worthless. They just aren't worth what they would've been in better condition. Based on these pictures I'd put them close to ten grand a piece."

"Just out of curiosity, what would they be worth if they were in pristine condition?"

"Are you sure you want to know?"

I hesitated for just an instant before replying, "Yes."

"Between thirty and fifty thousand per book."

I let out a low whistle and Sarah Murray nodded sympathetically. "I know, right? You wouldn't think those small things would detract so much from the value, but they do."

"I had no idea," I told her, regretting that I'd asked. Ignorance was bliss.

"Can I ask you something?" Sarah Murray looked at me expectantly.

"Sure."

"Are you working for the Dorsey estate?"

"How did you know?"

"Because I never forget a rare book. No matter who comes in here trying to either sell or buy I remember every single book since I took over the business from my dad when he died a decade ago. And I know these books. I recognize the markings and the wear and tear. I'm sure I sold one of these books to the Dorseys," she said, handing me back my phone.

"Does that mean that someone from the Dorsey estate was in here having these same books appraised?"

"Not to have them appraised. He came to try and sell them to me."

"Who?"

"Young guy about your age. Said he was a librarian working in the Dorseys' private library."

"Did he have permission from Martin Dorsey?"

"I seriously doubt it, which is why I contacted Martin Dorsey when he left. He told me that he had not authorized any sales from the collection."

"Did you know Lorraine Dorsey?"

"I didn't, but my dad did. She was a regular customer here. Anytime we had any classics by a black author, my dad called her first because she was building her collection and was interested. She was one of our biggest customers, at least while she was alive."

"Would you happen to know the name of the other librarian who was trying to sell the books?" I'm not sure why I was asking when I knew it had to have been Myles Patterson.

"That would be confidential information, Miss...?"

"Adams. Sabrina Adams."

"As much as I'd love to tell you, Miss Adams. I can't."

"Of course you can't. I'm sorry I even asked and thank you for the appraisal."

"Would you be interested in hearing when we get any books you might want to add to the Dorsey collection? I can make the same deal with you that my dad made with Lorraine Dorsey."

"Absolutely. And thank you."

I gave her my business card and was about to turn to go when she looked me straight in the eye and grabbed a notepad with the shop's logo on it from next to the register, then scribbled out something and handed it to me. It was an address.

"I can't give you a name. But you might find who you're looking for at this address."

"You remember his address after all this time?"

"I have an eidetic memory. I remember everything."

On my way home, I went to the address Sarah Murray had given me. It was a small run-down house in a neighborhood of mostly abandoned and run-down houses. There was a FOR SALE sign in the overgrown front yard. Whoever had lived here was long gone.

TWENTY
JARED

Detective Jared Green stared at his therapist impassively. He'd been seeing Dr. Rhonda Collier for a few years now and for the most part he liked and trusted her, which he couldn't say about most people in his life these days. Ever since he blew up at work and was told to get help or get lost by his sergeant, he'd upped his sessions with Dr. Collier. His anger management issues were threatening his job and had already ended a few of his friendships. He knew what the problem was but didn't want to admit it to himself. It was the guilt of all the ways he had failed the woman he'd loved, causing her to end their engagement and fall in love with the man who killed her.

"Jared, did you hear what I just asked you?"

"Yeah, I heard you." He looked down at his hands instead of at her because he knew she wouldn't let him off the hook until he answered her question.

"Jared?"

"I'm just tired, that's all."

"Of what exactly?"

"Of you and everyone else thinking I'm using Cherise's

death as an excuse to be angry at the world. Everyone thinking I don't want to accept the truth that her death was an accident."

Dr. Collier had asked him what he thought his life would look like now if Cherise hadn't died. Which was just another way of asking him if he was using his ex-fiancée's death as an excuse for everything that had gone wrong in his life. What was wrong with him wanting to know what happened to her? Why was he the only one seeking answers? After her funeral her brother, Elijah, had gone straight back to Korea where he'd lived for a decade teaching English. Her parents were so distraught that no one dared talk about her around them. That meant it was up to him, and him alone, to get the closure that no one else seemed to need. Dr. Collier's expression softened as she sat her notebook down on the table next to her.

"How's your personal life going? Have you started dating again?"

"If by dating you mean am I regularly spending time socially with the opposite sex, the answer is no." He wasn't about to tell her that his interactions with women since Cherise died consisted of casual encounters and situationships with women he had no serious interest in. That would have to be something they unpacked in another session.

"I thought we were making progress, Jared, but lately it seems like you're angrier than ever. What's happened? Because, frankly, I feel like we're almost back at square one."

Jared leaned back in his chair and put his hands over his face. "What happened is that I think what happened to Cherise is happening all over again."

"By happening again, do you mean you think Theo Dorsey will kill again?"

"Exactly."

"You're a police detective, is there any solid evidence for what you're feeling?"

"No. Not yet," he admitted reluctantly, thinking about how

he'd alienated the one person who had been willing to help him by lying to her. How could he ever get Sabrina Adams to trust him again? He needed her back on his side.

Jared already knew he sounded irrational. His colleagues at the station had labeled his obsession with Theo Dorsey as just that, an obsession. Jared had considered it a gut feeling. A cop's intuition or whatever else she wanted to call it, but he knew he was right. Just as he also knew that this time, he had to stop it. There wasn't much he wouldn't do to see Theo Dorsey pay for what happened to Cherise, even if it meant taking matters into his own hands.

TWENTY-ONE

SABRINA

With Luca's help, we were barreling through the shelves of dusty books at a much faster pace than if I had been doing it on my own. One of the reasons we were able to go so fast was because Luca wasn't a talker. Without small talk and banter, we were able to get so much more done. Luca's main focus was the books. She couldn't have cared less about me, and I knew it was because she was a teenager and considered me an old woman at twenty-nine. I could see so much of myself in her when I was her age. The awkwardness, the shyness, and the living in my own head most of the time. Spending time around her, I realized what other people around me must've seen when I had been so strange as a kid. Things turned out okay with me and I'm sure they would with Luca too. She only had a couple more years of high school and then she'd be free to do whatever the hell she wanted, but I remember being her age and thinking that day would never come.

I had returned to my desk to take a sip of the bottled water I always had with me while I worked because the air in the library was so dry and dusty, and I was always thirsty. I happened to look up and see Luca pulling something from

behind the books on the shelf that we were currently working on.

"Hey!" she called out, waving what looked like a dingy
canvas bag in the air. "Look what I found."

I walked over to where she was standing and took the bag
from her. It was a canvas tote bag, with brown leather handles
and two interlocking Cs on the front. I opened it up and inside
found a notebook, a pair of sunglasses, and a thin brown leather
wallet with the same interlocking Cs on it. As I flipped through
the wallet and found a photo ID, I quickly realized that it wasn't
interlocking letter Cs on the wallet and on the front of the tote.
It was an interlocking C and G. The bottom dropped out of my
stomach. I was holding Cherise Gamble's driver's license in my
hand. Jared Green's ex-fiancée, Cherise Gamble, had been in
this house. Not just this house. She'd been in the library.

Theo was in a very chatty mood at dinner. Regaling me with the
details of his day. I was barely paying attention because all I
could think about was the tote bag that I'd found, or rather Luca
had found, in the library hidden behind the books on one of the
shelves. Could the tote have been found in the woods behind
the property? Even so, who had hidden it in the library? I'd
locked the tote bag and its contents in my desk drawer in the
library, trying to figure out how I was going to bring up the
subject with Theo. There was no easy way to say *hey, I found
that dead girl's tote hidden in the library, the one you claim not to
have known.* Theo sensed my unease and had been staring at
me for I don't know how long before I realized he'd stopped
talking.

"Everything all right, Sabrina?" he asked casually around a
mouthful of prime rib.

As usual, the meal was amazing, fork tender and melt-in-
your mouth delicious, but it may as well have been sawdust for

as much as I was appreciating it. He waited for my response, and I had to dig deep to figure out how to explain my change in mood.

"I'm good," I assured him. "Just a bit of a headache. I think it might be allergies from all the dust in the library." It wasn't a complete lie. I wasn't feeling well, but not because of allergies. I was struggling with whether I should call Jared Green and tell him what I'd found. But he'd lied to me, and all his credibility had vaporized like mist.

"I can have Doc Hill write you a prescription for some allergy meds if you'd like. You do have healthcare through us for as long as you work here, remember?"

"I already have a prescription for allergy meds. They make me sleepy, so I only take it at night."

"Let me know if you change your mind. He's due back here to check on Belle next week and if you're still having problems, you should talk to him."

"I will, thanks." I forced down the rest of my food because the last thing I needed was Mrs. Manning side-eyeing me over an unfinished plate of food.

I was headed to my room after dinner when Theo stopped me. "It's a beautiful night. Would you like to go for a drive? I just got my Porsche serviced and want to blow it out on the back roads."

At first, I wasn't sure what to say. Had he somehow found out about us finding the tote bag? I didn't say anything, but Luca could have in a casual conversation.

"You don't have to come if you don't want to." Theo laughed and I realized I was being weird.

"No. I'd love to. I've never been in a Porsche before."

"Then let's go."

. . .

Theo was an excellent driver, handling the Porsche like a race car driver. Before I knew it, I was smiling and laughing as he raced up and down the hills making the bottom drop out of my stomach the way it did when Cami would take me for drives when I was a kid.

Once we reached a spot overlooking the river, Theo stopped and we got out. I'd grown up in Harper's Ferry and had never been to this spot. Then again, I never had a reason to come to this section of town, where all the elite families of Harper's Ferry lived overlooking the city. It was beautiful. The river was calm and still under a gorgeous full moon with the sound of crickets and the crunch of our footsteps through the gravel cutting through the silence.

"I've never been here before. This is gorgeous."

"Yeah, I come here a lot when I need to clear my head and think. Lately I've been here a lot."

"Is this about your sister?"

He nodded and continued to stare out across the river with an unreadable look on his face, half of it cast in shadow, since the only light illuminating the spot we were in was from the moon.

"Mrs. Manning still giving you grief about wanting to move Belle?"

"I haven't told her that I found a specialist for her to see in Louisville. She has an appointment next week. Now I just have to figure out how to get her there behind Mrs. Manning's back."

"I don't mean to sound like a snob, but doesn't Mrs. Manning work for you and your family? You have every right to do what you feel is best for your sister."

"It's a lot more complicated than that."

I waited for him to expand but he didn't, and something told me to leave it alone. Besides, I was still trying to figure out how to bring up what I'd found in the library. He needed to know that something that belonged to a woman killed on the road behind his estate was found in his house. Something was holding me back. I kicked myself because I knew exactly what it was. I was so attracted to this man I couldn't believe that he could've possibly done anything wrong to Cherise Gamble or anyone else. I remembered it was called the halo effect, from one of my psychology classes during my undergrad years at Ohio University. Today we called it pretty privilege where society is biased toward attractive people, assuming they have good qualities simply for being attractive. I was doing the same damned thing. It was a good thing I didn't feel threatened by Theo because here I was in the middle of the night several miles away from the estate, alone with him. But all I could think about was when he touched my cheek the other night, wondering what it would feel like if he'd done more.

"Sabrina? Earth to Sabrina."

"I'm sorry, what did you say?"

He laughed. It was a deep throated rumble that turned my insides to mush. Instead of answering me, he tilted my chin up and gave me a kiss. Not a sloppy groping tongue kiss, but a soft peck on the lips that left a lingering warmth behind just like his fingers on my cheek had.

"Sorry. I shouldn't have done that." He looked down at the ground, but he hardly looked sorry.

"No, you shouldn't have. I work for you, and I need this job. I can't have things getting complicated. Besides, Mrs. Manning would kill me."

I couldn't believe what had just come out of my mouth when a second before I had been fantasizing about him kissing me. But I wasn't wrong. Messing around with my boss could get complicated really quick, especially since he was seeing other women. Was that woman I saw him with the other night his girlfriend? He started to say something else when I held up a hand and stopped him and asked him what I should've asked him before I got in the car with him.

"I saw you with someone in your study the night I moved in. I didn't mean to spy on you, but I couldn't sleep and heard you in your study. Is she your girlfriend?"

He gave me an *I'm busted* look. "Yeah, about that. I thought I heard someone out in the foyer. I was hoping it wasn't you."

"Hey, you can do whatever you want in your house. You're a grown man, and besides you don't even really know me."

"You're absolutely right. In my defense, and you have absolutely no reason to believe me, I'd had a bit too much to drink and met that woman at a bar. I can't even remember what her name was, and I know that makes me look like a giant asshole, but we'd both had too much to drink. We didn't exchange numbers, and she went home in an Uber. And to answer your question, no, I don't have a girlfriend. I tend to shy away from relationships."

"Why?" But I was sure I knew. You can't be the CEO of a thriving company and not have women after you for your money and what you can give them, especially after what happened to his sister. Theo Dorsey had to be on high alert for gold diggers.

"Because I'm bad luck for any woman who gets too close to me," he mumbled without looking at me. From the way his jaw clenched, I could tell he hadn't meant to say it.

"Bad luck? What do you mean?"

"Never mind." He let out a frustrated sigh, and I let it go even though I was dying to know what he was talking about.

"Does that mean you've never had a serious relationship?"

"Just one," he said with a faraway look in his eyes. "Olivia King. We dated all throughout college and I proposed to her after her first year in med school while I was working on my MBA."

"What happened?"

"Honestly, I have no idea. One minute we were touring

wedding venues because she didn't want to get married at the house. The next thing I know, she's gone."

"What do you mean gone?"

"I mean she left me a note saying she couldn't go through with it, along with her engagement ring, and I haven't seen or heard from Olivia since."

"You didn't go after her?"

"Why? She made it very clear it was over."

"But she's okay, right? She didn't just disappear into thin air, did she?"

"As far as I'm concerned, she did. I have no idea what happened to her. She made a choice, and I respected her choice and stayed away."

Seriously? How could Theo's ex just be gone from his life, and he not try to find her? Unless he knew exactly what had happened to her. Could he have gotten angry when she'd tried to end it and made her disappear? The warm night air had turned cold, and I was anxious to get back to the estate. How could I tell him about what I'd found in the library now? But I couldn't help it. I needed to know more.

"What about Luca's mom? Was she one of those unlucky women who got too close?" If he was offended or insulted, I couldn't tell, but he did respond, which surprised me since it was none of my business.

"Heather Harris was my high school girlfriend junior year. We only dated for a hot minute because we quickly realized we made better friends. She got pregnant and left school, and we lost touch for a while."

"So, you're not Luca's...?" I let my voice trail off because the implication of what I was asking was clear.

"Father? No. We were sixteen and never progressed beyond making out. I didn't see Heather again until after I graduated college. She contacted me asking for money and when I met up with her, it was obvious that she needed it for drugs. Luca was eight years old, and I have no idea who her father is. Heather was in a bad way. Instead of giving her money, I got her into rehab. Luckily, she was able to get her life back together. She always had an amazing singing voice. She worked a lot of low paying jobs after rehab, but when Luca was ten, she got a good paying gig as a singer on a cruise ship. Her parents had disowned her when she got pregnant so sending Luca to live with them was out of the question. She left her with us, where she's been for the last six years."

"Is this going to be a permanent situation for Luca?"

"Trust me," he said, shaking his head. "Luca is much better off with us. Heather loves her daughter, but motherhood completely overwhelmed her. This is the best situation for both of them. She gets the freedom to do what she has always loved doing and Luca gets a stable loving home."

"Why isn't she in school?"

"She was for a while but didn't fit in and was being bullied so bad we were scared for her emotional state. She still attends classes online and both her grades and mental health are better for it."

"Poor kid."

"She's doing just fine now and in a couple years I think she'll be ready to go to college. Even if she isn't, she'll always have a home with us."

"Good. I'm glad to hear it. She seems like such a sweet kid."

"She is. Was there a reason you were asking about Luca? How are things going with her helping you in the library?"

"Great," I said honestly. "She's helping me out a lot."

"Glad to hear it. I was a little worried you'd be mad when I sent her to help you, but I'm glad it's working out. Luca's a loner and it's good for her to be around people on a regular basis. Have you started the book?" he asked, catching me off guard.

"Not yet. I usually read every night before bed, but I've been really tired." I wasn't about to admit I'd snuck a book out from the library. In all honesty, I was still so flattered about the gift and his confession, it would take me a while to stop smiling whenever I saw the book on my bedside table.

"No problem. Just let me know because I'm anxious to hear your thoughts. It's getting late. We should probably get going." He headed back to the car, and I trailed behind him.

The drive home was uncomfortably quiet. Theo's mood seemed to have changed, and we didn't speak again until we arrived back at the house. I was lost in thought myself and regretting I'd ever told Jared Green anything about Theo Dorsey. There was a good chance that Cherise had never even been in the house. She could've been trespassing on the property. The gatekeeper could've chased her, she could've dropped her tote as she was running and simply tripped and rolled down the embankment into the path of the car. But why didn't I believe that? So far, everything Theo had told me made perfect sense. Maybe that was what was bothering me. Maybe it made too much sense.

TWENTY-TWO

BELLE

She was stronger and didn't have to hide her pills underneath the sheets. Now she could shove them through a hole in her mattress, but she was worried they knew she was getting better. The nurse was staying longer than she normally did and Belle felt like she was being watched. It had been days since she'd been able to do her exercises and stretch her muscles. She worried she was going to lose every bit of progress she'd made. She wracked her brain trying to figure out if she'd somehow given herself away. Now the night nurse who used to just give her meds, check her vitals, and leave, was staying for more than an hour after she'd given her the medication. She could no longer pretend to take it and spit it out on the sheet.

The pills began to dissolve in her warm mouth until she felt herself drift away into nothingness. When she woke up hours later, sometimes the nurse would still be sitting in the chair reading a book or crocheting. But last night she was stunned to see him sitting in the chair by her bed when she opened her eyes. What was he doing there? He rarely ever came to see her. She could count on half of one hand the times that he had. Was he feeling guilty? He should. It was all his fault. Everything was his fault. He was asleep in the chair and could be there until morning if he didn't wake up.

She did her exercises with a watchful eye on him. She did everything short of lifting her arms and legs, too afraid the movement would cause the bed to creak and wake him up. But she had no choice. She couldn't stop now. She'd lose all the progress she had gained over the last few months.

By the time she was done, she was covered in sweat. As he stirred in the seat and began to wake up, she quickly closed her eyes, happy that the room was shrouded in darkness, and he couldn't see how her hair stuck to her damp forehead.

She heard him take a step closer to the bed. He stroked her damp cheek, and it took everything in her not to flinch. She heard his footsteps heading toward the door and the click of it closing behind him. Yet something told her, practically screamed at her, not to open her eyes. She lay there for five minutes unmoving when she heard another soft click of the door. She realized with horror that it had been a trap, and he'd just pretended to leave. She kept her eyes shut for another five minutes, almost falling asleep, as tired as she was from her exercises. Eventually, she forced herself to open her eyes and was relieved to find herself alone in the room. He was gone. But now she knew that he suspected she was no longer as sick and as helpless as she had been.

She needed to try to leave soon.

TWENTY-THREE
SABRINA

The decision on what to do with Cherise Gamble's tote bag was taken out of my hands when I arrived to work in the library the next morning. The tote was gone. I pulled out the drawer I'd put it in the night before, thinking maybe it had somehow fallen behind, but I knew even before I pulled out the drawer that the tote was gone.

Someone in this house had taken it. Was it Theo? Mrs. Manning? Because that would mean one of them had to have known it was there. Was I being spied on? Then the answer to my question walked in ready for work. I was about to launch into a diatribe accusing the kid of stealing, when I saw what was hanging off Luca's shoulder. It was a black canvas tote bag with brown leather handles. What I first thought were misshapen white polka dots covering the bag turned out to be tiny skull and crossbones.

"Look what my mom sent me from Greece." This was the first time I'd seen Luca this animated and happy. My urge to grill her about the tote instantly evaporated in the face of her joy.

"That is gorgeous, Luca."

"I know, right? I told my mom last month that I needed a new bag, but I didn't think she was paying attention. Guess I was wrong, huh?"

I didn't have the heart to bring up if she knew anything about the other tote going missing without making it sound like I was accusing her of something. Then I remembered, I'd taken pictures of the tote, and everything in it, before locking it in my desk drawer. After I got Luca busy working on the next set of shelves, I pulled up the pictures on my phone, happy that they were still there and I hadn't lost my mind and imagined the whole thing.

Later that night, after Mrs. Manning had retired for the evening, I approached Theo as he sat in the TV room watching the news. Most people I knew got all their news online from social media. I didn't know too many people who even got the newspaper anymore. But here Theo was, watching the news on TV like I remember my grandparents doing when they were alive.

"Look at you, Mr. Old School." I don't know why I was acting so lighthearted when I was about to bring up something that was anything but.

He turned to me and smiled, but things were still a bit awkward between us after what happened last night. This was the reason why you didn't mess around with the boss.

"Yeah, I know watching the news on TV shouldn't be relaxing but it is. At least for me. It's nice knowing that my petty problems are nothing compared to what's going on in other people's lives."

I sat down on the couch on the other side of the granite coffee table. I glanced at the TV screen to see the usual gloom and doom, lying politicians, murders, thefts, and natural disasters. I was just about to show him my phone with the pictures of the tote when the anchor, a grim-faced white man with a comb-over, introduced the next segment. A man named Danny Hampton was crying and appealing to the public for information about his missing wife.

Jennifer Lynn Hampton, thirty-seven, and a mother of two had been missing for five days. She'd gone out to a bar with some friends after work and hadn't been seen since. They showed a picture of Jennifer: she was an attractive woman with golden brown skin and curly natural hair. It was the description of her distinguishing features that made my blood run cold. Jennifer Hampton had a butterfly tattoo on her left shoulder. There was even a picture of the tattoo on her shoulder. I instantly looked over at Theo who was scrolling on his phone and not paying attention to the TV. Bile rose up in the back of my throat.

I got up and practically ran out of the room, barely making it to the bathroom before throwing up. Jennifer Hampton was the woman I'd seen Theo having sex with in his study. Was she the reason he wanted to sell the estate? First Cherise and now Jennifer? Did Jennifer even leave this house that night, could she still be here somewhere? Was that the real reason Theo had that scratch on the back of his neck? Did Jennifer put it there when she tried to fight back?

Once my stomach was empty, I looked at myself in the mirror and saw that my eyes were watery, and my face was flushed. I brushed my teeth and splashed cold water on my face. I left the bathroom and almost jumped out of my skin at seeing Theo waiting for me down the hall with a look of concern.

"What's going on? You ran out of the room like you saw a ghost."

I couldn't look at him. Instead, I rubbed my stomach. "Something obviously did not agree with me, but it's all gone now. I should go to bed. I didn't get much sleep last night."

"You sure? There's an urgent care about ten miles from here and I'm happy to take you if you need me to."

"Thanks, but I just need a good night's sleep. I'll see you in the morning. Good night." I quickly slipped into my room and shut the door behind me before he could say anything else. But I already knew I wasn't going to sleep tonight.

"I knew it! I knew he did something to her."

I was sitting across from Jared Green at the Cat's Eye Bar the next afternoon, still wondering if I was doing the right thing by showing him what I'd found. He stared intently at the pictures of the tote bag and its contents on my phone with a manic gleam in his eyes that scared me.

"There is absolutely no proof that anyone in that house did anything to Cherise."

"Are you insane? How else would her bag have gotten into that house if she hadn't been there?"

"Someone could've found it in the woods behind the house." I was playing devil's advocate because even though things looked bad for Theo, every angle needed to be explored and Jared had tunnel vision.

Plus, it was true; someone could have found her bag in the woods after the accident. What I couldn't explain was how it came to be hidden in the Dorseys' library, because people didn't hide things unless they had something they were feeling guilty about.

Jared let out a frustrated sigh and took a long swig of his beer. I could tell it was taking everything for him not to scream at me. I got it. I did. But once we went down this road, there was no turning back and we needed to be absolutely sure. Just like I needed to be absolutely sure that Theo had something to do with the disappearance of Jennifer Hampton, the woman I'd seen on the news last night.

I thought back on last night and realized the sound of the news anchor pronouncing Jennifer's name stirred absolutely no response in Theo, who had been scrolling on his phone at the time. Surely, he would've looked up and been shocked at the sound of her name if he had known what her name was? I distinctly remembered him saying that he didn't know her name and that it had been a drunken one-night stand. Was he telling the truth?

"Look," Jared said, lowering his voice above the din of the live band that had started to play. "I get that you're in a tough spot with this, but you need to be thinking about your safety. You could be in danger too."

He was right. Something might have happened to Theo's ex fiancée, Olivia King, too. No one seemed to know what had happened to the previous librarian, Myles Patterson, either. He was also in the wind, whereabouts unknown. Cherise Gamble had been struck and killed by a car on the road that ran behind the Dorsey estate. Now Jennifer Hampton, a married mother of two, who'd had a one-time hookup with Theo, was also missing. All of them were connected to the Dorseys, and all three women were connected to Theo. Common sense should've told me that I needed to start looking for another job if for no other reason than Theo Dorsey might be a serial killer, but I just couldn't wrap my head around that possibility. Jared leaned back in his chair giving me a disgusted look.

"You have got to be kidding me."

"What?"

"Are you screwing him too? Is that why you're so hesitant to believe that he's behind the death of my fiancée?"

Had I just heard this fool right? I sat back in my chair, arms crossed, and glared at him. "Whoever I may or may not be screwing is absolutely none of your business. To answer your question, no, I am not involved in any way other than professionally with Theo Dorsey. You need to watch how the hell you talk to me since I'm the only one who is willing to help you."

He shook his head and took another sip of his beer, and things were awkward for a few minutes before his face softened.

"I'm sorry. It's just that this is the first real lead I've had about what happened to Cherise since she died. I want whoever is responsible to pay for what they did."

We both knew that *whoever* meant Theo Dorsey. I wondered if he'd still want to hang Cherise's death around Theo's neck if she hadn't broken their engagement. How much of this was a search for justice and how much was need for validation to prove to himself that he was the better man, and that Cherise had made a mistake?

"Why did she break off your engagement? Are you one hundred percent certain that it was because of Theo Dorsey? Was she even dating him?"

Knowing what I knew about Theo and his dating history, it wouldn't have surprised me if Cherise had been a one-night stand who caught feelings and dumped her fiancé because she thought she had a future with Theo.

"Like I said, we were college sweethearts, and I wanted a home and a family with her. Cherise had worked hard in college while holding down more than one job. She told me that she just wanted to have fun for once in her life before settling down into a life of marriage and motherhood. After she gave me my ring back, I found out from one of her friends that she was seeing someone else. Then I went through her planner after she died and saw the appointment with someone whose initials were TD with those red hearts and flowers drawn all over it. And..."

His voice trailed off and I thought back to the photos Jared had sent me of Cherise's planner. I was so caught up in wanting to help this man when I thought Cherise was his sister, and sympathized with his heartbreaking grief, that I'd failed to realize that neither Theo's name nor address had been written in the planner. At least not in the photos he'd sent me. Jared was basing his theory solely on the fact that Cherise's body was found on the road behind the Dorsey Estate and his initials were TD. There were so many things pointing to Theo's guilt. But Jared Green was a liar with an agenda and his determination to see Theo held accountable for his fiancée's death made him unpredictable and possibly dangerous.

"You put two and two together and came up with Theo Dorsey being the reason why she broke your engagement. Did this friend specifically say she was dating Theo Dorsey?"

He wouldn't meet my eyes, and I had my answer. "I know I'm right and there's nothing you can say to convince me that he wasn't involved in this." The rigid set of his jaw told me not to waste my time trying to convince him otherwise.

There was no way that I could tell him about Jennifer Hampton. He'd be ready to arrest Theo in a heartbeat. I thought when I took the job with the Dorseys, I was well on my way to a better life and more opportunities, but my life was now just as complicated and screwed up as it was before I took the job.

"Now what? I'm pretty sure pictures of a tote bag that has gone missing aren't going be enough to reopen Cherise's case."

"I need you to find that tote bag, Sabrina. Please."

I didn't respond and saw an angry twist of his lips. I knew what was coming next. "How do I even know the tote bag is missing? How do I know you didn't get rid of it to protect your boss?"

I'd had enough and got up from the table, slinging my purse over my shoulder. "You don't know. Just like I don't know whether you were the one who chased your ex through those woods to her death."

He didn't try and stop me from leaving, but when I got to my car parked by the curb, I looked back through the bar's picture window and saw him staring at me with a look of regret. Whether it was regret over having insulted me and calling me a liar, or regret about what he may have done to his fiancée, I didn't know.

Luca was already hard at work by the time I got back from meeting with Jared. She had her earbuds in and had barely acknowledged my return. I, on the other hand, was surprised to see that I had a voicemail message from a woman named Sharon Claremont. True to his word, Kylie's fiancé Jack had given her my card and she needed someone to come for a consultation on her home library. There was nothing in my contract with the Dorseys saying I couldn't work for other people. I wasn't going to turn down an opportunity like that, especially if I had to quit this job, and quickly called her back and made a lunch appointment for Friday. Even though I had no intention of turning down this job, I wasn't going to do it on the Dorseys' time.

As I worked, downloading the software and unpacking barcodes to catalog the books, I heard soft talking. I looked up to see Luca talking into her phone and realized she was making a video. Here I was thinking she was shy. On a whim, I searched on TikTok until I found her account. She had just over 1,000 followers and her account consisted of book reviews, K-pop dance challenges, what she had to eat that day, and telling scary stories in the dark. Her last upload was her in the woods with the flashlight telling a story about a murder. When I saw how she was dressed, I realized she could have been the mysterious person I'd seen in the woods at least one of those times. It may not have always been Jared Green. Since I was pissed at him, I didn't feel bad about my mistake. I had no intention of contacting him with an apology any time soon.

"Hey, is this one of those rare books from that list you were talking about." Luca held out a worn-looking slim volume and I took it from her. It was a hardbound book with a white dust cover and writing on the front in lieu of a cover image. I gasped when I saw it was a signed first edition of Toni Morrison's *The Bluest Eye* in pristine condition.

I quickly consulted the inventory left behind by my predecessor Myles Patterson and noticed that it was not on the list and wondered why. His inventory listed the first thousand books, and Luca and I had only made it through maybe six hundred. So, why hadn't this been on his inventory?

Could this have been one of the books Sarah Murray had said Myles Patterson was trying to sell her? She said she'd called Martin Dorsey and told him about it. This must have been why he was fired, but where were those books now? The only person who knew the answer to these questions was Myles Patterson himself.

TWENTY-FOUR

SABRINA

Mrs. Manning was visiting a sick friend in the hospital, and God only knew where Theo was, so I took the opportunity to search his study for the tote. Once again, I found nothing. I searched through all the trash cans thinking maybe someone had pitched it in there and found nothing but trash. I searched the pantry, the laundry room, and all the spare empty bedrooms on the second floor.

Even though I had told myself I wouldn't search Theo's bedroom, I found myself on the second floor. I had no idea which room was his but figured it was probably the set of double doors at the end of the long hall to my left. The faint sound of a TV was coming from the other end of the hall to my right and I guessed it had to be Luca's room. From where I was standing in the hall, I could see that her door was slightly ajar and before I could talk myself out of it, I walked in the direction of her room. Before I could knock, I looked through the crack in her door to see her sitting at a desk in front of a flat screen computer with a headset on. She was gaming and I knew from living with my sister and her *Call of Duty* addicted husband, not to disturb a gamer while they were gaming.

I quietly backed away from her door and headed for my real destination. A quick glance at the crystal clock on the hall table leading to Theo's master suite told me it was a little after seven. I wasn't sure when Mrs. Manning and Theo would be home, and I certainly didn't want Luca to catch me and snitch. I wanted to get this over with as quickly as possible. I held my breath as I pushed one side of his set of double doors open onto a darkened bedroom. There was a large king size bed in the center with a burgundy bedspread and an abundance of pillows with a burgundy and blue paisley print. The room smelled like his cologne.

I got busy searching under his bed, only finding a bunch of his shoes, then moved on to his armoire and his chest of drawers. I searched his bathroom which was an opulent display of gray tiles and granite, with a huge shower that he could have had an orgy in and a toilet in a separate room. A search of all the bathroom drawers yielded nothing other than his surprising array of skincare for a man. Not that I was judging, but I'd never known a man who used more skincare than me. I refused to search through the luggage stored at the top of the closet and all of his shoeboxes. I crept back out of the room and down the steps to the first floor and ran smack into a woman I'd never seen before. It was on the tip of my tongue to scream, but I noticed she was wearing a nurse's uniform and I realized I had seen her before. This was the nurse I'd seen taking the delivery from the medical supply company a week ago.

"Jesus! You scared me."

"Sorry." She turned and looked up the stairs from where I'd come from and gave me an appraising look. "I'm Ms. Lawson, Miss Belle's night nurse. I was hoping you'd be able to do me a big favor." She was slender, brown-skinned, with blonde twists, and glasses with noticeably thick lenses.

"Yeah, I've heard about you. I'm Sabrina Adams. I work in the library." I held out my hand for her to shake, but she merely stared at it. I quickly dropped it realizing that because of her profession maybe she no longer shook hands. I certainly knew a lot of people who didn't anymore. "What can I help you with?"

"I need to zip out to the all-night pharmacy in town to pick up one of Miss Belle's prescriptions. It didn't get delivered today and she needs it. Would you be able to go up and sit with her while I'm gone?"

I didn't know what the hell to say. Mrs. Manning's instructions were very clear. I was not to go past the second floor. Ever. But surely, she didn't mean in the event of an emergency? It sounded like that's what this was. Ms. Lawson must've sensed my apprehension and let out an exasperated sigh.

"If you're worried about Mrs. Manning, don't be. I'll take the heat if she complains. I know she means well, but Belle could do with some more stimulation besides the two of us. I've been reading a book to her. It's sitting on the nightstand. I shouldn't be gone for longer than half an hour." She didn't even bother waiting for my reply and already had her purse hung over her shoulder and her car keys out, heading toward the garage door before I could protest.

"Her bedroom is at the end of the hall to your right on the third floor," she said over her shoulder.

"Shit," I mumbled under my breath as I went up to the third floor to meet Belle Dorsey.

Despite Mrs. Manning's ridiculous rules, I realized in that instant that I was very happy never to come to this floor. I was getting flashbacks from when I was taking care of my mother during her final days. Although I loved my mother, taking care of her was a challenge and it almost sucked every bit of life and light out of me. She was not ready to die and was understandably bitter, and I was resentful and angry at Cami for not being there. For some odd reason, I thought taking care of her would bring us closer together, but she was combative and noncompli-ant, and every day had been a struggle. The way she treated me made me feel like she was always angry with me, and it didn't hit me until after she'd died that a woman as independent as my mom was probably extremely angry at being dependent on someone else for her most basic needs. I remembered the night I got up to check on her and she had passed away in her sleep. I held her, sobbing like I've never cried before in my life.

I was thinking about my mother as I approached Belle's room, surprised to see that the door was wide open. When I stepped inside, I was even more surprised at how cold the room was. I'm not sure why I was expecting it to be kept hot, as if Belle Dorsey was an exotic flower. The room was spartan with basically just a bed and hospital equipment, and smelled like antiseptic and fresh flowers. I noticed a fresh arrangement on the table by her bedside.

I took a step closer to the bed and saw that the chair near the bedside table had a book lying face down on it. I gingerly picked it up and flipped it over to see the cover. It was *Waiting to Exhale* by Terry McMillan. The surly nurse had good taste in books. I sat the book back down on the chair and finally looked at the woman of the hour. Belle Dorsey lay so still, for a few seconds I wondered if she was still breathing. She had light brown skin and was thin almost to the point of being gaunt, with razor-sharp cheekbones and lips that looked even fuller than they were because of the sunken hollows of her cheeks. Her hair had been buzzed close to her scalp. I imagine it was easier to take care of that way. I wondered why, with all the Dorseys' money, they couldn't have hired someone to come and do her hair on a regular basis. On closer inspection I saw a smat-tering of freckles on her cheeks and across the bridge of her nose.

Her arms rested by her sides on top of the white sheet that was pulled up almost to her chest. Despite her not looking much like her photos in the family room anymore, Belle Dorsey was beautiful. A literal sleeping beauty. But it was her eyes that startled me to the point that I almost took a step back. They were open and stared at nothing. I noticed eyedrops on the nightstand by her bed and realized they were to keep her eyes moist because she didn't blink.

IV poles with saline solution and what I imagined to be some type of liquid sustenance were set up on the left side of the bed. I remembered the story that Mrs. Manning had told me about Belle's accident. It still didn't make any sense. Why would a man who'd snuck back to the house to rescue the love of his life from her tyrant father abandon her after a crash? The only person who knew the answer to that question was lying semi-comatose in a bed, and she wasn't talking.

After staring down at her for a few long minutes, I forced myself away from the bed and sat down in the nurse's vacated seat. I picked up the book, which was one I'd read many times before myself, and started to read aloud. I was on the section where Bernadine was selling all her cheating husband's things for a dollar each. I felt all the hurt and anger on Bernadine's behalf that I'd felt, along with millions of other women, like it was the first time I was reading it. Pausing, I wondered whether Belle Dorsey was aware and awake inside her head but unable to communicate. If so, how was she feeling about that scene in the book? Did it remind her of what happened to her and Myles, the man who'd claimed to love her only to run off and leave her at her most vulnerable?

I continued to read aloud to her, and several chapters later the nurse finally came back with some sort of liquid medication in a brown bottle.

"Thanks," she said, as she poured a measured amount of the liquid into a plastic cup.

She slid an arm under Belle's upper torso and effortlessly lifted her into a semi-sitting position. She put the plastic cup to her lips, tilted it and the liquid disappeared. The nurse wiped away the drop of medication that ended up on her lips and laid her back down. She turned to see me staring at her in shock.

"I thought she was non-responsive? I thought she was in a vegetative state?"

"She is. Most of her actions like opening her eyes and closing them and swallowing are all involuntary actions. She just can't chew and swallow food which is why she's on a feeding tube."

"Then why read to her?"

"Because I for one, and Mrs. Manning agrees with me, believe that she's still in there trying to find her way out. I read to her every day and so does Mrs. Manning. We want to shine a beacon for her to find her way back."

I remembered what Theo told me about getting more help for his sister. Even though he sounded like he wanted what was best for her, I didn't get the impression he thought she was still in there. Before I could ask her thoughts on Theo wanting to put his sister in twenty-four-hour professional care, voices drifted up from the foyer indicating that Theo and Mrs. Manning were home. At the look of alarm on my face, the nurse rolled her eyes and smirked at me.

"Don't worry. Just head to your left when you leave this room. You'll find a back staircase that will take you down to the laundry room. She'll never even know you were up here."

"Thanks." I appreciated her pointing me toward the path of least resistance, but I hadn't appreciated the sarcastic smirk she gave me.

I hurried out of the room, hanging a left until I got to the closed door at the end of the hallway. I quickly opened it and slipped through as I heard Theo and Mrs. Manning's voices arrive on the third floor. I took the staircase down into the laundry room, which was on a lower level, then went up another set of steps into the kitchen. This house had so many rooms, staircases, and back entrances. It was like a maze, and I wondered if that was one of the reasons why Mrs. Manning's rule said I shouldn't wander around the house at night. It was obvious that she was afraid I'd get lost.

Back in my bedroom, I'd just changed into my night clothes when there was a soft knock at the door. I opened it to find Mrs. Manning holding a plate with a thick slice of chocolate cake on it.

"I hadn't seen you all day and just wanted to say hi and bring you this."

I looked at the cake in surprise as she continued. "It's from a fundraiser that I attended tonight with Mr. Dorsey. I can't imagine that it tastes better than my chocolate fudge layer cake, but it seemed to be very popular and I thought you might like a piece. I'll allow you to eat in your room just this once. Please bring the plate to the kitchen in the morning."

"Thank you, Mrs. Manning." I gratefully took the thick slice of cake which probably could've been cut into two portions.

I said good night, took the cake back to the bed and dug in. Mrs. Manning had been right. While the cake was very good, it wasn't nearly as good as her chocolate cake, but chocolate cake was chocolate cake, and I ate every bite. When I was done, I pulled out my cell phone to give my sister a call, but she didn't answer, and I got a message that her mailbox was full. Feeling irritated because I was constantly having to tell her to empty it, I put my phone on the charger and climbed under the sheets. Within minutes, I was asleep and dreaming, although *dream* wasn't the word for what I had that night.

The nightmare was so real. My room was filled with smoke because everything around me was on fire. Smoke filled my nose and mouth, and I could barely catch my breath to scream.

Through the smoke I could see a figure, a dark shadow unfolding itself from the corner of my room and walking toward me through the smoke and flames. I was frozen as the shadowy figure kept getting closer and closer. Finally, when they were barely a foot away from the end of my bed, I let out a shriek that should have shaken the rafters.

Suddenly, all the smoke and flames were gone, and it felt like I was awake, but the shadowy figured remained staring at me from beneath a dark hood pulled over their head. It raised a single index finger to its lips and then calmly walked across my room and disappeared into my closet. I tried to lift my head off the pillow but couldn't. I closed my eyes for what I thought was only a few seconds, but when I opened them again, it was morning and no trace of my nightmare lingered. Still, I couldn't take my eyes off my closet door. I swung my trembling legs over the side of the bed and got up. Not knowing what I was expecting to find, I pressed my ear to the door momentarily before flinging it open to nothing except for my clothes hanging from the metal closet rod. In the cold, harsh light of day, I felt like a complete fool and looked over at the empty cake plate with only a few remaining chocolate crumbs to indicate what had been on it. I was groggy and out of sorts for the rest of the morning, causing Mrs. Manning to put a hand on my forehead in concern.

"Are you sure you're not sick? I knew I shouldn't have given you that cake last night. At my age I can't eat sweets that late, but you're a young woman and I thought it would be okay. I'm sorry if it made you sick."

"Who's sick?" asked Theo, walking into the room dressed to kill in a dark gray three-piece suit. He grabbed an apple from the bowl and put it in his pocket before devouring two pieces of buttered toast.

"I'm fine. I had a bit of a headache. I already took some aspirin. Once I get some coffee in me, I'll be good to go."

Theo and Mrs. Manning exchanged glances before Theo said goodbye and left for a day of meetings.

"Does Luca ever eat breakfast? She can eat toast, fruit, and oatmeal, can't she?"

"Luca stays up all night gaming. It's a miracle if she gets up before 10 a.m.," said Mrs. Manning as she cleared away my barely touched breakfast plate.

I could certainly relate. I remembered when I was her age and stayed up to all hours watching scary movies, at least that was the official excuse. I was really waiting for my mom to make it home safely from the bars, which didn't close until 2 a.m. In high school I made sure my first period was always study hall so I could supplement the four to five hours of sleep I got every night and took a nap when I got home. Did my mom appreciate me waiting up for her to make sure she got home safely? Possibly. I had no idea because she was usually too drunk to communicate by the time she got home. Ironically, she worked second shift and managed to get plenty of sleep.

By ten o'clock that morning, I had managed to clear another section of shelves. After cleaning the books, I lined them up on book carts for Luca to put away when she finally showed up. I was taking another much-needed sip of coffee when I got a notification on my phone. I hoped it was my sister calling to check in, but was met with a news notification. I'd set up notifications on Jennifer Hampton's name. I clicked on the link to see Greg Walters, the Harper's Ferry police chief, reporting that a car matching Jennifer Hampton's had been pulled from the river early that morning with a body inside. While there was no official confirmation that it was Jennifer Hampton, all indications pointed to it being her. This was the outcome I'd feared and suddenly I was cold; I was hoping I was wrong.

. . .

Luca showed up around 1:30 p.m. looking bleary-eyed, peeling an orange which quickly filled the library with its scent. It was what she was wearing that made me do a double take. She was dressed in black warm-up pants with a black hoodie pulled up over her head. I was instantly taken back to the hooded figure in my dream from the night before and my hands started to shake.

"Sabrina?"

When I looked up, she was staring at me like I was crazy, and I shoved my shaking hands into my sweater pockets.

"I think my blood sugar is getting low because I didn't eat my breakfast this morning."

"Here." She handed me another orange that she pulled from her hoodie pocket, and I quickly took it.

For the rest of the day, I kept checking the news to see if there was any more information about Jennifer Hampton. They hadn't officially confirmed that it was her body they'd pulled from the river, but I knew it was. I was so distracted I barely acknowledged when Luca brought me another one of the rare books from the inventory. It was a signed first edition of Zora Neale Hurston's *Mules and Men*. The dust cover was faded, and the edges were torn and raggedy, but the actual book itself was in pristine condition even though the pages had faded to a yellowish color. An online search estimated its worth at $50,000. Even in its less than pristine condition, it would probably fetch at least twenty to thirty thousand. So far, I'd found over $100,000 worth of rare books in this library and had so many more books to go through. Why weren't these books shelved together? Why spread them throughout the collection like this?

Even the excitement of finding another valuable book in the collection was dampened by the death of a woman who'd briefly spent time in this house with my boss, just like Cherise Gamble. And what had really happened to Theo's ex, Olivia King? None of this could be a coincidence, could it? What could I do about it aside from searching through this family's private things and risk losing my job? Was this job even worth holding on to anymore when I no longer felt safe?

I was so busy cleaning and entering books into the new inventory that I hadn't even noticed Luca had left. A quick glance at my watch revealed it was 3:30 and I figured she was probably taking her last class of the day. At least that's what I thought until I saw the tote her mom had sent her sitting on one of the chairs in the small reading room. I went over to retrieve it so I could take it to her, thinking it might have important school-work she needed. It was then I noticed a notebook which had fallen out of the bag onto the floor. I picked it up. It was open to a page of small, neat sentences that read: *Luca Elaine Harris-Dorsey*. The entire page was filled with that name. Suddenly, the notebook was abruptly snatched from my hands.

"What are you doing? You had no right to go through my bag!" Luca's face was red and the look she was giving me could've frozen water.

"I didn't. The notebook was lying on the floor, and I picked it up."

"You're a liar and a snoop! You think I didn't see you on the second floor the other day? You were snooping through Theo's room. I saw you go in there."

"Go in where?" Mrs. Manning had appeared in the doorway to the library, her gaze sliding between Luca and me, waiting for an answer.

My throat was suddenly dry. I didn't know what to say without completely gaslighting this kid. Luca must've realized what would happen if she snitched on me, and her lips clamped shut in a thin angry line before she turned on her heel and rushed up the steps, brushing past Mrs. Manning on her way out the door.

"What in the world was that about?" Mrs. Manning stared after Luca with a look of concern.

"She left her bag behind and her notebook had fallen out. I saw something she didn't want me to see." I had no idea Luca had seen me go into Theo's room. She'd not said one word to me about it.

"Let me guess," said Mrs. Manning, her face softening as she walked down the steps toward me. "You saw her greatest desire in that notebook, didn't you?"

"Greatest desire?"

"Luca is crazy about Theo. She's wanted to be a Dorsey since she moved into this house. Her greatest wish is that her mom and Theo will get married, and she'll get to be Luca Elaine Harris-Dorsey."

"I had no idea. Does Theo know?"

"Yes," she said with a sigh. "He loves Luca and tries to spend as much time with her as he can, but he refuses to lie to her. He and Heather are never going to be a couple again."

"Well, she's only sixteen. Hopefully, she'll grow out of it as she gets older." But would she? I was almost thirty and knew if I ever got married, there was no father, or father figure to walk me down the aisle and it made me sad.

Mrs. Manning looked around before stepping closer to me and lowering her voice. "Heather recently got engaged. She wants to be the one to tell Luca next time she's in town."

"Oh, wow. How do you think she'll take the news?"

"Not well."

Luca was still mad at me, so I was very surprised to find a note slipped under my door after dinner. It read: *meet me in the gazebo in the woods at midnight. I have something to tell you. Luca.*

I stared at the note in confusion, thinking back on the video that I had seen of Luca telling stories at night in the woods. She had to have been sneaking out of the house to do this because I couldn't imagine Theo or Mrs. Manning allowing her out of the house by herself. I wasn't allowed out of the house after midnight, and I was a grown woman. Had Theo given Luca the code to the security system as well? I somehow doubted it. I probably should've told Theo and Mrs. Manning about the note because Luca was a minor and they needed to know. They were both in Cincinnati attending yet another charity gala and would be gone until tomorrow afternoon, and I didn't know what else to do. I headed up to the second floor, surprised to find that Luca was not in her room. I searched the entire second floor, first floor, and the laundry area in the basement. She was nowhere to be found. The only other place she could possibly be was on the third floor and I wasn't about to go up there again. Instead of trying to track her down, I heated up some of the chicken and noodles that Mrs. Manning had left and sat in the kitchen to eat alone. Then I went into my bedroom, set the alarm on my phone, and read for a while until I fell asleep.

TWENTY-FIVE
SABRINA

My alarm woke me at 11:49 p.m. Feeling groggy, I looked around my darkened room, letting my eyes adjust to the darkness, and suddenly remembered the note. I jumped up and went to my window to see Luca dressed in black with her hoodie pulled over her head and a flashlight, heading into the woods. I thought it had been a joke. At least I'd hoped it was a joke, but it looked like she was serious about meeting me tonight. What could she possibly want to tell me in the woods? I grabbed my phone and keys, happy I didn't need to use the security code since Mrs. Manning wasn't home to set it at midnight. Outside, I was plunged into darkness as soon as I reached the tree line. In the distance, I could see the beam of light from Luca's flashlight.

"Luca!" I shouted into the darkness. But the beam of light in the distance never slowed and kept moving forward. "Shit," I mumbled under my breath as I headed into the woods with the flashlight on my phone to guide my way.

I could see about ten feet in front of me at a time clearly. Where was she going? Then I remembered that the note said something about a gazebo in the woods. Sure enough, five minutes of walking and I found it. It was a white gazebo or rather, formerly a white gazebo, because most of the paint had flaked off the lattice work. The steps were broken, and there was a big hole in the roof. I'm sure at one time it had been beautiful, but it had fallen into disrepair. The even bigger problem was that Luca was nowhere to be seen. I looked around wildly but could no longer see the light from her flashlight. That's when I realized I'd been made a fool of. She'd probably lured me into the woods because she was still mad at me over the notebook, and she was safely back in the house, but that didn't keep me from continuing to look for her.

"Luca!" My voice was swallowed up by the dark, dense woods. It only made me call out louder. "Luca! Where are you?"

Still no answer and still no more illumination from her flashlight. Angry and feeling like a fool, I started to head back toward the house. I hopelessly turned around, having no idea which way to go to get back to the house. What was worse, I'd forgotten to charge my phone that day and had less than ten percent charge. If I didn't find my way out of these woods soon, I'd be stuck here in complete darkness. Not wanting to have to hug a tree until daybreak, I slowed my rapid breathing and scanned my surroundings, when I heard the snap of a branch. Something was out there, but was it a person or an animal? I felt like I was being watched. With great effort, I remained still and silent, and listened. Someone or something was moving around. They were circling me.

"Who's out there? Luca, is that you?" The movement stopped. I strained to listen and heard something even more frightening than someone stalking me in the woods. It was the unmistakable sound of laughter. Soft at first, then louder. No, not louder. Closer. Whoever was laughing was getting closer to me. My already rapidly beating heart began pounding so loudly I could hear it in my ears.

"Luca! This isn't funny! Stop it right now or I'm calling Theo."

At the sound of Theo's name, the laughter stopped and a sharp pain exploded in my temple, driving me to my knees. Something had hit me in the head. Whoever was in the woods—and I was pretty sure it had been Luca—had thrown something at me. I touched my temple, and my fingers came away bloody. I heard running feet cutting their way through the woods along with the sounds of snapping twigs and rustling branches. Still thinking it was probably Luca running back to the house, I got to my feet, pain blossoming behind my eyes, as I followed the sound. Sure enough, I found myself exiting the woods. I'd expected to see Luca's figure cutting across the lawn to get back into the house, but there was no one else on the lawn. I was starting to feel faint, and stumbled forward, falling flat on my face. I must've passed out because when I came to, I was still lying on the grass outside the tree line of the woods with an older black man staring down at me. It took me a minute to realize who it was.

"Are you all right, Miss Adams? What happened?" Mr. Pearson, the nighttime groundskeeper, was looking down at me with concern on his face.

I tried to sit up and regretted it as Mr. Pearson gently pushed me back down onto my back.

"Don't move. I'm going to call an ambulance. They should be here soon."

"Ambulance? No, please don't. I'm fine." I sat up fighting the dizziness to show this man that I was fine, and he helped me to my feet.

"Are you sure? You're bleeding. You might have a concussion, and you need stitches."

"Can you drive me to the ER? I don't want to worry Theo and Mrs. Manning."

"What were you doing out here this time of night?"

"I think I must've been sleepwalking," I told him matter-of-factly, feeling a little too proud of myself for coming up with that lame ass excuse so quickly.

I wasn't about to snitch on Luca until I had a chance to talk to her and ask her what the hell she'd been thinking. Had she really thrown something at me?

An hour after Mr. Pearson dropped me at the ER, Theo arrived. I was still in the waiting room amongst about a dozen other people. By now, the cut on my temple had stopped bleeding, but I was left with a throbbing headache.

"Sabrina? Mr. Pearson told me what happened. Are you okay?"

"I'll live. I think Mr. Pearson overreacted. I'm fine." I hated how weak and shaky my voice still sounded, and I couldn't quite look him in the eye.

I knew I should absolutely tell him what had happened with Luca in the woods, but I didn't want to get the kid in trouble. I needed to talk to her first. If I was honest, I was also afraid she was going to snitch on me and tell Theo that I'd been snooping around in his bedroom.

"Mr. Pearson said you were sleepwalking and had an accident in the woods?"

I opened my mouth to reply when I was finally called to an exam room. Theo went with me despite my protests. After cleaning and bandaging my wound and giving me some aspirin for my headache, I was released, feeling highly annoyed because I could've done what they'd done myself. At least I didn't have a concussion. The ride home was silent and after ten minutes, Theo reached out and squeezed my hand.

"How are you feeling?"

"Embarrassed."

"How long have you been sleepwalking?"

"I really appreciate you coming to get me and waiting with me, Theo, but can we talk about this later? I'm fried."

"No problem. You just lay back and try and get some rest. We'll be home soon."

Once we were home, Theo walked me to my room. I glanced across the hall at Mrs. Manning's closed bedroom door, suddenly remembering that Theo and Mrs. Manning weren't supposed to be back until later that afternoon since it was now almost five in the morning.

"Oh my God! I ruined your plans, didn't I? You weren't supposed to be home until later this afternoon. I am so sorry, Theo." I was tired and achy, so it was no big surprise when my eyes suddenly filled with tears, and I buried my face in my hands.

"Hey, none of that. I promise you didn't ruin anything." He pulled my hands away from my face and pulled a handkerchief from his pocket to wipe away my tears. He opened my bedroom door and led me inside. After taking off my shoes and tucking me into bed fully clothed, he brought me a glass of water and some aspirin then kissed me on my cheek and turned to go.

"Theo." He turned to stared at me. "Thank you. And sorry for all the problems I caused tonight."

"You didn't cause any problems, Sabrina. I expect you to spend the day in bed today. I better not see you in that library."

"Mrs. Manning..."

"Isn't here. All you have to do today is get some rest. I'll check on you in a few hours to see if you're hungry. Don't get out of that bed. Got it?"

He closed the door behind him. Five minutes later, I was fast asleep. Before I was completely out, I'd glanced over at my mesh trash basket and could've sworn it was empty. The note Luca had slid under my door asking me to meet her in the woods was gone.

. . .

It hadn't been my imagination. When I finally dragged myself out of bed around noon, I immediately went over to the trash basket to find it completely empty. I even picked it up and looked underneath, scoured the floor and under my bed. The note was nowhere to be found. Had I imagined the note? I seriously doubted it. Most likely, Luca had snatched it out of my trash bin when she'd come back to the house. Speaking of Luca, I really needed to talk to her to ask her. After showering and pulling my braids back with a clip, I tossed on my comfiest warm-up suit, washed down a couple more aspirin, and went in search of something to eat, surprised that I had an appetite at all.

To my surprise, Theo and Luca were sitting at the dining table with soup and cucumber sandwiches. As usual Theo's face was buried in his iPad and Luca was listening to something on her phone through a set of old-school retro style pink and white headphones. Her eyes widened in surprise when she saw me.

"Whoa. What happened to you?"

It took everything in me not to lunge across the table at her. Instead, I sat down at my usual spot and grabbed a sandwich off the plate sitting in the middle of the table and took a bite, not trusting myself to speak. Theo spoke up for me.

"She had an accident in the woods last night."

"The woods?" Luca looked from me to Theo in confusion. "Is that what happened to your hair?"

"What?"

She gestured to an area on her head near her temple. My hand flew to the same spot on my own head, wincing in pain as I touched where I'd been hit, and noticed something I hadn't last night. One of my shoulder-length braids had been cut almost to the scalp. My fingers explored the now half-inch long piece of braid in confusion. When had this happened? I didn't remember the ER doctor having to cut my hair to treat my wound. Or did I just not remember?

"What were you doing in the woods last night? Nobody goes out there." Luca was looking at me like I wasn't too bright.

I eyed her closely. It certainly seemed like she had no idea why I would've been in the woods, let alone what had happened to me. But who else would've sent me on that fool's errand last night?

"I'm surprised you didn't hear all the commotion last night. Mr. Pearson took me to the ER."

Luca's eyes widened and just for a split second something flashed in her eyes that I couldn't decipher. Was it guilt or glee?

"Uh... I wasn't here last night." Her face turned slightly pink, and Theo's head whipped up from his iPad.

"What do you mean you weren't here last night? I don't remember you letting me know, let alone getting permission from me or Mrs. Manning, to be out after dark."

"I was at my RPG group meetup last night at the community college. Afterwards, we got pizza and hung out by the Riverwalk. I got dropped off around one this morning. Mrs. Manning didn't tell you I'd be out?"

Theo's face softened and he reached out and squeezed her hand. "Sorry, kid. Mrs. Manning's got a lot on her mind these days. She must have forgotten."

Luca's face fell and I started to ask what was going on with Mrs. Manning but deduced from their silence that it was something I wasn't meant to know about. Besides I was still digesting what Luca had just said. She hadn't been home. Was she telling the truth or covering her tracks for luring me into the woods and then attacking me? How could I even prove that was what had happened when the note that I had received was now gone? It was just like Cherise Gamble's tote bag. Of course there was another explanation, that I was losing my damn mind.

"Sabrina?" Luca looked genuinely concerned. Either this

kid was a good actor, or she had genuinely not been home last night. "You don't look so good. I think you need to go back to bed." Theo stood up and offered his hand, which I took. He escorted me back to my room, left and brought me some chips, fruit, and a couple of bottles of water.

"I better not see you outside of this room for the rest of the day and I'm locking the library so you can't get in there today."

"Yes, sir." I gave him a salute and watched him go.

The aspirin started to kick in. I propped myself up in bed after changing back into a night shirt, grabbed an apple and *The Conjure Man Dies*, and settled in for the rest of the day.

I drifted off, hovering in that strange spot between sleep and wakefulness when I became aware of someone in my room. I struggled to open my eyes to see who it was. Someone stroked my cheek and then I felt the unmistakable press of soft lips against my forehead. Yet when I opened my eyes, I was alone in the room and the sun was setting. It had felt so real, and I was momentarily confused until a knock sounded at my door, bringing me back to reality. It was Mrs. Manning with a dinner tray. I stepped aside for her to enter, and she set the tray on the bench at the foot of my bed: salmon, asparagus, wild rice, and crème brûlée.

"Mr. Dorsey told me what happened last night. How are you feeling?" She looked at my bandaged temple and winced.

Something seemed a bit different about Mrs. Manning tonight, but I couldn't put a finger on what it was. I was just happy she wasn't being a bitch to me because I didn't know if I could deal with her attitude after everything that happened last night.

"I'm fine. I should be back to work first thing tomorrow. Thank you for bringing me dinner. It looks delicious."

She must've really felt sorry for me because in bringing me

dinner to my room, she was violating the no eating in my room rule. I could tell she was thinking about that when she kept staring at the tray of food and then at me.

"I'll make sure to bring out the dishes to the kitchen when I'm done."

That seemed to do the trick, and she smiled at me. "Make sure you let me know if there's anything else you need." She turned to go.

"Hey, were you in my room just a little while ago?"

Mrs. Manning looked confused and shook her head slowly. "No, this is the first time I've been to your room since I got home a couple of hours ago. Why?"

"Oh, nothing. I think I must've been dreaming because I thought someone was in my room."

"Did you wake up right afterwards?"

"I did, why?"

"It's called false awakening. Used to happen to me all the time when I was younger. I would swear that I heard someone in my room or coming into the house, only to wake up and be home alone. I had been asleep the entire time. Do you think it could be connected to your sleepwalking?"

I could have kicked myself for telling that lie because now it was going to follow me around and label me as something that I wasn't. I had never sleepwalked in my life, not even when I was a little girl.

"That sounds exactly like what happened. Thanks, Mrs. Manning." I purposefully avoided making any direct connection with my sleepwalking. I hoped they would all forget about it soon.

The older woman smiled and left, closing my bedroom door behind her. I couldn't let what happened last night go. I needed to talk to Luca.

. . .

"You're saying you weren't in the woods last night?"

Luca stared at me like I'd just grown a second head. I'd gone to her room to talk to her privately. "Hello. Didn't you hear what I said at lunch? I wasn't here. Haven't you noticed I barely leave this house unless Manning or Theo make me? I don't even go to school. I take all my classes online. The only place I go to is therapy and my RPG guild gaming night once a month. I could do therapy online too, but Theo thinks it's good for me to get out of the house at least a couple times a month. The last place in the world I would ever go is into those woods." She made an exaggerated shivering move and rolled her eyes like I was the biggest idiot on the planet.

Was she telling the truth? I almost believed her until I remembered one more thing.

"I saw a video of you in those woods telling stories." I crossed my arms and stared at her, and she stared right back before finally sighing and getting up from her bed.

She walked over to the back wall next to her bedroom door where I could see a projector screen mounted near the ceiling. She pulled it all the way down to the floor, revealing it wasn't a projector screen. It was a fake backdrop screen for filming. It looked just like the woods behind the house. Next, she turned off the light in her room and sat down cross-legged on the floor in front of the backdrop and took a flashlight and beamed it up at her face. For anyone who didn't know any better, which was obviously me, it looked like she was sitting in a wooded area at night. My face burned with embarrassment.

"Sorry, Luca." I sat down on the edge of her bed feeling confused. "I'm just trying to figure out what happened to me last night. I could've sworn I saw you going into the woods."

"I overheard Theo telling Manning that you were sleep-walking. Was that a lie?" The teenager looked as confused as I was feeling.

"Yeah, I lied." I couldn't meet her eyes, and she instantly knew why.

"Were you trying to protect me over something I didn't do?"

"I wanted to talk to you first before I told Theo that someone had left a note in my room signed by you asking me to meet them in the woods. When I got out there, I got lost and confused and the last thing I remember seeing after something hit me is a figure running back toward the house, then I lost consciousness."

Neither of us spoke because I wasn't sure what else there was to say. I finally got up to leave. "I'm sorry, Luca. I was wrong and for the record, I was not snooping through your notebook the other day. So, I would really appreciate it if you didn't tell Theo you saw me in his bedroom."

"Why were you in his bedroom? Were you trying to hook up with him?" She said that last part in such a low voice I wasn't quite sure that I'd heard her right.

I recalled what Mrs. Manning told me about Luca wanting Theo and her mom to get together so they could be a family. I instantly felt a kinship with her. I remembered hoping that every man my mom dated would end up being my new father, and that my mom would stop drinking and we could be one big happy family. All the men my mom brought home were from the bar she hung out in, who stopped coming after a month or two. I remembered what Mrs. Manning told me about Luca's mom getting engaged and hated that I knew this, and she didn't. Everything I had been suspecting about Luca she'd easily explained away. Had she really been the one to lure me out to the woods to try and scare me away because she thought I was after Theo?

"No. I was looking for this." I pulled up the picture of the tote bag that she'd found in the library and showed it to her.

"Isn't that the old tote bag I found in the library? Why are you looking for it? I saw you lock it in your desk drawer."

I tried to keep the shock that she had known where I'd put the tote bag off my face. How had she known where I'd put it? She had already left the library for the day by the time I locked it in my desk drawer. Did that mean she'd come back and found it, then taken it?

"Well, it's missing now. It's very important that I find it. If you have any idea where it could be, please let me know."

"Yeah, sure, whatever." Her mask of surliness slipped back into place, effectively shutting me out. I wasn't going to get more information out of her.

"Hey, wait." I paused at the door and looked back at her. "What's so important about that tote bag?"

I was conflicted. Did I tell this kid the truth, risking her running back to tell Theo or Mrs. Manning? Because despite everything she'd just told me, I still wasn't completely convinced that Luca wasn't involved in what had happened to me in the woods.

"I know who it belonged to. And I know her family would like to have it back."

I left her sitting on the floor staring after me and wondered if I'd just made another huge mistake.

TWENTY-SIX
SABRINA

Sharon Claremont lived in a sprawling mid-century ranch three blocks away from the Dorsey estate. I arrived on her doorstep promptly at noon that Friday wearing the only professional outfit I owned, a tan pantsuit and black pumps that I'd worn to my interview at the public library three years earlier. A tan and red patterned headband held my braids back from my face, hiding the braid that had been cut until I could get an appointment to have my hair re-braided. When my host opened the door, I wondered why I'd even bothered when I saw that she was wearing workout clothing, black leggings with a matching crop top and Nike trainers. Had she forgotten I was coming?

"Sabrina, welcome. Thank you for coming." Sharon Claremont stepped aside so I could enter.

She was a slim, attractive white woman with an ash blonde bob and looked to be in her mid-sixties. She was the widow of Trent Claremont who'd been the president of Riverside Bank, the largest bank in Harper's Ferry.

"Thank you so much for contacting me, Mrs. Claremont. I'm so excited to see your library."

"Well, first things first. Since it's lunchtime I thought we could eat out on the deck by the pool. If you don't mind?"

She gave me an inquiring look and I knew immediately this was not a request. It was a command. We were eating lunch whether I wanted to or not and I regretted eating a sandwich before I came.

"Of course, Mrs. Claremont, that would be great."

I followed her through a bright, airy and minimally decorated home heavy on light colored wood and abstract art and out onto a sprawling deck that spanned the entire back of the house, overlooking an Olympic-sized swimming pool.

"Your home is beautiful," I told her truthfully, though it wasn't quite to my taste. I preferred a warmer, homier feel to a house. This place felt more like a showpiece.

"Thank you, and I hope you like Caesar salad." She gestured toward a glass table with an umbrella over it that was already laid out for two. A large, frosted glass bowl of Caesar salad sat in the middle of the table with a glass decanter of dressing alongside a pitcher of water with lemons floating in it.

"This looks delicious." I took a seat and Sharon Claremont took the liberty of heaping a pile of salad in the middle of a salad plate shaped like a frosted glass flower, before piling salad onto her own plate.

I poured myself a glass of water and was about to ask her how many volumes her library had, when around mouthfuls of salad, I discovered the real reason for this appointment.

"Tell me," she said, leaning forward and lowering her voice conspiratorially. "What's it like working for the Dorseys?"

Wow, I thought. She'd barely fed me, and rabbit food at that, and was already expecting me to put out. As quickly as the anger flared up over the time I'd most likely wasted on this appointment, I realized that if she wanted any information from me, then maybe I could get some from her too.

"I've really enjoyed my time at the Dorseys. They have a beautiful library."

Sharon Claremont rolled her eyes dramatically and speared a crouton with her fork. "Come on, I'm not talking about the damn library."

"Are you talking about what it's like working for the family?" Of course, I knew this was exactly what she meant, but if I was going to give up the goods, she was going to have to work for it.

"Are you from here? I mean, you know, are you Harper's Ferry born and raised. I'm not talking about where your people are originally from."

I almost choked on my salad because it never occurred to me that she would ask me where my *people* were from. "Yes, I was born and raised here."

"Then you've already heard about Martin Dorsey's reputation then, right?"

"I've always heard he was a very shrewd businessman, which didn't always make him a very nice man." That was the absolute truth. I wasn't gossiping about the man because anyone who had any kind of encounter or knowledge of Martin Dorsey knew what kind of a person he was. It was common knowledge.

"Ah," said Sharon with a smirky smile. "You're very diplomatic and discreet. I like that." She shook her fork at me. "I would expect the same if I were to hire you."

I gave her a thin smile because we both knew that she wasn't planning on hiring me for anything. She had lured me over here under the pretense of employment so she could grill me about the Dorseys. I had to tread lightly with this woman, or she could derail my business before it even got off the ground with one bad word to her friends.

"I'm assuming because of your late husband's line of work you probably traveled in the same social circles as the Dorseys?"

"More or less. After his wife's death he shut himself away with his kids and we rarely saw him unless it was some charitable event. He was very charitable."

"Do you know Theo Dorsey?"

"Only in passing. I'd sure like to know him better. He's gorgeous."

"That he is," I replied dryly and took a quick sip of water to mask my sudden discomfort. Sharon laughed.

"Oh, don't look like that. I'm just kidding. He's young enough to be my son. I think he may have even gone to school with my daughter, Chloe. But any way is it true what they say about his sister? What's her name? Brie?"

"It's Belle. And what is it they say about her?"

"That they locked her away in an institution because she had a breakdown after her father died."

It shouldn't have surprised me that the gossip mill had gone into overdrive about Belle. Theo told me they were able to keep her accident out of the papers. Coupled with the fact no one had seen her publicly in years, it was only natural for misinformation to spread when there was a lack of facts. But what she'd just said was just plain shitty and I felt an inexplicable need to protect my boss's sister.

"An institution?" I let out a laugh and shook my head. "She's in Europe." I'm not sure how Theo would feel about the lie I'd just told, but I didn't really care. Belle living her best life in Europe sounded a whole lot better than her locked away somewhere, and infinitely better than her true circumstances.

"Europe?" Sharon's eyes narrowed, but I continued to smile at her when it became apparent that she'd rather believe the rumor. "Well, I guess that makes more sense than her being institutionalized given the fact that Theo is running things in her absence."

Now we'd reached the point where I either had to pretend

to know what she was talking about to maintain my façade that I was knowledgeable about my employers, or ask what she was talking about and reveal that I knew nothing about the people I worked for, thus stopping our flow of information. As much as I wanted to know what she meant, I opted for the former.

"I think he's doing a great job, don't you?"

"Oh, absolutely. Dorsey Snacks shares have soared in recent years under Theo's leadership. But I must admit, when Belle was named CEO of the company after Martin died, many of the shareholders, me included, thought she'd run that company right into the ground. I'm happy she's letting her brother run it in her absence."

Belle was the CEO of Dorsey Snacks? Why hadn't I known that? Probably because it wasn't relevant to my life, and I had no interest in business. My mom's, and now my sister's, only interest in the company they worked for was the salary and benefits it provided. But why had Martin Dorsey done it? Why Belle and not Theo?

"I think it's great when we're aware of our limitations," I said absently as I pushed the now wilted salad around on my plate, dangerously close to reaching my own limitations with this appointment.

"I'm glad the Dorsey siblings have remained close in spite of those horrible rumors."

"I know. Wasn't that horrible? People can be so cruel." I was very aware that she was fishing to see if I'd tell her they weren't close, which by everything I could tell, they weren't. Not when Theo could hardly stand to see his sister in her current condition.

"Well, I never believed Theo Dorsey hurt his sister so he could become CEO of Dorsey Snacks."

"Hurt his sister?" I blurted without meaning to, causing Sharon Claremont to raise an eyebrow. "I mean he'd never hurt anyone," I replied, recovering quickly.

"I know, right? People are so stupid. Theo Dorsey wouldn't hurt a fly. Besides, why risk hurting her? If she dies, the entire estate goes to charity, and he gets nothing. If anything, he should be making sure she's very well taken care of... wherever she is." Her smile was as sweet as saccharine, and I smiled back, desperate to leave so I could digest this new information in private.

She stood and gathered our plates. "Dessert?"

"Yes, please."

She returned with two slices of New York cheesecake and a small silver bowl with cherry sauce. "I don't mind eating light if it means I can have dessert."

"It's delicious. Did you make it?"

"Me? God, no. I can't cook to save my life. It's from Dorsey Snacks' new line of cheesecakes. I'm so happy to see them expanding beyond chips, cookies, and pretzels."

"Did you know the Dorseys' previous librarian?" I was ready to change the subject from Theo and Belle but still wanted to know what else this woman knew. Sharon thought for a minute before replying.

"Previous librarian? Oh, you mean that sweet young man they say was stealing from them?"

And there it was again. That accusation that Myles Patterson had been stealing from the Dorseys. Anytime I asked anyone about this man, all I heard about was the stealing, not the romance with Belle Dorsey. I wondered if that was what Martin Dorsey had intended for my predecessor, to be labeled a thief, something that would follow him around for years to come.

"That must be him. I heard there were some issues with him, and I just wondered if you knew him."

"I didn't. But you should talk to his aunt Grace Pruitt."

"Grace Pruitt?" This was the first time I'd heard that name.

"That's right. Grace was the school librarian way back in

the ice age when I was in school. She's got to be well into her eighties by now. If anyone would know about that young man, it would be her."

"And she's still alive?"

"If she is, she's probably still over on Tipton. That street's gone to the dogs. But she refuses to move. Her house is the old caretaker's cottage next to the Dumare mansion. You can't miss it. It's got a big rosebush out front."

I spent the next hour going through Sharon Claremont's so-called library, a small room with two empty bookshelves and an entire back wall filled with boxes of old cookbooks she'd inherited from her mother. She asked me to give her an estimate of what it would cost to turn the room into a library. I was looking at a few hours of work, tops. It was a project she could've probably done herself, but I was happy to take her money if she wanted to pay me. I told her I would email her an estimate and then left, certain I would never hear from this woman again.

Tipton Lane had seen better days from when it used to be one of the most affluent areas in town back at the turn of the century. Now, the once magnificent old Victorian mansions had been split into apartment rentals, most of which had fallen into disrepair or had sat empty and abandoned for decades. Grace Pruitt's house was one of the better maintained houses on the street. As I approached the house, I could see an elderly lady with curly snow-white hair wearing denim overalls and well-worn Birkenstocks pruning a large rosebush next to her front steps.

"Excuse me, Mrs. Pruitt?"

She turned to me and smiled. "Yes, may I help you?"

"Hello, ma'am. I don't mean to disturb you. I was wondering if I could talk to you about your nephew, Myles."

To say the woman looked shocked would be an understatement. Her head jerked back like I'd punched her, and her eyes widened in excitement. "Myles? Do you know where he is?" She quickly stripped off her gardening gloves and set her pruning shears down on one of the steps before walking over to me.

I'm not sure why it hadn't occurred to me that she may think I might have information about her nephew, and I could've kicked myself. I was about to disappoint her.

"No, ma'am. I am so sorry. I was wondering if you knew where he was."

By now the smile that she had given me was gone, replaced by suspicion, and her bright blue eyes had turned hard.

"And *you* would be?"

"My name is Sabrina Adams, and I work as a librarian for the Dorsey family. Myles was my predecessor, and I was trying to get in contact with him about the work he'd done for the Dorseys."

"The Dorseys." She spat the name out like it tasted bad. "They ruined my nephew! He could never get another job in his field after he worked for them."

"I am so sorry. I didn't realize. I should probably go." I took a step back, but she gestured me forward.

"You'd better come in. I'm going to need a drink if I'm going to talk about this."

I followed her up the front steps past two swinging benches mounted to the ceiling on either side of the door into a modestly decorated home that smelled of roses and cigarette smoke. The living room was small, and the furniture was worn, but it had a cozy, lived-in charm that no interior decorator would've been able to replicate.

"Have a seat. Sabrina, was it?"

"Yes, ma'am." I sat down on a floral couch while she headed into the kitchen and emerged two minutes later with a pair of stemless wine glasses that turned out to hold Moscato wine.

Grace Pruitt sat in a leather chair opposite me and took a sip of her wine before turning her attention to me, and I did the same, surprised at how refreshing and light the wine was.

"You work for the Dorseys, huh? And how's that going?"

"So far so good," I said, shrugging before taking another sip of my wine. Grace let out a snort of laughter.

"Liar. Because if everything was good, you wouldn't be here asking about my nephew who I haven't seen in years. You want to know what I think, young lady?"

I didn't want to know what she thought, but the only way to get information out of her about Myles was to let her vent. "I'm sure you'll tell me whether I want to know or not."

Grace let out another snort of laughter and drained her wine glass. "Damn straight. I'm too old to mince words. What I think is you've probably encountered some of the same shit my nephew did, and you want to talk to him to get his take on how to deal with those freaks, am I right?"

Now it was my turn to laugh as I realized just how much I liked this woman. After dealing with all of Mrs. Manning's moodiness and bullshit rules, Grace Pruitt was a breath of fresh air.

"You're not one hundred percent right, but close. Did your nephew ever confide in you about what he experienced while working for the Dorseys?"

"He did in the beginning. Talked about all the rules and regulations and weirdness. Talked about what a cheap and controlling bastard Martin Dorsey was. And then he stopped. Clammed right up and I couldn't get any more information out of him. Probably right around the time he was trying to get in Belle Dorsey's pants." She got up and grabbed my now empty wine glass and went back to the kitchen to refill them, this time bringing the rest of the bottle with her.

"I heard about that. I also heard he was fired."

"That he was fired was never in doubt. It's why he was fired that's always been the real mystery."

"You mean there was another reason besides his romance with Belle?"

"Depends on if you believe the rumors or not."

I remembered what Jo had told me about him stealing rare books. I wanted to see if his aunt had heard the same rumor.

"Myles was a lot of things. Smart as a whip, charming, and ambitious, but those Dorseys tried to make him out to be a thief and I refused to believe it. Even though my nephew was book smart, he lacked common sense. That didn't make him a thief."

"Not unless you counted Belle Dorsey's heart," I pointed out and thought I'd overstepped, but then she laughed again.

"Last time I looked, it took two to tango, young lady. Everyone likes to make Martin Dorsey's daughter out to be some kind of flower withering on the vine. I'm sure she knew exactly what she was doing with my nephew. And if the gossip around town is anything to go by, she was desperate to get away from that father of hers. If my nephew was using her as a stepping stone to the good life, she was using him to get out of that house and had convinced herself she loved Myles when she probably didn't."

"He never talked about her to you?"

"Nope. He knew better than to tell me he was risking his job over a woman."

"Why was that?"

"Because I'm the reason he became a librarian. We'd always been close when he was growing up. He was an only child and became the son I never had. I was a school librarian for the Harper's Ferry city school system my entire career. I encouraged Myles to get an MLIS. I was so proud of that boy. First when he got his job at the public library and then when he got on with the Dorseys. But that ended up a shit show."

"Was he really not able to get another library job after they let him go?"

"Could never prove it, of course, but he always knew that Martin Dorsey had black-balled him. He applied for library jobs here in Ohio, Indiana, and Illinois. No dice. No one would hire him. How in the hell is that possible if Martin Dorsey hadn't used his influence to see that he never worked in the library field again?"

"How did he support himself?"

"He was on unemployment for six months. Then he was a substitute teacher for about five years. But he was miserable."

"You haven't seen or spoken to him in years? Did he move away?"

"Honestly, young lady, I have no idea what happened to my nephew. Over time he just stopped coming around until I realized that it'd been months since I'd seen or heard from him. My brother and sister-in-law hadn't heard from him either. Then I saw in the paper one day that Martin Dorsey had died and figured things would look up for him since that horrible man was gone. I remember trying to get a hold of him for a week before his cell phone was just shut off. I haven't heard from him since. I just hope he's finally living the life he's always wanted to live."

"He was never declared missing?"

Her lips tightened in disapproval. "I blame his parents for that."

"Why?"

"Myles was always very ambitious and wanted more for himself than his parents could provide. My brother and sister-in-law were plain, hardworking folks. They were happy with the life they had and Myles kind of looked down on them for not wanting more. They became estranged, so it wasn't a big surprise when they stopped hearing from him. I think they just figured he'd finally found the life that he wanted, and it didn't include them."

"What do you think?"

"I think something happened to him, but I have absolutely no way of proving it and the last time I looked, the police don't base their investigations on an old lady's gut feelings."

"You think the Dorseys are involved?"

"Do flies love shit? Of course, I think they're involved." She gave me an indignant look like it should've been obvious that they were involved.

I'd met another person who thought something had happened to a loved one at the hands of the Dorsey family. This couldn't be a coincidence. Could it? As much as I'd been looking forward to talking to this lady, I wanted to go. I drained the last bit of Moscato from my glass and sat it down on her coffee table.

"Thank you so much for talking to me about Myles, Ms. Pruitt, but I should get going. I've taken up enough of your time."

"Wait," she said, getting up from her chair. "I've got something to show you."

She disappeared down a hall near the door and came back with a photo, which she thrust at me. It was of a handsome young white man in his mid-twenties, with sleepy light brown eyes. His dark hair was cropped close on the sides and the back, and was longer and wavy on the top. His lazy smile revealed a slight gap in his front teeth. If this was who I thought it was, no wonder Belle Dorsey had lost her mind over this man.

"Myles?" I asked, and she nodded, staring fondly at the photo before clearing her throat.

"I want you to take a good hard look at my nephew. Remember his face. You seem like a nice girl, but there's something wrong with those Dorseys. And I'd hate to have to read about you in the papers."

"I won't forget it. Thank you for talking to me," I told her as a shiver ran down my spine.

On my way home there was a breaking news alert on the radio about Jennifer Hampton's death. What had originally been thought to be a tragic accident had now been determined to be a homicide based on the result of her autopsy, which hadn't been released yet. What I'd just heard was horrifying, but not as horrifying as realizing that she might still be alive if she hadn't come home with Theo that night.

TWENTY-SEVEN
BELLE

She decided it was the perfect time to move on to the next phase of her recovery—finally getting out of this bed. She pushed herself into position, elated by the fact that it was getting easier, and her arms were getting stronger. But the effort wore her out and she had to rest for ten minutes before she moved on to the next part. She pulled back the covers and twisted into position but had to grab her legs to move them off the side of the bed. She couldn't remember the last time she had her feet on the floor. It felt amazing. She took her time to get acclimated to the feeling of pressing her soles into the cool hardwood and flexing her toes.

She braced her arms, locking her elbows in preparation for something she hadn't been able to do in months. She chocked up what happened next to overconfidence and impatience. Instead of standing when she pushed up off the bed, she slid into a heap on the floor. Panic caused sweat to form on her brow. She could not let them find her on the floor. She could not let them know how far she'd progressed and how close she was to escaping. She managed to twist her upper torso so that she could see the clock on the wall and realized she had about five hours to try and get herself back into bed.

She struggled for about two hours, only managing to get herself closer to the bed and lift her arms up to the side. But she wasn't strong enough to pull herself back up onto the bed. Her last memory, before pain and exhaustion caused her to pass out, was resting her head on the side of the bed as sweat poured down her face, soaking her nightgown. When she came to a few hours later she was shocked to discover she was back in her bed. She was alone in her room and minutes after she woke up and sunlight began streaming through her closed curtains, the housekeeper came in with her morning meds, giving no indication that she'd been the one who'd found her on the floor. That only meant one thing. *He* had come in and found her and put her back in bed.

He knew she was trying to leave.

TWENTY-EIGHT
SABRINA

Based on the statement from the Uber driver who'd picked Jennifer Hampton up at the front gate, it finally hit the papers that she had spent time at the Dorsey estate the night she died. News crews were parked outside the gate that led up to the estate and Mr. Gaines had to prevent the media from following me through the gate when I arrived home. Jennifer's death and Theo's link to her had made national news and the only reason he wasn't considered a person of interest was because Mr. Pearson had been the one to walk Jennifer to the Uber and see her off.

Judging by the comments on the article, many people thought he had followed her back to the Parkwood Hotel. The hotel's security cameras weren't working that night and hadn't worked for months. Surveillance footage from nearby businesses showed Jennifer's car leaving the hotel parking lot, but the footage was too grainy to see who was driving. I read the article online in my room before I came to dinner. While I was relieved that Jennifer Hampton had left this house alive, I was at a loss as to what to say to Theo who looked tense and miserable.

"You've seen the news?" he asked, staring at me intensely.

"Yes. There are news crews camped out by the front gate."

"We need to call the police," said Mrs. Manning from the doorway of the dining room. "Those people are trespassing. The property starts when you turn onto the lane, not at the gate. They have no right to be there." The look she gave Theo could've frozen water, which shocked me because usually she acted like butter wouldn't melt in his mouth.

I looked at Mrs. Manning and wondered what she was thinking, knowing that Theo had brought a stranger here that had resulted in a young mother's death and unflattering attention directed at the Dorsey family. I knew she would probably have a lot more to say if I wasn't here. As justified as she may be in those feelings, they weren't helping anybody, least of all Theo.

When neither of us responded, she turned on her heel and went back into the kitchen.

"I'm sorry, Sabrina. Between trespassers on the property, your accident, and now this, you probably wish you'd never come here."

Did I wish I'd never come here? That wasn't really the question. The question I was asking myself was, was being here worse than being where I'd come from? The answer to that was a resounding no.

"Why didn't the police question me?" I replied, ignoring what he just said. "I was here that night and I saw the two of you together. The brief glimpse that I caught, you weren't hurting her. I didn't see her leave, but I could have told the police that I didn't see you behaving violently toward Jennifer Hampton. Combined with Mr. Pearson's statement, I don't understand why the media are here harassing you."

"Because he's the wealthy CEO of the biggest employer in the area, Miss Adams." Mrs. Manning had come back into the room with a pitcher of iced tea, and topped off both of our glasses. Her tight lips and hard eyes when she looked at Theo told me exactly what she thought of his current predicament. But if her disapproval bothered Theo, he wasn't letting it show in front of me.

"Thanks, Sabrina, but Mrs. Manning is right. My guilt or innocence doesn't matter. As long as my connection to a murder victim exists, the media is going to use it to sell papers and increase viewership of the news."

"It goes without saying that we don't want you talking to the media." Mrs. Manning reached out to take my plate and annoyance flared up in me.

"You don't have to tell me that. And I'm still eating." Her hand froze halfway to my plate, and she looked startled before quickly snatching her hand back.

"I'm sorry," she said, looking contrite. "I'm feeling a little on edge. As a matter of fact, I think I'm going to go lay down. Can you two clean up after yourselves?" She didn't wait for a response before turning on her heel and heading toward her bedroom.

When she was gone, I gave Theo a sheepish look. "I shouldn't have snapped at her. And of course I won't be talking to the media."

To my surprise, Theo reached out and grabbed my hand and gave it a squeeze. I became hyper aware of the warmth of his skin on mine and wanted to pull away but couldn't. I thought back on our kiss and even though getting involved with him was a bad idea, I wasn't ready for the contact to end.

"She's got a lot on her plate right now. Maybe she'll tell you about it herself, but right now just give her a little space. This whole mess isn't making it any better. I blame myself for putting her on edge."

There wasn't a whole lot more to say, and although I had plenty of questions for Theo, I could tell he wasn't in the mood to answer them. Once we finished with our dinner, he helped me clear the table and put away the food.

"Since when does a millionaire CEO of the biggest employer in the area know how to load a dishwasher?" I was attempting to lighten the mood and was happy when Theo laughed. But as soon as the word CEO had left my mouth, I was reminded of what Sharon Claremont had told me.

Once I'd left Grace Pruitt's house, I'd checked out the Dorsey Snacks website. Unfortunately, the site hadn't been updated in a long time and only listed Martin Dorsey as the founder. There was no information on who the current corporate officers were.

"Well, I haven't always been the millionaire CEO of the biggest employer in the area," he deadpanned. "I spent five years in boarding school and four years in college and two in grad school. I learned very quickly how to take care of myself."

"How old were you when you went to boarding school?"

"I was thirteen. I wanted to go to school around here, but my dad wasn't having it. He always said public schools were for the workers and private schools for the CEOs."

"He went to public school, right?"

"And state college. I think after he became successful, he became obsessed with how to get me to where he was faster. He believed private schools and spending time around other successful people would help me attain that goal quicker."

I wasn't about to say what I was thinking, which was that everything I'd heard about Martin Dorsey painted him as a horrible human being. No one was all good or bad. After all, he built his wife the beautiful library that I was currently working in. He couldn't have been completely unredeemable. I also noticed he didn't seem to have the same ambitions for Belle that he'd had for Theo and wondered why he'd named her CEO.

"Did you always want to run Dorsey Snacks?"

"Hell, no. I wanted to flip houses."

"Flip houses?" I let out a laugh thinking he was joking but could tell he wasn't.

"I'm serious. Do you know how many abandoned castles and chateaus there are in France? I'd love to buy one and restore it. Not just hire someone to do it either. I want to do as much of the work as I can myself."

He had a gleam in his eye that I'd never seen before, especially not when he left for work every day. "Then why don't you?"

He shrugged and the gleam was gone. "Things happen and you have to step up and do your duty. Maybe one day."

Was he talking about Belle's accident? Had he been thrust into a role he hadn't wanted because of what happened to his sister? It occurred to me that Sharon Claremont had probably told me rehashed gossip she'd gotten second- or third-hand, and I was suddenly embarrassed and ashamed I'd been so quick to believe it.

"What about you? I know very little about you, Sabrina Adams. I'd like to know more."

I gave him a quick look to see if he was kidding because I was the least interesting person I knew. The earnest look in his eyes made me smile. His question reminded me of the conversation that I'd had a week ago with Mrs. Manning when she had asked me the same question. I was also fully aware of the fact that her bedroom was only down the hall, and it wouldn't surprise me if she had her ear to the door trying to listen to what we were talking about.

"Why would that be?"

"Why do I want to know more about you? That should be self-explanatory. I mean you do work for me and you're living in my home. You already know a lot about me. I think it's only fair that you tell me who Sabrina Adams really is."

I'm not sure why his words shocked me. Perhaps because I

didn't think he really wanted to know who Sabrina Adams was. I wasn't sure I knew who Sabrina Adams was.

"I'm Harper's Ferry born and raised. I have a degree in English from Ohio University, and MLIS from Kent State University. My mom passed away from liver cancer and I'm the younger sister of Camille Adams Mitchell, an army vet. I love all things chocolate, I'm allergic to cats, and I read about one hundred books a year. My last relationship was with a guy who dumped me via text message while he was on a first date with the woman he ended up marrying." Now why had I told him that? Then again, he said he wanted to know about me, and my crappy love life was a part of my history that the few friends that I had laughed about regularly.

"That guy was an idiot."

"No, that guy cut me loose when he realized he had a connection with his future wife before he wasted more of my time. And yeah, dumping me via text message was shitty, but I preferred that to him stringing me along for months or even years."

"How very glass half-full of you," he said, laughing. "Are you always this positive about other people's horrible behavior?"

"Only when I learn something in the process, which is rare. Mostly people are just assholes." I'm not sure what I said to wipe the smile off his face, but he leaned back against the kitchen island lost in thought.

"Hey." I reached out and poked him in the forearm. "Where'd you go?"

"Sorry. But..."

"But what?"

"You know I didn't hurt Jennifer Hampton, right? I mean, I know the fact that she was even here was inappropriate. I should've never allowed myself to get that drunk, let alone let a stranger drive me home, but what happened between us was consensual. I would never hurt anyone."

I wondered why it was so important to him that I knew this. I desperately wanted to tell him that I believed him. But there was still the matter of Cherise Gamble and the tote bag that I found in the library.

"Sabrina? You do believe me, right?"

Fortunately for me, we were interrupted when Luca came barging into the kitchen on a food run while she was on a break from gaming. The teenager instantly noticed the tension in the room and her eyes narrowed suspiciously. She looked from me to Theo, and I was reminded that Luca wanted Theo and her mom to get together. I purposefully went over to the sink and got busy scrubbing it, so she didn't get the wrong idea.

"What's up with you guys? Why are you cleaning up the kitchen. Where is Manning?"

"She's not feeling well and decided to turn in early," I told her.

Luca's eyes immediately flew to Theo and all the color drained from her face.

"She's just a little stressed out over everything that's going on. She'll be fine." Theo walked over and put an arm around Luca and walked her back upstairs to her room. By the time he came back, I had already started the dishwasher.

"Is she okay?"

"Luca's at a place in her life where she wants to hold on to everyone the way she was never able to hold on to her mom. She acts like Mrs. Manning gets on her last nerves, and I'm sure she does, but if anything happened to her, Luca would be devastated."

"Have you talked to her about what's going on now?" The way he looked away from me gave me my answer.

"Not yet. I already feel horrible that this is even happening and even worse for that poor woman's family. Did I tell you I spoke to her husband, Danny?"

"Jennifer Hampton's husband? When?"

"This morning. He showed up at Dorsey Snacks demanding to speak with me. We had a nice long chat in my office, and I told him everything that happened that night. I even sent him the security footage that showed her leaving."

"How did that go?"

"He was angry, but not at me. According to him he and Jennifer weren't in a good place in their marriage. He cheated with an old girlfriend and even though Jennifer decided to stay with him, she was still very angry and had started having affairs of her own to get back at him. If anything, he was mad at himself for creating the situation in which this happened. Now the media have found out that she died after hooking up with another man, they're victim blaming her in the press. A lot of them are saying whoever did this to her was probably angry after they found out she was married."

I read that in the comments on the news article online about her death and had been disgusted. None of what this woman had done made what happened to her okay. She didn't deserve to be killed, leaving her husband forever regretful and her children motherless. She was a mother, a wife, a sister, and a daughter, she was so much more than a woman who had a one-night stand. If she was guilty of anything, it was being in the wrong place at the wrong time.

Theo looked so miserable that I wanted to hug him and almost did but thought better of it. I knew if I touched him, I wouldn't want to stop and the last thing either of us needed was the complication of an impulsive encounter. He had enough problems because of his last hookup. I didn't want to be any port in a storm.

"I've hired extra security to patrol the grounds so those idiot people from the press don't sneak onto the property through the woods."

"Thanks. I'm sure this will all blow over in a week or two.

Are the police going to release the footage of her leaving here in that Uber?"

"It would sure help me out a lot if they did." He looked beyond fed up and tossed his dish towel on the counter in frustration.

I didn't know what else to say to him, especially questioning his innocence. "Well," I said, folding my dish towel and setting it on the counter next to the sink. "I'm going to turn in. Good night."

"Thanks for listening, Sabrina. I really appreciate it. I don't have many people to talk to and it was nice of you to listen."

"I'm happy to listen anytime you need to talk. You know where I live," I said teasingly. He gave me a smile and turned to go.

"And, Theo." He looked back and I gave him a smile. "Of course I don't think you did anything to Jennifer Hampton."

The relieved look on his face made me glad I'd just lied to him.

TWENTY-NINE
JARED

Jared had to call in a favor to get a copy of the recording of Theo Dorsey's interrogation by the Harper's Ferry PD. He was still on desk duty back in Cincy and damned lucky to still have a job. There was no way they'd have let him sit in on this interview since he had no jurisdiction here. He sat in his car, clicked the link in the email he'd been sent, and watched the video that popped up on his phone screen. On it, Theo Dorsey, dressed in an expensive gray three-piece Brooks Brother suit, was sitting at the table with his lawyer, a bespectacled middle-aged white man named Foster Grimes. Two homicide detectives, a white man named Sam Clark and a black woman named Pam Trent, entered the room with a tape recorder. Trent sat it down on the table, turned it on and identified herself, and stated the date and time and who they were interviewing.

Det. Clark: "We'd like to thank you for coming in, Mr. Dorsey. We know you're a very busy man."

Dorsey: "Anything I can do to help, detective."

Det. Trent: "Glad to hear it. Let's get started. Now, do you still contend that you did not know Jennifer Hampton prior to meeting her at the Parkwood Hotel bar and taking her home with you?"

Dorsey: "That is correct. I was pretty drunk, and she was nice enough to drive me home."

Det. Clark: "Then can you explain this?"

He slid a photo across the table at Dorsey, who glanced at it briefly.

Dorsey: "It's a picture of an employee training we did last year."

Det. Trent: "And who's the figure standing in the back of the room by the buffet table?"

Dorsey looks again and does a double take and then looks over at his lawyer, clearly at a loss. His lawyer nods at him to answer the question.

Dorsey: "It looks like... Jennifer Hampton, but I don't understand."

Det. Clark: "It looks like Jennifer Hampton because it is her. Her and her husband's catering company, J&D Catering, catered no less than five events for Dorsey Snacks. Do you still insist you didn't know her?"

Grimes: "My client runs a Fortune 500 company with over a thousand employees and numerous contractors. He can't be expected to know every single person his company employs."

Det. Trent: "Be that as it may, Mr. Grimes, but we don't need to know about over a thousand employees. We only need to know about one. So, again, Mr. Dorsey. Do you still contend you did not know Jennifer Hampton?"

Dorsey: "Detective, I don't handle any of the details of our company trainings. Our events coordinator schedules all of that, including the caterers. From what I understand, we have a list of about a dozen we use. I usually come in and introduce whatever trainer is conducting the training and leave. I'm not denying that Mrs. Hampton's company was hired by Dorsey Snacks, or that I may have met her in passing."

Det. Clark: "Then what are you saying, Mr. Dorsey?"

Dorsey: "I'm saying I did not know Jennifer Hampton personally prior to our encounter that night."

Grimes: "Are we done here, detectives? Because unless you're planning to charge my client for not knowing everyone his company employs, we're done here.

The interview ended after that, and Jared sat back in his passenger seat in disgust. They'd been way too easy on him because of who he was. If Jared had conducted the interview, he'd have gotten a confession out of him, even if he'd had to beat that pretty face of his to a pulp. But that was why he was on desk duty. He willed himself to calm down. Of course, that asshole would deny knowing Jennifer Hampton. Just like he'd denied knowing Cherise. But if nothing else, Jared knew exactly what he had to do. He looked through his contacts list until he found the contact he was looking for, *The Harper's Ferry Gazette*.

The Jennifer Hampton case was all over the news for the next two days with each article giving more and more information. Like the fact that both her phone and wedding ring were missing, and she had died from blunt force trauma to the head before she'd even gone into the water. The biggest shock came when one journalist connected Cherise Gamble's death to Jennifer Hampton's, theorizing that Theo was responsible for both. I wondered if Jared was behind the news story. He'd been blowing up my phone with texts for two days, wanting to know if I'd found Cherise's tote bag.

I hadn't answered because I was still pissed at him and had nothing new to tell him. I thought he'd get the hint. Apparently not. And now Cherise's death had made the news again. Jared had to be behind that story, and I was terrified Theo would find out I'd agreed to help him. The more I thought about it, the less sense it made. If Theo had truly been responsible for Cherise's death, why not just throw the tote bag away in the trash? Why hide it in the library? Even if Cherise had been in the house, that still didn't mean Theo had chased her through the woods to her death.

Theo was handling the media's fixation on him by burying himself in work. He decided to work from home and spent all day locked in his study. Mrs. Manning spent her days cooking and micromanaging the staff to the point that one of the cleaners had quit on the spot. As for me, it was business as usual in the library. I was finding more rare editions that had not been listed on Myles Patterson's inventory. Had he purposefully left these editions off the inventory because he'd stolen them, or had he just not had the chance to include them? There was no rhyme or reason to his inventory, and I couldn't tell where he had started or finished before his untimely dismissal.

Luca didn't show up to help me the day before and I was told her mother and her mother's fiancé had arrived to take her away to Cincinnati for the weekend. I was glad that they were getting her away from all this drama but felt a little stung that no one had bothered to tell me she wasn't coming, let alone introduced me to her mom who I would've loved to have met. Then I had to remind myself that I was a member of staff. Why in the world would they go out of their way to introduce me to Luca's mom? I was not a part of this family, and I needed to remember that.

I'd just taken delivery of a large glass display cabinet to house all the rare editions when Theo showed up looking out of sorts and on edge.

"Is there anything I can do to help you? Because if I have to sit in that office for another minute, I'm going to lose my mind."

"What's wrong? Did something else happen?"

"Seems like something is happening every ten minutes. Have you seen the news lately? Now they're saying I'm responsible for the death of that girl who was killed on the road behind the estate. Mrs. Manning is afraid they're going to show up here with a search warrant."

"Don't they have to have evidence for a search warrant?" I was trying to figure out how I could ask him more questions about Cherise Gamble when he spied the display cabinet which had been delivered unassembled.

"I can put this together for you if you want."

"Really?"

"Yeah, really." He looked more relaxed as he walked over to the large box on the floor and leaned over.

"Hey, can you do me a favor and get my toolbox? It's in my study in the bottom right drawer of my desk."

"A toolbox in your study. How very handy of you," I teased, heading up the library steps. He laughed.

"What can I say? I was a Boy Scout, and we're always prepared."

I found Theo's toolbox right where he said it would be. But also noticed a file folder shoved all the way in the back of the drawer preventing me from closing it all the way. I pulled it out. It was a manila folder labeled, Misc. I glanced toward the door to make sure no one was coming and opened the folder. There were only a few sheets of paper inside. It was a letter of resignation from his job as CAO of Dorsey Snacks dated February 9, 2015, three months before his father died.

Dear Members of the Board,

I hope this letter finds you well. After much consideration, I am writing to formally announce my resignation from my position as Corporate Administrative Officer of Dorsey Snacks, effective June 30, 2015.

The decision to step down wasn't an easy one, but I have decided to pursue new opportunities that will allow me to continue growing and evolving. This choice comes from a place of excitement and optimism about the future.

It has been a pleasure working with the talented and dedicated team at Dorsey Snacks. I deeply value the experiences and knowledge I've gained during my time here, and I am grateful for the trust and support the board and the organization have extended to me throughout my tenure.

I look forward to seeing the continued success of Dorsey Snacks and remain committed to assisting in a smooth transition in any way I can. Thank you once again for the opportunity to serve in this role, and I am confident that the company will continue to thrive.

Sincerely,
Theodore Martin Dorsey
Corporate Administrative Officer
Dorsey Snacks

Theo had planned to leave Dorsey Snacks but hadn't. Was it because his father died? That was the only thing that made sense to me. I quickly closed the folder and shoved it back into the drawer. There were brochures all over Theo's desk and I absent-mindedly picked one up. It was for Hilltop Mental Health Hospital, a long-term mental health facility in Louisville, Kentucky. I flipped through it and saw they offered long-term health care and figured it was one of the places he was researching for Belle. But it still seemed odd. Why a mental health facility?

I was heading out of the study when I heard a loud beep. It was Theo's phone. I couldn't help myself and picked it up to see a text flash on his display screen.

> You know I'm always here for you if you need to talk

The message itself didn't surprise me. It was who it was

from that made me do a double take. It was from Olivia King, Theo's ex-fiancée.

Dr. Olivia King agreed to meet me in the cafeteria of Saint Ann's hospital in Cincinnati where she was a pediatric surgeon. As she approached me in her powder blue scrubs, I wondered why he had lied to me about never having heard from Olivia since she broke their engagement. She'd certainly been in the area, and she was certainly beautiful, but not in an over-the-top way enhanced by lots of makeup. She was beautiful in an effortless no makeup, glowing dark golden skin, and gorgeous smile way of the type of women who made me very self-conscious. But the warmth of her smile instantly put me at ease. I bet her patients loved her.

"Sabrina?" As she approached me, she held out her hand, which I shook.

"Nice to meet you, Dr. King. Thank you so much for meeting me. I know how busy you are, so I'll make this quick."

"You said this is about Theo? Is he okay?"

"Have you seen the news recently?"

Her eyes widened in understanding, and she gave me a brief nod. "Let's go sit over here where we could have a little more privacy."

I followed her over to an empty seating area next to the cafeteria and we sat ourselves on the leather couch. After I'd seen the message from Olivia on Theo's phone, a quick internet search led me to where she worked, and I reached out to her. I had to promise I wasn't from the media to get her to agree to meet me, but never told her exactly who I was. She must still care a lot about him to have agreed to meet a total stranger.

"I saw the news and I feel horrible for him. Theo would never hurt anyone." As an afterthought, she added, "Wait... are you his girlfriend?"

"No. I'm not. I work for Theo. I was hired to restore his mother's library."

"Well, you two must be close if you're contacting me." The brief narrowing of her eyes told me that her guard was suddenly up.

"I'd like to think we've become friends, and I know I have no right to ask you this, but why did you break off your engagement?"

She looked completely taken aback by my question but relaxed when I added, "I suspect the police are going to want to question everyone close to him any day now. I think Theo's a good guy, but I haven't known him as long as you have. I just want to make sure I'm not wrong about him."

"Well, what did he tell you about our engagement?"

"You left him your ring and a breakup letter, and he hadn't seen or heard from you since."

"That would be true except for the not hearing from me. I still text Theo Happy Birthday every year and on every holiday, but he's never texted me back."

"You obviously still care about him. Why break up with him?"

"Breaking our engagement wasn't a decision that I made lightly, and it was a long time coming."

"Did something happen? Did he cheat?"

"No, nothing like that. I'm not sure how I can explain this in the way that you'll understand, but if you're working for him, can I assume you've met his family? Spent time on the estate?"

"I'm living on the estate. My room is across the hall from Mrs. Manning's."

Olivia let out a breath, leaned back against her chair and gave me a look. "So, you've felt it, haven't you?"

"Felt what?" But I knew exactly what she was talking about.

"That lurking, lingering feeling of dread like you know

there's something not quite right in that house but you just can't put a finger on what it is."

I looked away from her and didn't quite know what to say, because she had hit the nail on the head. I nodded.

"I kind of thought it might've gone away since we split up, but if you're here asking questions, I can only assume nothing has changed, right?"

"Is that the reason why you broke off your engagement?"

"No, but it was a big reason. That and his father."

"You didn't get along with his dad?"

"Theo was a different person around his father. Things would be fine between us. We'd be getting along well. Then either his father would call, text, or stop by his apartment and when he was gone, Theo would fall into this funk for days. I've never seen a man with such a tight hold on his children. He'd punish Theo whenever he did something he didn't like."

"How?"

"Theo was the heir apparent. But his father would change his will in favor of Belle whenever he was mad at him. It was sadistic."

"What was Belle like?"

"I never really saw much of her because their father kept her so busy. She was basically his flunky. He treated the house-keeper better than her. But the few times we talked, she was a little... odd... but sweet."

"And Mrs. Manning?"

"She was nice enough to me. I had no real issues with her, but she seemed hella uptight and was always watching me like I might steal something."

"What was the final straw?"

"We were growing further and further apart. Every time I told him he needed to stand up to his father, he pushed me away, but the final straw was what happened after his mom's memorial service that year."

"Memorial service?"

"Yeah, every year on the anniversary of her death they would have a private candlelight service in the Dorsey family mausoleum. Have you been in there?"

I merely nodded, anxious for her to continue.

"Martin Dorsey would have a priest come and perform a service. That year I was invited because Theo and I were engaged. I'd never been invited the entire time that we'd been dating. It was a brief service and afterwards we were going to have dinner at the house. After we left the mausoleum, I realized I forgot my phone and ran back to the chapel to get it. By the time I grabbed my phone and went to leave, someone had turned the lights off and locked me in."

"What?" My hands flew to my mouth as the horror of being locked inside a mausoleum made my stomach knot up.

"I must've pounded on that door screaming for at least twenty minutes before someone finally came and let me out. It was the gatekeeper. I can't even remember the guy's name. By that time, I was crying and hysterical and just wanted to go home. And Martin Dorsey treated me like I was some silly child who'd overreacted. Right then and there I knew there was no way in hell I was marrying into that family."

"Did you ever find out who locked you in?"

"No. None of them would admit to locking me in and Theo acted so strange I wondered if maybe he'd done it."

"Why would he have done that to you?"

"Honestly. I think he wanted me to break our engagement. I think he was trying to save me."

"From what?"

"I have no idea. I didn't stick around to try and figure it out. I got up early the next morning and left him the letter along with my ring, and I haven't seen Theo since. I wasn't trying to be some tragic Gothic heroine who met her end at the hands of some fucked-up family."

"He made it sound so cryptic like you disappeared off the face of the earth and no one had heard from you since."

"I think he was probably saving face telling you that. I'm not sure I would've admitted what really happened to anyone."

"You've been in Cincinnati all this time?"

"Yes. Which is why I wondered if Theo was the one that locked me in that mausoleum to scare me away because if he'd wanted me back or wanted to know why I left beyond what I'd written in the letter, he knew where to find me. But he never came after me."

We were silent for about a minute before I asked the real question I wanted the answer to.

"If you think he's the one that locked you in the mausoleum, do you think he's capable of murder?"

"You're asking me if I think he killed Jennifer Hampton?"

"Yes."

"Honestly, the Theo I knew wasn't capable of murder. That was several years ago. I don't know the man he is today, but I do know this."

"What?"

"We're all capable of murder under the right circumstances."

I thanked her and left. As I was heading toward my car in the parking lot, I spotted someone I knew in the distance heading into another brick building adjacent to the hospital. It was Mrs. Manning carrying a large vase of flowers that I recognized from the foyer. Then I noticed the name on the building she was walking into: Brightman Dialysis Center. I figured she was there donating flowers and started to follow her to check to see if she needed help but stopped myself. I didn't want to have to explain what I was doing there. So, I left.

I tried calling my sister on the way home to see if she wanted to have dinner with me. I was surprised with everything going on that she hadn't called to see if I was okay or to tell me I told you so about working for the Dorseys. Once again, I got the message that her voicemail box was full and hung up. Then my phone rang, and I answered, figuring it was Cami. It was Jared Green.

"Why are you avoiding me, Sabrina?" he asked in lieu of a greeting. His voice was tense and angry.

"Why are you harassing me, Jared?" I snapped back. "I told you I'd contact you if I found the tote bag. And I haven't contacted you, so what does that tell you?"

"It tells me I'm not sure if I can trust you anymore because I don't know whose side you're on."

"This isn't about picking sides. I always keep my word. I said I'd contact you if I found the tote. I haven't found it."

"Are you even looking for it?"

"Are you the reason why the media is connecting Jennifer Hampton's death to Cherise's?"

"I guess that means you're not looking for it and, yes, I may have sent a journalist friend I know an anonymous tip. Don't worry. I never mentioned your name, so what are you worried about?"

I had to calm down before responding because I was ready to explode. "You are a police detective. Why am I having to tell you of all people that linking Cherise's death to a current murder muddies the waters and just adds to the leads your colleagues have to chase down to solve Jennifer Hampton's murder. You've let this vendetta against Theo Dorsey cloud your judgment."

"Wow. So, you are screwing him."

"You know what? Screw *you*, Jared!" I hung up on him and blocked his number.

THIRTY-ONE
BELLE

She was too afraid to try again. Too afraid of what would happen if he caught her. But she needed to leave soon. Last night she'd overheard the nurse talking on her phone, telling someone her job would be ending soon because Belle was being sent to a long-term care facility. She didn't believe for a single second he was sending her anywhere that would aid in her recovery. She remembered their last conversation before she'd ended up in this bed, and he'd called her crazy. If he was sending her anywhere, it would be a psychiatric hospital because his life would be so much easier without her, and no one would ever believe her about what he'd done. Whatever his plan was, she had no intention of sticking around to find out.

The clock was ticking, and she finally realized she needed help. As she lay in the dark, her eyes scanned the room, and she saw that the nurse had left the book she'd been reading on her bedside table. It was *Waiting to Exhale*. Then she saw something else, an ink pen lying next to the book. Getting the pen into her hand wouldn't be a problem. She could easily turn over and reach the book and the pen. The question was, could she write with the pen? Her fine motor skills were taking longer to recover as was her voice. If she could talk, she could just ask the nurse for help. This was the best and only plan she could come up with on such short notice.

She turned on her side and reached out.

THIRTY-TWO
SABRINA

Raised voices from the foyer greeted me when I emerged from my room the next morning. A tall rail-thin white woman with wavy auburn hair was with a shorter light-skinned black man in the foyer, with a very concerned-looking Mrs. Manning.

"Are you sure she's not here?" The redhead was looking around the foyer and poked her head into Theo's study while her companion and Mrs. Manning stared at her in alarm.

"What's going on?" All three sets of eyes swung in my direction, but it was Mrs. Manning who responded.

"Luca ran away." She glared at the redhead who visibly flinched, and then turned her attention to me as the source of her discontent.

"Who is this? How many people are living here? What's going on in this house?"

"This is Sabrina Adams. She's our librarian and has been working to restore the library, and Luca has been helping her," replied Mrs. Manning before I had a chance to.

"Calm down. We're going to find her," said the black man, putting his hand on her back to try and calm her down.

The redhead flinched away from him. "Don't tell me to

calm down. My daughter is missing, and no one seems to care. She's only sixteen! She could be anywhere. Don't think I haven't been reading the news, a woman was murdered in this town."

"This is Heather Harris, Luca's mom," said Mrs. Manning when Heather didn't introduce herself. But I wasn't about to hold that against her. She looked frantic.

"I don't want to hear one word, Mrs. Manning. I know I messed up! I should've told her months ago that I was engaged, but you know what she's like and I was afraid of how she'd react."

"So, you showed up here with the fiancé that she knew nothing about and expected her to be happy for you? I thought we agreed that you were going to tell her before you arrived." Mrs. Manning was looking at her in confusion.

"I was going to. I swear I was. I've just been so busy, and it just slipped my mind, and I didn't think it would be a big deal just showing up here. She could see how great Carter is and how good we are together, and be happy."

"How well did that work out for you?"

Heather let out a disgusted snort and threw up her hands. "I'm done talking to you. Where is Theo? He should be here."

Heather stormed up the steps and made a left-hand turn. For someone he claimed he was no longer involved with, I noticed she knew exactly which direction his bedroom was in. I instantly shook off that thought because it was not a good place to be in emotionally over a man I'd barely shared a kiss with, and who was also my boss. Mrs. Manning trailed up the steps behind her, leaving me alone with Heather's fiancé.

"Sorry about that," he said, and gave me an apologetic smile. "I'm Carter Elliot. I'm Heather's manager and fiancé. I'm sorry that we're meeting under these circumstances." He held out a hand and we briefly shook.

"What happened? Last I heard, you guys were spending the weekend in Cincinnati."

"We were in Cincinnati for the day. Then we rented an Airbnb in Newport so we could go to the aquarium today. Things seemed to be going fine. I mean, Luca was quiet, especially after she found out we were engaged, but it seemed like she was starting to warm up to me. When we woke up and checked her room this morning, she was gone. She'd left a note saying she wasn't feeling the whole future stepdad thing and that she was going back home. But she's not here and Heather's freaking out."

"This is a big estate, Mr. Elliot. Has anyone checked with Mr. Gaines at the front gate to see if he let her in this morning?"

"No, but that sounds like a great idea. I think I'm going to head down there, thanks."

I watched Carter leave just as Heather came back down the stairs trailed by Mrs. Manning.

"Well, she's not in her room. I have no idea where she could be."

"I told you when you called that she wasn't in her room." Mrs. Manning and Heather looked ready to kill each other.

"How would Luca have even gotten back here? Did she have money?" I asked, not realizing I'd just fanned the flames.

"Theo gave her a credit card when she turned sixteen. But he told her it was only for emergencies and to always keep it with her when she wasn't at home."

"He gave a sixteen-year-old a credit card. Why wasn't I informed about this?"

Mrs. Manning stared at her until Heather let out a harsh laugh. "Oh, I get it. I had a drug problem and you two were afraid I was going to take my daughter's credit card to try and score some meth. You are unbelievable, lady."

Not in the mood to watch these two going at it, I decided to look around Luca's room to see if there could be any clue as to where she could be.

"I'm going to look around to see if she's hanging out in some other part of the estate. This is a big place and she could be anywhere. Your fiancé went down to check with Mr. Gaines to see if he remembers her coming back." They both ignored me.

After a quick check of the library came up empty, I went up to the second floor and could hear Heather and Mrs. Manning continuing to snipe at each other in the foyer. I wondered if I should call Theo, but before I did, I wanted to do a thorough search of Luca's room while I could. Because now I had an excuse to do so.

Luca's room was much neater than it had been the last time I'd been in here. The bed was made and the clothes that had been all over the floor were gone. However, her desk with her computer where she took her classes and did all of her gaming was littered with empty pop cans, chips bags, candy wrappers. No wonder the kid never joined us for meals. She was too full of junk.

She was also clearly not in her room. But as I looked around, I noticed something I hadn't realized before. Luca's bedroom had the exact same layout as mine. Right down to the large window with the window seat overlooking the backyard and facing the woods. As I walked toward the window seat, I noticed that something was sticking out from under the bench and remembered that it had storage space underneath.

I lifted the window seat and was stunned by what I saw. On the underside of the bench seat Luca had attached a corkboard with pictures and printouts of news articles about missing people and homicide stories pinned to it. Also, inside the storage space was something very familiar. It was Cherise Gamble's tote bag. I hadn't wanted to think that Luca took it, and I distinctly remembered waiting for her to leave before locking it in my desk drawer. She must've been spying on me after she'd pretended to leave. Or she'd come back to the library later that night and found it in my desk. It wouldn't have taken much to open the lock on my drawer. If she lied about taking the tote, did she also lie about luring me into the woods, and what were all these printouts and news articles for? I looked closer and saw she'd pinned a note to the top of the pinned items on the corkboard. It read: *Midnight Caller cases.* I suddenly remembered that was the name of her TikTok account, the one where I saw her reading ghost stories in what I thought were the woods. I glanced over at the wall to see the backdrop was still mounted to the wall. When I pulled up her channel on my phone, I realized I had it wrong. She wasn't reading scary stories in the fake woods to her viewers. She was recounting true crime cases. This was a true crime podcast channel.

All the cases were crimes against women and the episodes had names like, the girl in the lake, the girl in the desert, the girl in the barrel and the last one really caught my attention. It was a preview for an upcoming episode called the girl in the road. The preview was less than a minute long and recounted the story of a young woman named Cherise Gamble who mysteriously died after being struck by a car in the road behind the estate of a wealthy family.

My mouth was suddenly dry. What made Luca decide to cover Cherise's case? Was it because she was a local woman? Or did Luca have her own suspicions about the unfortunate Miss Gamble? I searched through the rest of the items in the storage space and found files. There was a file that corresponded with each episode of her podcast channel. I grabbed the one called *the girl in the road* and stood at the door and paused to listen, relieved that Heather and Mrs. Manning had taken their argument into the garden. I used the notes app on my phone to scan each page of the file before putting it back where I'd found it, and rejoined the search for Luca.

. . .

An hour later, Theo arrived home with the missing teen who had taken an Uber from Newport to Theo's office in downtown Harper's Ferry. Luca stood behind Theo as Heather went off on her daughter for running away, before breaking down into tears. Luca looked like she wished the earth would open and swallow her and save her from her mother's tirade.

"I'm sorry!" Luca burst into tears and pushed past all of us to run upstairs into her room, and we all heard her slam the door.

"Did you put her up to this?" Heather rounded on Theo whose face was suddenly hard as stone, causing all of us, especially Heather, to flinch. I'd never seen him so angry. Heather took a step back.

"We need to talk." He didn't even raise his voice. He just cut Heather a look and she instantly shut up and followed him into the study, leaving Carter, me and Mrs. Manning staring after them in the foyer.

"Have you eaten, Mr. Elliot? Let me fix you some lunch." Mrs. Manning headed back to the kitchen and Carter Elliot trailed behind her, leaving me alone in the foyer.

I went upstairs and knocked softly on Luca's door. Hearing muffled crying on the other side, I decided just to walk in.

"Luca? Do you want to talk about it?"

She was lying face down on her bed and her shoulders were heaving. I remembered what it was like to be sixteen and have no control over my life. I sat on the side of the bed and rubbed her back until she finally stopped crying and turned a red tear-stained face to me.

"Two years," I told her.

"What?"

"Two years until you can do whatever you want whenever you want with whoever you want. I know that seems like a long time right now, but trust me, it'll fly by and then you'll be eighteen and no one can tell you what to do anymore." I'd just told her the same thing Cami had told me during one of her rare visits home from the military when I was sixteen and Mom and I were at each other's throats. She'd been right. Those two years had flown by, and I left for college and never looked back, until my mom got sick.

"But what do I do right now? Mom wants me to come live with her and that Carter guy after they get married. But *this* is my home! I don't want to leave."

"When's the wedding?"

"Next spring."

"Well, you still have time. Talk to your mom, maybe you can make a compromise and split your time between here and her house."

"They're moving to Florida. Mom hates Ohio weather, and Carter..." she said, making exaggerated air quotes around his name, "is spineless and goes along with whatever she wants."

"That's kind of harsh, Luca. You barely know the man."

"He eats his fries with... mustard." She shivered in disgust. "That's all I need to know."

We both burst out laughing. Luca rolled over, sat up and wiped her eyes with the back of her hand. I was trying to figure out how to bring up what I'd found inside her window seat when a knock sounded at the door.

Heather was standing in the doorway with a contrite look on her face. "Can I come in?" She gave her daughter a cautious smile and I instantly got up to go.

"I'll let you guys talk." As I walked past Heather, she mouthed *thank you* and I was happy to see that she looked much calmer and more reasonable than she had earlier.

Downstairs, the sounds of Theo's, Carter's, and Mrs. Manning's voices in the dining room told me they were having lunch. I wasn't hungry and headed straight for the library. They had things to work out and I had work to do. I got busy cleaning the glass display cabinet that Theo had put together for me and hadn't even heard Heather come in until I saw her standing at the top of the steps looking around.

"Let me guess, you had no idea there was a library in this house, did you?"

"I barely know what's in this house." She walked down to where I was, and I tossed my dirty cleaning cloth onto my desk. "Luca told me how much she enjoys working in here with you and I just wanted to check it out."

"She's been such a big help. I think she might have a future as a librarian."

Heather let out a snort of laughter that set my teeth on edge. "I can't think of anything worse than being buried in books for a living, but if it gets her out of that room and amongst the living, I'm all for it."

"I can think of worse ways to earn a living."

"Oh God. I'm sorry." Her hand flew to her mouth. "I'm such a bitch. Thank you for being the voice of reason earlier. Mrs. Manning drives me nuts. She's never liked me and when Theo and I reconnected, she shit a brick."

"She can be intense. But she means well." I wanted to ask her what, if anything, had been worked out with Luca, but realized it was none of my business.

"If you say so," she said, clearly unconvinced.

Heather continued to wander around the library, looking bored, and finally plopped down in a leather chair in the reading area. She pulled out her phone and began scrolling. I shook my head. She had no interest in this space or the fact that her daughter was working here with me. She just wanted a place to hide.

"Is lunch over already?"

"Oh, I never eat lunch," she replied absently, still scrolling. "But they're still eating."

"I think I'll go up and join them." I was about to walk up the steps when Heather jumped up, her face reddening.

"Don't leave me here alone." She practically ran over to where I was standing.

"Why? What's wrong?"

"This house is haunted." Her voice was barely above a whisper, and I couldn't figure out why since we were the only two people in the room.

"Haunted?"

"I know it sounds crazy but look at this." She pulled back the sleeve of her gauzy green blouse and showed me a thin whitish jagged scar on the underside of her forearm. It was about half an inch long.

"A *ghost* did that to you?" My raised eyebrow and skeptical look made her immediately pull her sleeve down.

"I know how it sounds, but that's the only explanation I can think of. And before you ask, no, I wasn't high. I've been clean for eight years."

"Then what happened?" I know she claimed to have been clean for eight years, but her eyes were fever bright and she was suddenly fidgety.

She crossed her arms and leaned against the stair railing. "Two years ago, I was here visiting Luca and went out into the garden to take a call. I was in the garden alone when someone pushed me from behind and my arm got cut on the edge of the fountain when I tried to catch my fall. There was no one in the garden with me. Everyone else was inside."

"Everyone?"

"Everyone except Theo. He hadn't gotten home from work. Not that he was any help. He found the heel of my high-heeled sandal stuck in one of the cobblestones near the fountain. It had broken off and Theo was convinced that's the reason I fell, because my heel broke. But I'm not crazy. I felt hands on my back."

Carter suddenly appeared in the doorway of the library. "Babe, I booked us a hotel room in town. We need to go check in. I'll be out front." He left and Heather turned to go.

"You guys aren't staying here? There are four guest bedrooms."

Heather whirled around. "Didn't you hear what I just told you?" she hissed. "This place is haunted. My daughter may be a big fan of this house, but I'm not staying here, and I thought you of all people would understand."

"Me? Why?" What was she talking about?

Heather touched her index finger to her temple and gave me a sympathetic look. "Looks like the ghost got you too."

I touched the wound on my temple, now covered by a brown flesh-colored Band-Aid and resisted the urge to blurt out that I thought her daughter had done this to me as I followed her out of the library and watched her leave. Theo was back behind his locked office door and Luca was in the kitchen with Mrs. Manning. A platter of sandwiches was on the sideboard, and I spied something familiar sitting next to it. It was a hardback copy of *Waiting to Exhale*. It looked like the same one Belle's nurse had been reading to her. Why was it here? I'd last read it for my modern black classics class in college and a reread was in order. I grabbed it and put it in my purse in my room to read during my appointment to get my hair re-braided tomorrow.

I couldn't catch Luca alone again until after dinner. She was in her room packing snacks into a backpack and when she saw me, she made a face.

"They're making me come with them. I have to stay with my mom for the next few days while she's in town."

"We need to talk." I walked over to her window seat and

pulled it up, revealing the corkboard and all the articles and photos.

"Hey! That's private! What is your problem?" She rushed over and tried to close the window seat, but I'd already grabbed Cherise Gamble's tote and pulled it out.

"You lied to me. You had this all along. Why did you take it? For some podcast?"

She reached out and tried to snatch it away from me, but I held it out of her reach.

"Answer me, Luca."

"All right! Fine." She went over and sat down heavily on her bed while I stood, still holding the tote bag.

"You want to know one of the main reasons why I stopped going to school?"

"I heard it was because you were bullied."

"But do you want to know why I was bullied?"

"Why?" I figured it was because she was different. A shy, anxious loner. In other words, an easy target. At least that's what I thought she'd say.

"It's because kids at school said Theo was a murderer. They said he killed a girl on his property, then pushed her down the embankment into the path of car. I know that's not true and I'm going to prove it."

"How?"

"The same way all good true crime podcasts do, research, and witness interviews."

"Witness interviews? There were witnesses to what happened to Cherise Gamble?"

"Well, no," she admitted, looking down at her feet. "But I found a couple of people who knew her when she was alive, and they had a lot to say about what could've happened to her and neither one of them think Theo did it."

"Who are these people? No, let me guess, her barista and her first-grade teacher."

"No. Her best friend and her brother." Her smug smirk instantly put me in my place.

"Isn't her brother in South Korea?" I asked, wanting to make sure Jared Green hadn't approached Luca pretending to be her brother like he had with me.

"Yeah, so what?"

"You interviewed them both?"

Luca nodded and smiled, proud of herself. I had to admit I was impressed. As much as I pride myself on my research skills, I would've had no idea who to even contact for interviews.

"Did you know whose tote bag that was when you found it in the library?"

"Uh... yeah. About the tote bag." She looked at her feet again.

"What about it?"

"I didn't find it in the library. I was the one who hid it in there because Manning is always searching my room whenever I'm out to make sure I'm not hiding kilos of cocaine under my pillow. When you saw me with it, I panicked and didn't know what else to say. Then you wouldn't let me have it and I had to get it back."

"You cannot be serious right now," I said through gritted teeth. "Where did you even get it?"

"Luca!" Heather's voice sounded from the foyer. "We're ready to go!"

Luca rolled her eyes and gave me a pained look. "I have got to go with Mom and Colonel Mustard. But listen to my podcast. I already recorded and uploaded it and it's going live in an hour." She grabbed her backpack and darted out the door before I could stop her leaving me standing in her empty room.

You're listening to The Midnight Caller podcast with your host Luca Harris. And in tonight's episode we're going to be talking about the mysterious death of Cherise Gamble. We're also going to be talking to two guests who knew Cherise better than anyone, her best friend, Risa Logan, and her brother, Elijah Gamble. But first: Who was Cherise Gamble?

I had ten seconds to spare before pulling up Luca's podcast channel on my phone. I'd spent the hour since she'd left sitting in my darkened room and staring at the wall, unable to believe that for a week, I'd suspected Theo Dorsey of killing a woman based on finding her bag in his house. I'd even involved the dead woman's ex-fiancé who was now convinced her death was at the hands of my boss, and had tipped off the media. All because I was a coward and hadn't shared any of this with Theo, and because a teenager was afraid to tell me the truth. What was the truth? Where had Luca gotten Cherise's tote bag?

I listened as Luca described Cherise's backstory, most of which I'd already heard from Jared, leading up to the day of her death, and the introduction of her first guest, Risa Logan. The screen suddenly split showing Risa, a pretty plus woman of about thirty with light brown skin, and perfect makeup rocking a shaved head. She was sitting in a room that looked like a home office.

Luca: Thank you for coming on the show, Risa.

Risa: Thanks for having me.

Luca: How long were you and Cherise friends?

Risa: About five years. We met in college.

Luca: What was she like?

Risa: She was smart, funny, kind... an amazing friend. I've never had a friend like her and probably never will again.

Luca: Can you take us back to the day she died? Did you see her that day?

Risa: Just briefly. Her car was in the shop, and I gave her a ride to campus that morning. She told me she didn't need a ride home and that she'd call me the next day. But... (crying)

Luca: I'm so sorry. Do you need to take a break?

Risa: No. I'm okay. It's still so hard to talk about her. I still can't believe she's gone.

Luca: Did you know what her plans were for that day?

Risa: She had an appointment with the place she was doing her internship. But she never said where it was, and I didn't ask because I was running late for work.

Luca: Did Cherise have a boyfriend?

Risa: She had a fiancé named Jared. But he cheated on her, and she broke up with him. That asshole really broke her heart.

Luca: How did she find out?

Risa: The other chick DMd her.

I sat up in bed. I'd caught Jared in another lie. Cherise hadn't broken up with him for another man. The real reason he was so obsessed with finding out what happened to his ex, and so determined to blame Theo, was because he'd cheated, and the guilt was eating him alive. By the time I turned my attention back to the podcast, Luca was asking Risa her last question.

Luca: To your knowledge, did Cherise know Theo Dorsey?

Risa: If she did, she never told me. I have no idea why she was on the road behind his property.

Luca thanked Risa for being on the podcast and took a break to talk about the episode's sponsor, an energy drink called Buzzy. While she talked about how Buzzy gave her energy and focus, I scrolled through the scanned photos on my phone that I took of the contents of the file she had on Cherise's case. Nothing jumped out at me at first. It was just copies of the same photos and articles she had pinned to the window seat corkboard. But there was something else, an aerial photo of the road behind the estate with an x marking the spot where Cherise had been hit. It also showed the embankments on either side of the road as well as the woods and the buildings on each side.

To the left of the map beyond the woods was the Dorsey estate, and on the right side was a historic home whose parking lot butted up to a wooded area. When I saw the name of the home, my stomach turned inside out. The Thomas Duncan House. Thomas Duncan had been the founder of Harper's Ferry, and his home was a museum. TD. Cherise's appointment had been at the Thomas Duncan House, not with Theo Dorsey. Since her death was ruled an accident, no one had bothered to investigate when Jared had shown them the appointment with TD in her planner. She'd fallen down the embankment from the opposite side of the road.

"Way to go, Luca," I mumbled to myself.

I immediately unblocked Jared and called him. He needed to know about this new information. It didn't solve Cherise's case. At least now he'd be looking in the right direction for answers. There was no answer, and I hung up and texted him.

We need to talk. ASAP. It's important!

A minute later, he texted me an address in Cincinnati. It was already after eleven thirty and it would be close to midnight when I got there, but this couldn't wait. I glanced at Luca's podcast again in time to see the real Elijah Gamble, who was the male version of his sister, thanking Luca for retrieving his sister's tote bag for him from where it had sat in storage for years at her old apartment building, and agreeing to mail it to their parents.

THIRTY-THREE
JARED

When she arrived, Jared stepped aside so she could enter. His hands tensed with the urge to wrap them around her throat and squeeze. She eyed him with the same haughty *butter wouldn't melt in her mouth* look she'd given him when they'd first met all those years ago. Back then it had turned him on, challenged him even. Now it just made him sick.

He'd never been into older women, and looking at her now, didn't understand what he'd once found so appealing. When he'd spotted her photo in the newspaper that morning, he'd been stunned. How had he not known who she really was? It all made perfect sense. But it was also validation that Cherise's death had been all his fault, and he'd sagged to the floor, sobbing with guilt and regret. Once he'd calmed down, he went to his bedroom and searched his closet until he'd found the burner phone he used to use to call her.

"I'm here. Now, what do you want?" She looked bored and gazed around his condo with a frown as if it were a shack.

"To see you in prison for the rest of your miserable life. You murderer."

"Name your price."

"I can't be bought," he spat, and noticed her eyes widen in shock as he pulled out a set of handcuffs and lunged for her.

She was surprisingly quick for an older chick and narrowly dodged him, almost escaping his grasping hands. But he got a handful of her shirt, nearly ripping it from her back, and pulled her to him. She threw her head back, catching him in the mouth and splitting his lip. He let out a grunt and shoved her away from him. She stumbled and almost fell, before heading into the kitchen and grabbing the smallest of his set of red ceramic kitchen canisters from the counter and throwing it at him. She missed, hitting the wall. The canister exploded. They both stood staring down at the contents lying on the floor amongst the ceramic shards. There was a clear plastic bag with a rose gold iPhone with a broken screen and a platinum wedding band. She quickly snatched up the bag and flipped it over. The back of the phone case was a photo of a smiling Jennifer Hampton with her two beautiful little girls.

"I really wish you hadn't seen that." His dull voice was devoid of emotion. He'd been planning to arrest her. Now she had to die because she knew he'd killed an innocent woman.

He'd met Jennifer while he was at a bar in Newport one night and they'd hit it off. He'd brought her back here to his condo. It was the best sex he'd had in a very long time, and he wouldn't have minded seeing her again, but she was gone by the time he woke up. He kept going back to that bar for weeks, but she never came back. Months later, he'd spotted her again in the Parkwood Hotel while he was following Theo Dorsey. He'd watched her take off her wedding ring and how it fell on the floor when she tried to hastily shove it in her purse.

He'd overheard her telling the older white businessman who was buying her drinks that her name was Amber, and she was a graphic designer. She'd told Jared the night they'd met that her name was Mira, and she was an accountant. He couldn't have cared less that she was married. But when she made a beeline straight for Theo Dorsey and then left with him, it enraged him. Another woman he'd been with who wanted that rich bastard instead.

It was irrational thinking on his part, but he didn't care. He'd picked up her ring from the floor and waited for her to come back to her car. He hadn't meant to kill her. That hadn't been his plan. He thought she'd be grateful he'd found her ring and maybe come home with him, but she'd looked right through him when he finally revealed himself. She didn't recognize him at all. He noticed her face fall when she realized he wasn't Theo Dorsey. Filled with pent-up rage, he snapped.

Afterwards, he kept her phone and wedding ring with plans to plant it on Dorseys property. But he'd hired more security after Sabrina called the cops on him, and now Jared's plan was on hold.

"Wow," she said, throwing her head back and laughing hysterically. "Talk about the pot calling the kettle black. Then again, you've always been a hypocritical bastard, haven't you?"

He lunged for her, but she pulled her own surprise from her back pocket. A butcher knife. She plunged it into his chest and as he sank to the floor, he wondered briefly if he'd finally get to see Cherise again. His visitor pulled the knife out, straddled his chest, and got to work.

THIRTY-FOUR

SABRINA

Jared lived in a condo complex where every unit had the same taupe colored vinyl siding but with different colored front doors. When I arrived, I was surprised to see his navy-blue door slightly ajar and knocked.

"Jared?" I pushed the door open and stepped inside the condo to find myself in a small foyer with steps that led up to the living area.

A small glass table sat along the wall to the right of the door with a ceramic bowl sitting on it that held a set of car keys next to a framed photograph of a smiling couple. It was Jared and Cherise, and from the way they were dressed and their pose with her right hand over his showing off a heart-shaped engagement ring, I figured it was their engagement photo. But it was what was hanging around her neck that made me pick the photo up to get a better look.

Cherise wore a thin gold chain with a turtle pendant hanging from it. The turtle's shell was inlaid with mother of pearl. It looked exactly like the turtle charm I'd found under my bed in my room at the Dorsey estate. How did it get under my bed? And why was I right back to where I'd been before Luca's podcast? Did this mean Cherise had been in Theo's house, after all? I sat the photo back down and took a deep breath to resist the urge to punch the wall. Shit!

"Jared!" I walked up the steps into his living room. It was dark. The only light that was on besides down in the foyer was coming from the kitchen, which had a long counter with barstools separating it from the living room. I walked toward the kitchen and was startled by the sound of heavy breathing.

"Jared?" I walked into the kitchen and saw what had been obscured by the kitchen counter.

Jared Green was lying on his back on the kitchen floor with the lower half of his face and the front of his shirt stained in blood. His eyes were open and staring. His mouth was open, too, revealing half his tongue was gone. And the person crouched over his body with his hands covered in blood was Theo.

The neighbors must have heard me screaming. I wouldn't be surprised if people back in Harper's Ferry heard me screaming. Someone called the police and by the time they arrived, I'd taken Theo's arm and quickly guided him out of the condo. But not before noticing a plastic bag lying on the counter with an iPhone face down and a wedding band. My heart leaped into my mouth as I recognized Jennifer Hampton's photo. This was her missing phone and wedding ring. Why were they here? Were they here when Theo arrived or did he bring them with him?

"He was like this when I got here. I didn't do that to him." Theo's voice was pitched a good two octaves higher than normal and his eyes were wild. He touched the back of his head, and his fingers came away bloody.

"Hold still." I looked at the back of his head and found a cut.

"Someone hit me and ran out."

"We'll get this all figured out once the police get here." But would we? What was going on? My car was parked closest, so we headed toward it.

"Hey, wait. Are you okay? Why did you text me to meet you here?" he asked as he sat in my car's driver seat with the door open and I put pressure on the back of his head with a napkin from my glove box. The flashing lights from all the police and emergency vehicles arriving lit up the night sky.

"What are you talking about? I never texted you to meet me here."

He pulled his cell phone from his inside blazer pocket and handed it to me. "I was out having drinks with some business associates, and I got this." On his screen was a message from me that read: *please meet me at this address it's an emergency* followed by Jared's address.

"I swear I didn't send this to you." I pulled out my own phone and handed it to him. He scrolled trying to find a text that wasn't there. In fact, I could only ever remember texting Theo a few times the entire time I'd known him.

"Then what are you doing here? Do you know that guy?"

Here came the complicated part. How was I going to explain how I knew Jared Green? But now was as good a time as any to at least try to explain. So, I did and watched Theo's face go from concerned to angry and finally resigned. He wouldn't look at me.

"Theo, I am so sorry," I said when he still wouldn't say anything or look at me. "I know I should have come to you when he first approached me, but I..."

"You thought I was guilty? That's why you didn't tell me when some dude you didn't even know asked you to help him prove I was responsible for a woman's death."

"No, I..."

"Let me get this straight." He stood up and snatched the bloody napkin out of my hand. "You've been living in my house, eating my food, taking my money, and smiling in my face while plotting against me with a stranger who holds me responsible for his fiancée's death? Are you fucking kidding me?"

What could I say to make him understand when I didn't even understand myself why I'd handled this so badly. But he was right. There was a part of me that thought he could have been responsible.

"Mr. Dorsey?" A tall, middle-aged black woman with a salt and pepper bob walked up to us. "I'm Detective Alison Raines. Can you answer a few questions for us?"

"Sure."

"And, ma'am, we'll need a statement from you as well. What is your name?"

"Her name is Sabrina Adams," said Theo, giving me a contemptuous look. "She *used* to work for me," Theo told her before turning to walk away.

He made it all of five steps before crumpling to the ground.

Theo was in the ER being examined. He could have hired an Uber to get him home, but the least I could do was give him a ride so he wouldn't have to get Mrs. Manning out of bed at this hour. Plus, he'd been there for me when I'd been in the ER. I should have known I was going to screw up this job when lying had cost me my last job. Not that my having been fired was the biggest thing on my mind. Jared Green was dead. Someone murdered him and cut out his tongue. It was so brutally specific. Did that mean he'd lied to someone else besides me? That was a stupid question. Liars lie to everyone, including themselves. I knew that better than anyone.

I'd given a brief statement to Detective Raines, promising to come in later today for a more in-depth interview. He may have been an obsessed liar, but I felt bad that Jared had died thinking Theo had been the cause of Cherise's death. Now he'd never know the truth. And what was the truth? I thought that after what Luca had dug up, Theo was in the clear. But why had Cherise Gamble's turtle charm been under my bed? And who had lured us both to Jared's condo?

I'd been waiting half an hour when a slender dark-haired young white man wearing a blue warm-up suit with a brown leather messenger bag slung across his torso approached me.

"Miss Adams?"

"Yes?"

"Hi. I'm Gabe Sanders, Mr. Dorsey's assistant."

"Right. I remember talking to you on the phone. It's nice to finally meet you."

"How's Mr. Dorsey doing? He called and said he needed a ride home."

"I haven't heard anything yet and he must not know I'm waiting for him."

"Um..." began Gabe, suddenly looking uncomfortable. "He wanted me to tell you that you can leave. It's late and this isn't the greatest neighborhood after dark." His face reddened in embarrassment, and I knew Theo had told him he'd fired me.

"If you don't mind, I'd like to stay. Just to make sure he's okay."

Gabe nodded and went to get us coffees. I settled in for a long wait, pulling the copy of *Waiting to Exhale* from my purse. I opened it to the first page, noticing the edge of a bookmark near the center and opened to the section with the bookmark to find someone had drawn all over the page in black ink. At first, it looked like a series of random squiggles down one side of the page. The pen had left deep grooves that had broken through to the page beneath in some parts. What in the world? Did the nurse do this? And why? Or did she have a toddler at home that had gotten hold of a pen and marked up the book? But when I turned the book horizontally, I could see the squiggles were letters.

He l p me. Tra p pe d. Be ll e

Help me. Trapped. Belle. I jumped up, grabbed my purse, and rushed out to my car.

"Miss Adams? Where are you going?" Gabe called out after me. But I didn't stop.

I had the book in my hand when I arrived on the third floor and my mind was racing. Why had Belle written that message in the book? Was she being abused, hurt? Were they keeping her from leaving? The door to Belle's room was open. I rushed inside without hesitation to find myself in a room with an empty bed. Belle's hospital bed was empty and the machines that had been connected to her were gone. Dread flooded my body as I looked at the lone woman standing by the window. It was Mrs. Manning.

"Where is she? Where's Belle?"

Mrs. Manning turned to look at me and noticed the book in my hand.

"I wondered where that had gotten to. I left it in the dining room. Why did you take my book?" She took a step toward me, and I took a step back. What the hell was going on? Where was Belle and why was Mrs. Manning here? She was looking at me with a much more relaxed expression than I'd ever seen on her face. But relaxed wasn't the right word. She looked peaceful.

"Your book?" I looked down at the book in my hand with its vibrant colors on the cover and then back at Mrs. Manning in confusion. "I came up here because I found a message from

Belle in this book saying she needed help and that she was trapped."

Mrs. Manning chuckled softly before reaching out and taking the book from my hand. She opened it to where I found the message. "This was my book. I wrote that message back when this was my room, and *I* was trapped here."

"I... I don't understand."

She let out a slow sigh, like she was in pain and put a hand on her stomach, still staring at the book. "Well, I guess there's no reason to keep this secret any longer."

"What secret? What do you mean?" I took a step closer to her when she suddenly swayed on her feet.

"I'm dying, Miss Adams. And I need to get this off my chest before I do."

I looked at her, really looked at her, and realized she wasn't wearing makeup. Her skin was dull and washed out and her hair was thinning. She'd been wearing wigs. She had been doing a very good job of hiding being sick. But now she looked worn out. I realized the signs had been there all along. Her constant absences, seeing her at the Dialysis Center, and Luca's concern. I tried reaching for her hand, but she snatched it away, the proud look on her face letting me know she didn't need my pity.

"Do you like your name, Sabrina?" she asked, surprising me. Why was she asking me this?

"Yes... I do," I replied slowly. I actually hadn't liked my name until I was in college.

"Well, I've always hated my name, Annabelle," she said with a soft chuckle and a shake of her head. "Still do. Hated everyone calling me Anna or worse yet, Annie B. But my best friend Lorraine Collins called me Belle, like the heroine of *Beauty and the Beast*. She hated that everyone called her Lori. So, I called her Rainey," she said, her face lighting up at the memory. "We met at Harper's Ferry Community College when we were both flunking the same math class. We weren't ready for college back then and only went to make our families happy. The end of our first year we dropped out, got an apartment together, and got jobs working the line at Dorsey Snacks. This was before your time, but there used to be a show that came on back in the eighties about two best friends who were roommates and worked at a brewery."

"*Laverne and Shirley*." She looked surprised that I knew about that show. "I used to watch reruns with my mom."

"Well, that was us. But even though she called me Belle, Rainey was the beauty. She was *that* girl as they say today, and it didn't take long for Martin Dorsey to notice. I'll never forget the day we had a line inspection, and he came down personally from his office and saw Rainey. He couldn't take his eyes off her. Within a week, he pulled her from the line and made her his secretary. Within the year, they were engaged and six months after that they were married. That was the beginning of the end of our friendship."

"Why?" But I knew why. I'd dated a guy like Martin Dorsey once, controlling and demanding of my time and attention.

"Because he hated anyone and anything that Rainey loved that wasn't him, especially me. Before I knew it, we slowly lost touch. I was so hurt over that at the time. But now I realize he isolated her and made it impossible for her to maintain her friendships."

"I don't understand. What do you mean you were a prisoner here?"

Mrs. Manning wouldn't be rushed and stared off into space and I had to wait several long seconds for her to continue.

"The year after Rainey got married, I got married myself. To a wonderful man named Theodore Manning. Ted was the safety manager at Dorsey Snacks, and he wasn't a flashy man or the richest man. But he was a good man, and he treated me like a queen."

"Mom, you told me my dad abused you." Theo was

standing in the doorway to Belle's room. How long had he been there? And what the hell had he just said?

"*Mom?* She's your... mom? But..." I looked from Theo to Mrs. Manning, but I may as well have not even been in the room.

"I told you that so you'd stop asking questions about your father I couldn't answer." Mrs. Manning's voice was devoid of emotion, and she looked beyond tired.

Theo walked over to his mother and put his arm around her. She leaned into him, looking like she wanted to hold on to that moment with her son forever, but she had a story to tell and turned back to me.

"Belle and I had always promised we'd name our firstborn daughters after each other and when I found out she'd named her daughter Belle, I realized she still loved me like a sister. But I couldn't return the favor because Ted and I struggled with infertility for ten years before I finally got pregnant with our miracle baby." She smiled up at Theo who smiled back. "Then four months before my due date, Ted was killed in an explosion at Dorsey Snacks."

Mrs. Manning's husband was the man that was killed in the explosion that blinded my mom. It had never even occurred to me to wonder who that man had been.

"But how did you end up trapped here in this room?" I asked, still so confused.

"Because Martin Dorsey paid out a lot of money in settlements to everyone hurt in the explosion, but he refused to pay me the settlement I'd been awarded for Ted's death. All he did was pay for the funeral. I really didn't want his damned money. I just wanted to clear my husband's name because Martin Dorsey lied and said my husband was the reason why that machine exploded. He lied and said Ted had submitted phony safety reports, but I had copies of Ted's original safety reports that the piece of machinery was faulty and needed to be replaced. As much as I wanted to clear his name, I needed money. I was pregnant and had no family to help me since both of my parents were dead and I was an only child. I was having a difficult pregnancy and had no healthcare because I'd been cut off Ted's health insurance once he died. I was desperate and I contacted Martin Dorsey and told him I had the original safety reports and that if he didn't pay me my settlement, I was going to the police and the media with the reports."

"What did he do?" asked Theo, and I realized this was the first time he was hearing about any of this too.

"Invited me over for dinner to talk. Told me how happy Rainey would be to see me." Tears instantly filled Mrs. Manning's eyes, and she buried her hands in her face and sobbed. Theo and I exchanged glances, and Theo rubbed her back until she pulled herself together enough to continue.

"Was she happy to see you?" I asked as I took a step forward and took her hand, surprised that she let me.

"Rainey was dead. She'd died in childbirth along with their son two days before. I hadn't even realized she'd been pregnant again. That bastard took me to the Dorsey family mausoleum where her casket was laid out. My best friend in the whole world was gone."

So that's why Lorraine Dorsey's crypt had the name Martin Edward Dorsey Junior etched under hers with no birth or death dates. Martin Dorsey Junior had been the son who'd died with her in childbirth.

"That mother…" whispered Theo through gritted teeth, his voice trailing off before he could finish what he'd wanted to say, echoing what we were all thinking.

"It was such a shock I went into premature labor right there on the spot. During labor I had a stroke. He kept me here." She gestured around the room. "And provided me with minimal care while he passed my son off as his own to the world and played the grieving widower. No one except me and Dr. Hill knew that Rainey and their son had died. I laid in this room rotting for months, determined to get my strength back, to get my son and get the hell out of this house. It took me six months to get the strength to even get out of this bed."

"You didn't leave. Why?" I asked.

But Mrs. Manning was staring off into space like she'd disappeared into that distant memory.

THIRTY-FIVE
BELLE

It didn't take Belle long to realize no one was coming to save her. Despite the message that she'd written in the nurse's book, she was still a prisoner. And Martin Dorsey was planning to send her to a long-term care facility. Once she was out of this house, she'd never be allowed back, and she'd be cut off from the one thing that truly belonged to her. She would need all her strength to do what needed to be done. It was after midnight before she swung her legs over the side of the bed, listening to the sounds of the house as she'd done a million times before. She'd gotten so good at being able to tell where people in the house were, but the only person whose location she needed to know always was Martin Dorsey's. She planted her bare feet on the hardwood and rocked up from the side of the bed into a standing position. Her legs were still weak, but she was more determined and had more motivation than the last time she'd tried this.

She broke down what she had to do into small goals. Standing up was goal number one. The next goal was reaching the end of the bed. She was able to use the bed itself to reach that goal, and she dragged her feet to the end of the hospital bed, gripping the railing at the foot of the bed for dear life. For her next goal it took a while to get up the courage to push off from the railing at the foot of the bed and launch herself in the direction of the door. But with wobbly legs like a toddler learning to walk, and with her arms outstretched in front of her, she managed to make it almost to the door before falling heavily against it.

She held on to the doorknob as sweat poured down her face and back, dampening the cotton nightshirt that she'd lived in for six months. She could smell her own body odor but couldn't be bothered about that. After what seemed like an eternity, and when she finally caught her breath, her next task was to grip the doorknob tight enough to twist it open. Her hands were slick with sweat, and it took her several tries to grip the knob tight enough to pull the door open. Once it was open a crack, she pressed her eye to the opening. But all she could see was sporadic light illuminating the dark hallway, and she could hear the faint sounds of music.

She opened the door enough to squeeze her thin frame through it and looked both ways to figure out where the music was coming from. Clinging to the wall, she took slow, agonizing steps toward the sound of the music. As she got closer, she could hear it was a lullaby, "Twinkle, Twinkle Little Star". She paused just beside the open door to catch her breath and rest. She was so close, and she wouldn't be denied now. Pressing herself up from the wall, she swung around until she was standing directly in the doorway looking inside, and what she saw shocked her.

Martin Dorsey sat in a wicker chair by a crib in a beautifully decorated nursery. Lions, tigers, elephants, and giraffes frolicked across the walls in patterned wallpaper. The source of the lights was a carousel lamp on a table that played "Twinkle, Twinkle Little Star" as it cast animal shaped lights all around the room, including the ceiling. A beautiful, brown-skinned baby boy of about six months old was cradled in Martin's arms. Her baby. The room smelled like baby lotion and talcum powder, and once again she was aware of her own stench. The stench that she'd been allowed to wallow in while this man played father to her son. When he finally looked up at her standing in the doorway, he didn't seem shocked. In fact, he looked like he'd been expecting her. He stood up.

"Belle, welcome. I wondered how long it would take you to reach this room. Although I'm surprised you got here at all."

"Give... me... my... s-son." It had been so long since she'd spoken, and her tongue felt thick and useless. Her words were slow, slightly slurred, and halting but had a quiet power behind them that was reflected in her steely gaze when she looked Dorsey in the eye.

"Of course, have a seat." He stepped aside, still holding the baby, and making no attempt to help her across the room and into the chair. He just stood there watching her to see what she would do.

She lurched forward, lost her footing, stumbled, and fell onto her hands and knees. She lifted her head up and glared at him. She realized what he was doing. This was a test. This had always been a test. He'd cut her off from the one thing in the world that was hers, then sat back to see how hard she would work to get it back. He wanted to see what she was made of and what it would take to get herself into that wicker chair. She reached out on her left-hand side and grabbed ahold of the changing table with the intention of pulling herself into an upright position. But the changing table tilted threateningly, almost falling on top of her. She instantly let it go. There was nothing else to grab onto and Martin Dorsey stepped back even further out of her reach.

Her arms and legs were screaming with pain and exhaustion from the effort it had taken her to get to this room. She crawled on her stomach, pressing her sweaty hands against the carpet and painfully pushing herself forward inch by inch. When she finally reached the chair, she had to lay her head down to catch her breath. But she didn't dare rest for too long or she might pass out and wake up back in that bed. She grabbed the chair legs and hoisted her torso across the seat, then braced her feet against the floor to push herself further up into the chair. Panting heavily, and with sweat running into her eyes and blurring her vision, she turned painfully until she was in a seated position.

"My... s-son. N-now." She held out her arms.

Martin Dorsey laid her baby in her lap, and he stared up at her, grinning with a toothless smile like he'd been waiting for her his entire life.

She broke down and sobbed, burying her face into the baby's soft neck and breathing in his heavenly baby scent. She had been robbed of the first six months of his life and she drank in every inch of him.

"You can stay here with him you know. Raise him. He'll always know that you're his mother."

Belle's head jerked up and she stared at him.

"Of course, you'll have to burn the safety reports that you were threatening me with when you came here."

"Why... w-would... I... d-do that?"

"Because like it or not, we need each other. You have nothing and no one and you still need to get your strength back. You're in no shape to raise a child. And I need an heir."

"Lit-tle... B-Belle." Was all she could get out as she referred to the daughter of her best friend and this sorry excuse for a man.

"Is just like her mother, I'm afraid. Head in the clouds, nose in a book, living in her own little world. Absolutely no head for business. Zero backbone. It would be different if that's all she was. But she's always been... off." He said it with a look of distaste on his face. "Belle's not quite right in the head. I could never leave her in charge of Dorsey Snacks. But little Martin Jr. here will have all the advantages you and your husband would've never been able to give him. He'd be a Dorsey as far as the world was concerned. He'll have the world at his feet. And you could work for me. My housekeeper Mrs. Crane is retiring. You could take her place managing my household and taking care of the children. You'd both have a beautiful home and all the things that money can buy. But if you leave this house and release those safety reports to the press and the police, I'll make sure you never see your son again."

Belle laid her head back against the back of the chair and closed her eyes. She had the reports in a safety deposit box at the bank. She had leverage, or so she'd thought. But Martin Dorsey had money and a stable of lawyers at his disposal while she could barely walk or talk, let alone get to the bank to get those papers. She looked down at her son and stroked the soft skin of his cheek while he babbled, and knew she would do anything for him. Even accept a deal from this bastard.

"In... wr-writing?" She glared at him.

"I'll have my lawyer draw everything up in writing just like any other legally binding agreement. So, we have a deal then?"

Belle nodded and he turned on his heel to leave the room when she called out.

"His... n-name... is... Th-Th-Theo." Belle knew there was little she could do to clear her husband's name. But at least his son would have *his* name.

THIRTY-SIX

SABRINA

Belle Dorsey had been moved to a smaller room and was safely asleep three doors down with her nurse sitting by her bedside watching the small flat screen TV and crocheting. The nurse never looked my way as I passed by on my way to my room to pack, giving Theo and his mom some much-needed privacy to talk.

"Sabrina, wait." Theo caught up with me at the top of the stairs. "Look, I'm sorry about what I said earlier. It was a... shock after finding that guy dead like that with his..." He shook his head and grimaced. "Then finding out you knew him."

"I know." I could barely look at him. Man, this was awkward. "How's your head?"

"Aside from a headache and some stitches, I'll live. Can we talk in the morning?"

Technically, it was the morning. I wasn't sure what there was to talk about because if we didn't trust each other, there was no point in me staying here.

"Are you sure you don't need to be with your mom? That was pretty heavy back there. Did you have any idea about any of that?"

"Honestly, no. I mean I always knew Martin Dorsey wasn't my real dad, but I also knew it was a secret I couldn't talk about, and my mom wasn't big on answering my questions. She would shame me for not being grateful for the life I had any time I asked."

I guess I couldn't blame Mrs. Manning for that since she'd been through so much to ensure Theo had a privileged life. But at what cost? "I need to go back to Cincy to give my statement later this morning and I'm fried. Can we talk when I get back? I have something to tell you about Cherise Gamble's death."

"What about it?" He was instantly on guard again. I reached out and touched his forearm.

"I promise it'll be something you'll be happy to hear about."

He gave me a half smile and nodded, then headed back down the hall.

It was nearly five in the morning when I kicked off my shoes and laid across my bed fully clothed only to discover I couldn't sleep. How could I? I rolled onto my back trying to wrap my head around all that had happened in the last twenty-four hours. Luca's investigation unknowingly uncovered where Cherise Gamble had really died, Jared Green was brutally murdered, I'd been fired, Theo was Mrs. Manning's son, and Mrs. Manning revealed her tragic past. Talk about shit getting real. Finally, my eyelids began to droop, and I closed my eyes falling into a dreamless sleep.

Music woke me up. I slowly rolled over and looked at the clock on my bedside table. It was 6:15. I groaned. Who was playing music at this time of the morning? By the time I'd pulled my comforter over me and tried to go back to sleep, the music had stopped. Then I noticed something else. The light in my closet was on. When had I turned the closet light on? I struggled to remember as sleep tried to reclaim me once again. I was almost out when the music started up again. This time I realized it was coming from inside my closet. My heart quickened as I strained to hear the music. With my heart still hammering in my chest, I threw back the comforter and got out of bed and slowly headed toward my closet door and the faint glow of light emanating from it.

I opened my closet door and realized I'd been right, the closet light was not on. Where was that light coming from? I parted the clothes hanging on the rod to press my ear against the wall. Sure enough the music was coming from behind the wall, as was the thin strip of light. There was a room behind my closet.

I flipped on the closet light so I could get a better look at the back. Feeling around on the wall, I quickly found the seams to a door but no doorknob or latch to pull the door open.

I remembered the door to the library which sat flush against the hall wall in which it was located. This appeared to be a similar type of door. I used a press pad daily to get into the library, so I started pressing around both sides of the door not knowing which way the door would slide open. Finally, about three inches from the edge of the door on the left-hand side was a circular indentation I'd never noticed before because I had no reason to look for it. The music was still playing. I couldn't tell what the song was as it was muffled, but once I pressed the indentation, the door slid open and the music stopped again.

I was at the bottom of stairs leading up to a landing. Why would there be a secret room accessible through my closet? Who was up here? My first inclination was to think it was Luca. But why? She had her own room, she had no need to sneak around secret rooms in the house. Besides, I got the impression that when she wasn't taking her online classes, recording her podcast, or gaming, searching around for rooms and passages wasn't something she had time for. I started to walk up the steps and found myself in a loft like space.

Along one wall was a table with an old-fashioned wooden card catalog sitting on top, with six drawers. Next to it was a record player playing a vinyl record. It had been turned down low, but I could now tell that it was Whitney Houston's remake of "I Will Always Love You". Underneath the table was a large trunk about four feet high and six feet wide. But it was what was in the far corner of the opposite end of the room that made my heart almost stop. Sitting in the chair slumped forward was Belle Dorsey. She was nude and from what I could tell from where I was standing, she was unconscious.

"Belle!" I rushed over, kneeling in front of her still form. As soon as I touched her shoulder, she fell forward from the chair and on top of me. The first thing I noticed was how heavy she was. There was no warmth, and the elasticity of her skin felt off, which made sense when I realized that I was, in fact, holding a life-size doll. As I struggled to extricate myself from the doll, laughter filled the small space. I saw a woman staring down at me with a demented look on her face as she continued to laugh. I scrambled to my feet. With her close-cropped hair, slender build and light brown skin, the woman looked familiar.

"Who are you?"

"You know who I am. You met me, remember?" She looked down at the doll and back at me, the demented smile still on her face.

I looked at her again and finally remembered who she was. She was the night nurse who'd asked me to sit with Belle while she went and filled a prescription, only her hair was different, and she wasn't wearing the thick glasses. Then something else became apparent and I stared at her in horror. With her graying cropped hair, and the creases in her forehead and around her eyes, she looked just like a middle-aged Belle Dorsey... because Belle *was* a middle-aged woman. When I'd seen her that night for the first time, I'd thought about how beautiful she'd looked lying there like Sleeping Beauty. But that wasn't how Belle would look in real life.

It had been the doll I'd seen in the bed that night.

"You're... Belle?"

"See," she said, making a sucking noise with her teeth. "Now you look disappointed." She bent down and grabbed the doll by its foot and dragged it back to the corner draping it over the chair with its ass in the air, making it look obscene. The doll was anatomically correct, complete with pubic hair, and I looked away.

"How long have you been..."

"Awake?" She looked proud of herself.

"I was going to say fooling everyone. Or do Theo and Mrs. Manning know you've been faking it?"

"I have no clue what that brother of mine does or doesn't know. He avoids the third floor like the plague. We were never close. Our father made sure of that. And all Mrs. Manning cares about is appearances and not embarrassing the family. I became the doll that came to life at night. I became the night nurse and would tuck doll Belle into my bed, and then creep out and have adventures. Not every night, just when I wanted to escape for a while. That doll was damned expensive. Had it custom made. Turns out there's a lot you can do when you're a ghost."

"But it was... breathing. I saw you giving that thing medicine." I glanced over at the doll like it was about to sneak up on me.

"You saw me pour medicine into its mouth. There's a compartment inside to catch... fluids. And doll Belle can breathe." She went over and pressed a button on the back of the doll and its chest began to gently rise and fall which, given its position over the chair, made it look even more ridiculously obscene. "Trust me, the company I bought her from caters to a lot of lonely guys, so they pride themselves on how realistic these things are."

"I... I need to go." This woman was so clearly not in her right mind. For all his faults, Martin Dorsey hadn't been lying. Something was very wrong with Belle. But I didn't care about anything in that moment, I wanted out of that room and away from her and that creepy doll.

I immediately headed toward the stairs, but she pulled a knife from her hoodie pocket and blocked my path. The knife had rust all over the blade. No, not rust. Blood. My hands flew to my mouth.

"Belle? What are you doing? Why do you have a knife?"

"Because you're being rude." She spat the words out at me. "You're trying to leave without even seeing *my* collection."

"What... are you talking about?"

"My collection." She grabbed me, pressed the knife against my side, and dragged me over to the table with the card catalog.

For the first time I noticed that each one of the drawers were labeled. The first drawer was labeled *Tears of the Devil*. With the knife still pressed against my side, Belle reached out and opened the drawer, pulling out a small glass vial of clear liquid with a cork stopper. She pushed it right into my face. "This was the first piece that I'd ever collected."

"What is it?" Sweat was trickling down my back and I was frozen to the spot in fear.

"Just what it says. These are my father's tears. He caused all my tears during his lifetime. I thought it only fair that I collect his. When he was dying of cancer and in so much pain, I would sneak into his room at night because it was next to mine. I'd already had my accident when he got sick so you should have seen the look on his face when he saw me sitting next to his bed." I let out a gasp and she laughed.

"He'd come into my room at night and tell me I deserved to be where I was because I'd disobeyed him by trying to run off with Myles again. I bet that bastard thought I was a ghost coming to collect his soul. He was in such agonizing pain that he was on a morphine drip controlled by a button whenever he needed it. I would tape the button to the wall out of his reach and he would cry because he was in so much pain. I started collecting his tears in these glass bottles. She pulled out the entire drawer and I could see that it was filled with several vials of tears. "I could've collected an ocean's worth of that bastard's tears, and it would never equal the tears he made me cry."

"Belle, I..."

"Next, we have *Screams of a Banshee*." She opened the drawer and pulled out a small cassette recorder and pressed the play button. The screams and pleading of a woman whose voice I recognized as Olivia King filled the small space: *Help me! Is anyone out there? Let me out! Please, can somebody hear me! Hey! Let me out!* On and on it went.

"You're the one who locked her in that mausoleum? And you recorded it?"

"You know about that, huh?" She let out a harsh laugh. "You went snooping around in my brother's business and found Olivia."

"How could you do that to her?" My voice was wobbly with fear.

"Let me guess, she told you all about how she left her phone in the mausoleum and had to go back and get it. I bet she didn't tell you she had her phone all along and just went back to call a friend and tell them all about how weird and creepy our family was and how once she and Theo were married, she'd make sure he cut us off. So, hell yes, I locked her ass in! Backstabbing bitch was always smiling in our faces and sucking up to my father. If it were up to me, her ass would still be in there."

I tried to pull away from her, but she grabbed the front of my hoodie again, pulling me to the next drawer labeled *Blood of a Siren*. She reached inside the drawer and pulled out a white handkerchief trimmed in lace with a rusty red stain the size of a quarter on it.

"Is that... blood?"

"Yes. But whose blood? Think!" she screamed in my ear when I stared at her in confusion.

"I... I... I don't know."

"What do sirens do, you idiot? You're a librarian. You should know this shit!"

"Sing?" Then I got it. "Heather? Luca's mother? So, you're the one who pushed her in the garden."

"I'm also the one who wiped her blood off the cobblestones." She put the handkerchief back in the drawer.

"What did she do to deserve that?"

"She's a shitty mother to Luca. That whole visit I watched from the shadows while she ignored that kid. She was always on her phone. I like Luca. She used to come read to me sometimes. My own brother barely came to visit, but that kid would." She was lost in the memory, and I used her distraction to push away from her and make a run for the stairs.

"Oh no you don't." She caught me by my hair, yanking me backward, and quick as a flash, like a snake sinking its fangs into flesh, punctured my side with the knife. She clamped her hand over my mouth, muffling my scream. "Don't do that again," she whispered hotly in my ear, "or I'll ram this knife into you up to the hilt. Got it?" I nodded as tears flowed down my cheeks and warm blood oozed down my side, soaking my hoodie.

"Yes." I pressed my hand to my side to try and slow the flow of blood.

"Moving on." She opened the next drawer labeled *Love of a Cherry* and pulled out a long thin gold chain. I instantly knew what it was.

Cherise was French for the word cherry and the chain in her hand was the necklace Cherise Gamble had been wearing in her engagement photo.

"I know where the turtle charm is," I blurted without thinking. That got her attention, and she froze and stared at me unblinking. "A... a... collection isn't complete without all the pieces, right? It's in my room. I found it under my bed. Why don't you let me go get it for you?"

"Why don't you shut up? Stop being so rude, and let me finish."

"You killed her, didn't you? You're the reason she fell down that embankment." I should have shut up but couldn't help myself. Belle sighed and rolled her eyes.

"Okay. You like books as much as I do. So, here's a story for you. Once upon a time Sleeping Beauty got bored pretending to be asleep and snuck out of her house while everyone was sleeping. She went into town and ended up at the only place that was open, which was a bar where she meets a handsome prince named Jared."

I let out an audible gasp. Belle glared at me and stopped talking. "I'm sorry. Go on."

"Anyway, Sleeping Beauty lied and told the man her name was Elle. They hit it off right away and hooked up in his car. Sleeping Beauty fell hard for Prince Jared and kept sneaking out to hook up with him until one night he stopped showing up and wouldn't answer her calls or texts, and the bartender told her Prince Jared's secret. He was engaged to another woman and told Sleeping Beauty to forget about him. That night our heroine snuck into her brother's study and used his computer to look up Prince Jared and found his Facebook page and saw all the pics of him and his pretty fiancée, Lady Cherry. Sleeping Beauty messaged Lady Cherry and told her she'd been hooking up with Prince Jared."

"You're the reason they broke up?"

"Didn't you just hear what I said? Are you going to let me finish or not?" Her face contorted in anger, and I nodded my head for her to continue.

"Lady Cherry ended it with Prince Jared, but he couldn't let her go. Sleeping Beauty saw Prince Jared again at the bar and he told her he regretted ever meeting her and never wanted to see her again. But Sleeping Beauty knew if Lady Cherry was gone for good, she'd have her prince back."

"You lured her to that house and chased her to her death."

"I did it all. I wrote Lady Cherry the letter offering her the internship at the Thomas Duncan House in their archives. I sabotaged her car. I pretended to be an Uber driver and picked her up and drove her to the house. And I was the one who ripped this necklace off her when she tried to get away from me in the car."

"And you were the one who chased and pushed her."

"Guilty as charged," she said in a soft menacing voice. "Not that it made any difference. Prince Jared still loved Lady Cherry, and she became a saint in his eyes when she died."

"You killed Jared too? Why?"

"That was his fault."

"How?"

"When that woman got herself killed and the media made a connection to Lady Cherry's death, they ran a pic of our family in the news and Prince Jared recognized me and started putting it all together. He called me on the burner phone we used to communicate years ago and told me he knew who I was and what I'd done. Can you believe the nerve of that man? Accusing me of murder when he was the one who'd killed that woman. He was going to frame my brother and arrest me for what happened to Lady Cherry. He could have killed you too. Prince Jared was an angry guy. I had no choice. I had to kill him. But I got a lovely souvenir." She pulled open the next drawer labeled, *Lies of a Prince*, and pulled out a glass jar.

I already knew what it would be but the sight of Jared Green's pink, bloated tongue floating in formaldehyde made me retch. Thinking I was about to vomit on her, Belle shoved me away from her and I fell backward onto my ass making the pain of my wound vibrate through my body and bringing tears to my eyes. I stared up at her, breathing hard as I clutched my side trying to staunch the flow of blood, and then I smelled it. Bacon. Mrs. Manning was up cooking breakfast.

"Help! Mrs. Manning!" I screamed. Belle fell on me, slapping me hard across the face and then grabbing two handfuls of my braids, slammed my head hard against the floor, knocking me out cold.

THIRTY-SEVEN

SABRINA

My head was killing me when I woke up and could taste blood in my mouth from my split lip. I was also sweating because it was hot in the windowless room. I was lying on the floor and Belle was gone, probably back in her room pretending since the sun was now up. I tried to get up, but my side was on fire. Thankfully, it had stopped bleeding. Slowly, I made it down the steps only to find I was sealed in and there was no panel on my side to let myself out. How did Belle get out? How was she getting in for that matter? I pounded and yelled until I was hoarse, but no one came and I instantly thought about Olivia King. I went back up with the intention of feeling around on the walls for another hidden opening when I spied Belle's collection and realized she hadn't opened the last two drawers.

I walked over and pulled open the one labeled *Crown of the Interloper* and was shocked to find a single braid. My braid. Belle was the one who'd lured me to the woods and attacked me. Why? The label said it all. I was an interloper, someone who was involved someplace I wasn't wanted and didn't belong. Belle was threatened by my being here. Did she know Theo wanted to send her away? Did she think I had something to do with that? Either way, she'd be found out.

I shoved my braid into my pocket and yanked open the last drawer that didn't have a label to find a gold skeleton key. Could this key unlock a hidden door? Scanning the room, I could see no lock to insert it in until I saw the trunk under the table with a shiny brass keyhole on the front. I winced as I bent down and pulled on one of the side handles. I had to rest between each pull, but finally managed to get the trunk free of the table. The trunk was made of leather with brass nails studding the corners. I knelt painfully in front of it and inserted the key. At first, I thought I had the wrong key as the lock was stiff and wouldn't budge, but after wiggling it around, I heard a click. I pushed up the lid and the thick odor of mildew that escaped almost made me gag. It was filled to the brim with books and as I removed each one, I saw more than a few with Lorraine Dorsey's name in them that hadn't been on Myles Patterson's inventory. I had several stacks of books piled up around me and noticed how stained and smelly they were. I was disappointed when I got to the bottom and wondered why Belle had brought this trunk up here, then remembered my room had once been Myles's room, and he probably hid this trunk up here when he was stealing books.

The heat combined with my blood loss made me light-headed and I had to lie down for a minute. I laid on my back staring up at the ceiling wondering how I was going to get out. I knew that Belle couldn't keep me alive after revealing every-thing that she had done. Was her plan to leave me up here to starve to death? Would she add the rest of me, along with my braid, to her collection? I had to find a way out of this room. I was just about to roll over and push myself to my feet when I noticed something on the ceiling, a handle. It looked like the one at my sister's place that pulled down a set of steps leading into the attic.

Slowly and painfully, I got to my feet and stared up. Yes, it was a handle I was looking at. But how was I going to get up there? Could I use the trunk? I closed the lid and climbed on top, reaching my arms up. But I miscalculated the sturdiness of the lid and my own bodyweight. One of my feet went right through the lid, landing heavily on the bottom of the trunk, or what I had assumed to be the bottom of the trunk because as soon as my foot hit it, a drawer popped open from the back. If I thought the smell of mildewy books in the main compartment was bad, it was nothing compared to the smell that emanated from the hidden drawer. I pulled my leg out and bent to look inside. What I saw made my head snap back in terror. Inside, curled into a fetal position, was the mummified remains of a body. Its skull was caved in on one side and its mouth was slightly open, showing a slight gap between the yellowed front teeth. I had found Myles Patterson.

I passed out.

I dreamt about waterfalls, specifically standing under a waterfall with my mouth open drinking the crystal clear, cold water and relieving my extreme thirst. Then I woke up to find I was lying on my back with Belle pouring a bottle of water onto my face. I immediately opened my mouth, and she poured a little water inside before twisting the cap back on the bottle, grinning down at me. The room was much cooler than it had been. Had the sun gone down?

"I see you met your predecessor."

"Did you kill him too?"

"Well, he didn't crawl in there and die on his own, now did he?"

"I thought he ran away and left you after the crash when the two of you tried to elope?"

"That's what I wanted everyone to think. I should've done it the first time he screwed me over and took money from my dad to dump me. But then he came back and wormed his way back into my life."

"Why did you let him back in?"

"Because I was still waiting for the damned prince to come save me. When Myles showed up again, I thought I'd been wrong about him. We were going to elope, but I caught him stealing more books from the library. He was up on the third level, and I shoved him over the railing. Then I panicked and didn't know what else to do because his car was parked on our property."

"He was never in the car with you, was he? You tried to get rid of his car and got into an accident and let everyone think he'd left you there."

She nodded enthusiastically, like I'd gotten an answer right in class. "What better way to never have to answer questions about where your missing boyfriend could be than faking being in a coma. But guess what?" she said with a harsh, humorless laugh. "No one ever came looking for him."

She was silent for a long time before pulling the knife from her back pocket, grabbing me by my hoodie, and pulling me to my feet. My legs buckled and I almost fell, but she jerked me up like a puppet on a string. She zip tied my hands behind my back and shoved me in front of her.

"Let's go."

"Where are we going?"

"Don't act like you don't know how this ends."

She dragged me over to a section of the wall and pressed a panel near the top. The door opened to more steps leading up. We walked up three flights of steps, each flight with its own landing that I'm guessing connected to other bedroom closets in the house, until we came to a panel in the ceiling which she pushed up and out. I stumbled and fell, but the night air quickly cooled my overheated skin. I looked around. We were on the roof surrounded by a waist high railing.

"Why are we up here?" But I knew. She was going to shove me over the side and make it look like I had taken my own life, and I had no intention of making it easy for her.

I swept one of my legs out into the back of her ankles, making her fall. I managed to get to my feet, and sprinted toward the opening we'd just come through, when she tackled me to the ground. My hands were still tied behind my back, and she turned me over and punched me in the face. My weakness from hunger and blood loss made me no contender for her and I helplessly laid there as she dragged me over to the railing.

"Please... don't." I knew she wasn't listening. But she couldn't ignore the voice that came from behind us.

"Belle, stop!"

I twisted around, stretching my neck so I could see over my shoulder and behind me. It was Mrs. Manning in a bright white nightgown, looking like an angel.

"Why? Why should I stop?" snarled Belle.

"Because I'm the one you should be mad at."

"Shut up! You can't save her! She's the reason Theo wants to send me away!"

"Look at me, Belle!" Belle glanced back at her but quickly looked away. "I know you can see that I'm dying. I have end stage kidney disease, and I've stopped my treatments. I should be in hospice care, but I want to be here with my family, and there's something I need to tell you before I die."

Mrs. Manning walked closer, standing by the railing to catch her breath. I could tell she was in pain and wondered how she'd made it up all those flights of steps to the roof. Belle stopped pulling me and turned to face the woman who'd been like a mother to her.

"What?" I could tell by the sound of Belle's voice that it was thick with tears.

"Your father is not the one that made Myles go away. I was the one who paid him to leave. I was the one who told him that if he didn't take the money and go, I would have him arrested for theft. He loved you. He never would've left otherwise, but I poisoned the household against him because you were so sheltered and naïve. I didn't want to see you get hurt."

Belle looked stunned, her mouth falling open in shock. "You had no right to make that decision for me."

I had managed to get to my feet as Belle glared at Mrs. Manning. Over Belle's shoulder, Mrs. Manning met my gaze, and I knew what she was doing. She was lying to redirect Belle's rage toward her because I was sure she'd done none of those things. She'd done something much worse. All her rules about wandering the house at night, locking myself in my room at midnight, not being allowed on the third floor, and being so freaked out over me calling the police meant Mrs. Manning had known what Belle was doing and had turned a blind eye, which made her an accomplice.

"Is that why you've been covering for her all these years?" I blurted out, causing both women to turn in my direction. "Did you help her hide Myles's body in that trunk? How could you?"

Mrs. Manning broke down in tears. "She's my Rainey's baby girl. My namesake. I couldn't let them take her away, not when it was all that bastard's fault."

I couldn't tell if she meant Martin Dorsey or Myles Patterson, but it hardly mattered when it was still so messed up.

"What about all the others? Cherise Gamble, Jared Green, and what she did to Olivia King and Heather? Not to mention what she was just planning to do to me. How could you turn a blind eye to all of it? She's clearly not in her right mind." Belle's face contorted in rage, and she lunged at me.

"Stop it!" Mrs. Manning shrieked as she pushed herself away from the railing, getting between me and Belle and looking panicked, as well she should. But I saw something else in her eyes that I had never seen before: terror.

It hit me all at once. Theo's resignation letter that I found in his desk drawer. Olivia King saying that Martin Dorsey was constantly changing his will. The promise that Martin Dorsey made Mrs. Manning about Theo never wanting for anything and becoming the Dorsey heir.

"This was all about Theo, wasn't it?" I took a step closer to the older woman, still keeping an eye on Belle.

"I have no idea what you're talking about."

"What *is* she talking about?" Now it was Belle's turn to look uncertain and confused as she stared between me and Mrs. Manning.

"I found Theo's resignation letter. Theo wanted out. He wanted his own life. He never wanted to run Dorsey Snacks."

"That's not true," said Mrs. Manning, leaning back against the railing, but there was no conviction behind her words because she knew what I was saying was the absolute truth.

"Martin was sick, and he was furious at Theo for wanting to leave and changed his will in favor of Belle just to scare him into changing his mind, thinking that if Theo thought you all would be left with nothing, he would stay. And he was right. Theo stayed because he felt it was his duty."

"He left Dorsey Snacks to... me?" Belle whispered, incredulous.

Mrs. Manning couldn't look at her and stared at the ground instead.

"You mean she doesn't know? She doesn't know that all of this," I flung my arm out, gesturing to my surroundings, "including Dorsey Snacks, belongs to her?"

"It was never supposed to be like this," said Mrs. Manning with tears streaming down her face. "He was just trying to teach Theo a lesson, but his cancer got worse before he could change his will back. There was a clause in the will stating that only the heir had access to Martin's fortune, properties, and company. The rest of us were left with nothing. Theo could only run Dorsey Snacks if Belle was deemed incapable, but it wasn't supposed to be Belle in the first place. Martin drafted that will with Theo in mind, knowing he would always take care of me and his sister. He knew she wasn't fit to inherit."

I opened my mouth to point out that Belle was not Theo's sister, but looking over at Belle, I shut my mouth. She looked ashen. All the color had drained from her face, and I didn't know how she'd react to that revelation. They may not have been blood siblings, but they were still family.

"You... made me... hide myself away," Belle began in a halting voice thick with tears. "And lurk around in the shadows like a rat pretending to be a fucking vegetable because you didn't want me knowing I own... everything? Everything!"

"Belle, please," said Mrs. Manning, holding up her hands feebly, like she was trying to shield herself from the younger woman's wrath.

"That's why she turned a blind eye to everything you've done and let you roam around at night wreaking havoc. She gave you the night so she could keep you compliant and in the dark during the day. So, you'd never find out." The irony that she'd done the same thing to Belle that Martin Dorsey had done to her blew my mind.

"You told me Myles's aunt contacted you regularly to check up on me, to see if anything had changed, and that's why I had to keep pretending! You said she suspected I was the reason he'd disappeared and that she was an old lady, and we had to wait until she died before I could make a recovery."

"That's a lie," I blurted out. "I spoke to Myles's aunt, and she despises this family and wants nothing to do with any of you. She wouldn't even know how to get in contact with Mrs. Manning."

Belle deflated like someone had stuck a pin in her. She

stared at Mrs. Manning with tears rapidly filling her eyes. "You ruined my life. I thought you loved me."

"I do love you!" the older woman insisted. "All I've ever tried to do was keep this family together, secure Theo's future, and keep you out of prison or an insane asylum. And because I love you, I agreed with Theo to put you in a place where you can finally get some help before you hurt anyone else. You need help, Belle. More help than I can give you." Mrs. Manning looked at Belle with pity and then at me. I looked away because I knew she was purposefully provoking her again. And I was right.

Belle let out an anguished cry as she charged toward her namesake with a lifetime worth of rage coursing through her veins. Mrs. Manning held her arms out, clasping Belle around her middle right when she crashed into her, before leaning backward causing the momentum to send them both tumbling over the side.

Amidst all the chaos of police cars, ambulances, the coroner's van, and the glut of media that descended on the Dorsey Estate, I fled. Once I'd been freed from the zip tie, I got into my car and sped through the gates like the devil was after me. I needed to be free of that house of horrors. I needed my sister. She was sitting in the kitchen when I arrived, and when she saw the state I was in, bloody and disheveled, she instantly got up.

"Brina, what the hell? What happened to you?"

"Where have you been?" I screamed at her. "I've been calling you for days. Why aren't you answering my calls?"

She held out her arms and I flew into them, buried my face in her neck, and sobbed.

That's how Theo found me hours later, on the couch pouring my heart out to my sister, happy she was finally listening to me and being sympathetic.

"Sabrina? Are you all right? Why did you leave? You need to be in the hospital."

"I'm fine," I said, and could tell he knew I was anything but.

"Who were you talking to?" His red-rimmed eyes were fixed on me and filled with concern. He'd just lost what was left of his family and here he was comforting me.

"My sister. Cami, this is..." I began. But when I looked over at my sister, she was gone. She had just been there seconds before, but now she was gone.

"Sabrina," Theo said in a soft voice as he sat on the coffee table in front of me and grabbed both my hands. "Your sister is dead. Gabe ran a background check on you when I hired you and it pulled up your sister's obit. Don't you remember? She and her husband died in the garage fire seven months ago. I never asked you about it because I was afraid the memory was too painful for you."

"Liar!" I yanked my hands from his. "Cami! Cami! Where are you! I need you!"

I jumped up and ran from room to room screaming my sister's name before Theo caught me in the hallway and gathered me into a tight embrace, sagging to the floor with me as I lost control. I let out the tears I'd held back for months because letting them out meant they were really gone, and it was all my fault.

I knew they were dead. Somewhere in the recesses of my mind I had always known. But if I kept them alive in my mind, I didn't have to deal with the guilt and the grief. So, I chose to keep them both alive. Every conversation I'd had with both Cami and Bruce for the past several months had been rehashed and reconfigured conversations I'd had with them when they were alive.

I still remember the day it happened. It had been my first day working at The Book Barn, two months after I had moved in with them at my mom's house. I hated it and was desperate to leave. I'd been an hour into my workday when Cami called me ranting and raving that a strange woman had showed up at the house looking for Bruce. Some chick he'd been gaming with online and who he'd given the impression he was single and living with his sister. He had planned her visit before I'd moved in and timed it to when Cami had been away on her army reserve weekend. But her flight had been delayed and she arrived in town after my sister had gotten home.

I was already nervous about my first day and spent the rest of my shift irritated. When I arrived home, Cami and Bruce were in the backyard. Cami was pacing and chain smoking, something she always did when she was upset. Her asshole husband tried to convince her that she was overreacting, and that he had no idea who the woman who'd shown up at the door earlier was. They were so loud that some of the neighbors were starting to come out onto their porches. I remembered telling Cami and Bruce to either lower their voices or go back into the house. Cami had screamed at me to mind my own business.

I was tired and fed up and told them if they wouldn't come back into the house, to finish their argument in the garage away from the prying eyes of the neighbors. I watched them head into the garage and happily went inside and got into the shower. I'd been in there for less than ten minutes when someone pounded on our front door. It was one of our neighbors. I could barely hear what they were saying as smoke caught my attention. The garage was on fire. I ran outside and tried to run to the garage, but one of the neighbors knocked me to the ground and pinned me there. The garage was engulfed in flames. It had already been too late to save them by the time the neighbor had knocked on the door.

From what the Fire Marshal was able to figure out, the large piles of mulch from Bruce's defunct landscaping business had combusted. They weren't sure if a spark from my sister's cigarette caused them to ignite or if it was simply bad timing.

But they had exploded, engulfing the garage in flames, killing both my sister and her husband. I had told them to go in there because I'd been worried about what the neighbors thought. And now my sister was gone.

The story poured out of me like lava, flowing out of my mouth, my brain, my consciousness, hot and violent, burning a path out of me that I couldn't stop. When I was finally finished unburdening myself, I could barely see through the tears blurring my eyes. Theo continued to hold me and let me sob.

"It's not your fault, Sabrina," he whispered into my hair. "It's not."

On some level I knew it was true, but I wondered how long it would take before I believed it.

EPILOGUE
SABRINA

Loire Valley, France
One Year Later

I sat on the steps of our mobile home and drank my morning coffee, mentally going over everything I needed to do that day. It would be a day of deliveries, cleaning, supervising the crew of workers who'd be there within the hour, and tackling a mile long to-do list. I looked over at the 17th-century château I co-owned with pride. Theo and I were now business partners and over the course of the past year, had become so much more. According to Martin Dorsey's will, upon Belle's death, the Dorsey fortune was to be distributed amongst several charities, and that's exactly what happened.

But unbeknownst to him, Mrs. Manning had been quietly buying up shares of Dorsey Snacks which she had passed to her son, giving Theo a majority share in the company. Theo sold his shares and with the proceeds from the sale of the house I'd grown up in, along with life insurance from my sister and his savings, Theo and I had gone into business together creating Adams & Manning Restorations. He'd also legally changed his last name to Manning. I had my own division specializing in library restoration.

Theo was due to arrive back later that afternoon. He'd gone to Paris to pick up a chandelier from an auction house we'd bought for the entryway. I'd have gone instead, but I still didn't have my French driver's license, and somebody had to be here to meet the workers.

Luca was still living with us. Heather and Carter broke up and there were no more plans to move to Florida. She was currently in her last year of high school, still attending online, but was excited about attending college in person. Theo and I are helping her navigate the college application process as well as accompanying her on college tours. The day I found Luca looking under my bed was the day she'd been snooping around and had found Belle's collection. Of course, she had no idea what it was, and thankfully never looked inside the trunk. My braid and Jared Green's tongue had yet to be added, but she'd looked through all the drawers and found the necklace and took the turtle pendant, only to drop it on the way out of my closet and was not able to retrieve it before I walked in. As it turned out, every room in the Dorsey house had a network of hidden rooms accessed via the closets because Martin Dorsey loved spying on his wife and children, and used it to keep them under his thumb.

I finished my coffee and headed inside, impatient for Theo to get home. If you would've told me when I was a little girl growing up in Harper's Ferry that I would be living in a château in France one day with a man I loved, I'd have thought you were crazy. I navigated around boxes down hallways full of debris from all the demolition, into the library that I'd be working in for the foreseeable future. It was an immense 2,000 square foot space with faded wallpaper, ancient light fixtures, crumbling crown molding, and a buckling wooden floor. Large casement windows looked out onto a garden that would be another other project and there was a fireplace big enough to stand up in. It was beautiful in all its dilapidated glory.

I got busy unpacking boxes and glimpsed movement out of the corner of my eye. Two people were standing outside the door to the garden. It was Cami and Bruce. It had been a while since I'd seen them, which coincided with whenever I was upset or stressed out. They were standing side by side staring at me, their faces devoid of emotion. I resigned myself to the fact that I would see them for the rest of my life and thought back on their last day and what I never told anyone. Not even Theo. We had our own life now and it was a good one. I won't let something that can't be changed, ruin it. I closed my eyes against the memory, trying to block it out. But it wouldn't be denied and suddenly I was back there again, following Cami and Bruce into the garage.

In an attempt to get my sister to kick Bruce to the curb for good, I'd told her he'd been hitting on me. I knew she'd be angry, but I wasn't prepared when my sister turned on me and stood up for the asshole she'd married by telling me that I was just jealous.

"What did you just say?" I'd asked her, confused, because I wasn't sure I'd heard her right.

"You heard me, Sabrina!" She'd gotten right in my face like she wanted to fight me. "I finally found someone who puts me first and you're just jealous and making up lies. Go find your own man."

"Puts you first. How is cheating on you putting you first, Cami? And I'm not lying! You're barely out of the house for five minutes and he's starting in on me! And what do you mean you finally found someone who puts you first?"

"Mom," she spat out.

"Mom? What does Mom have to do with this?"

Cami let out a bitter laugh and looked at me and shook her

head like I was stupid. "For fifteen years it was just the two of us, Mom and me. Then you came along, and Mom changed."

"Changed? Changed how?" What was she talking about?

"She got sober," she said bitterly. "But you didn't know that, did you? She fell back off the wagon over and over again. But she *tried* to be better... for *you*. She never did anything like that for me. You have no idea how many times you probably thought she was at the bar, but she was really at AA meetings."

I couldn't believe what I was hearing. There was no way Mom had tried to get sober for me and me alone. She'd loved both of us. But the pain I saw in Cami's eyes that day was real, and I knew there was no use trying to change my sister's mind when she was so determined to be the victim. How long had she felt this way?

"Is that why you hardly ever came home? Because her cancer got worse when you turned your back on us? You didn't even come home for Christmas the year before she died. Then you went and replaced us with this waste of space who probably saw you coming a mile away and told you everything you wanted to hear!" I gestured toward Bruce who was standing a few feet behind Cami with a shit-eating grin on his face. He knew better than to say a word.

"Shut up!" Cami's hand flew out and cracked me hard against the side of my face.

My hand flew to my cheek and my eyes filled with tears. "So that's it? You don't believe me? You're choosing him over me?"

"He's my husband! And you know what?" She shook her head sadly. "This isn't going to work. I want you out of the house tonight."

"You can't put me out. This house is half mine," I'd insisted.

"I don't care if I have to take out a second mortgage, I'll make sure you get your half. But this isn't going to work and you need to go."

"Where am I supposed to go?" My voice was barely a whisper.

"Sleep in your car! I don't care. Just get out!" She shoved me and I fell back against the door.

I'd been so overwhelmed with hurt and anger I could barely see through my tears as I left the garage to the sound of Bruce's mocking laughter. But my anguish evaporated as I walked out into the afternoon sunshine, and quickly turned into rage. I lost it and wasn't thinking straight, then did something that changed everything.

Theo was right. I wasn't responsible for the fire that killed them. But it was my fault they couldn't get out.

My sister chose her husband's lies over my truth. So, as I pulled the door shut behind me when I left the garage, I locked it, trapping them inside. I'd planned on letting them out as soon as my car was packed. Fate had other plans. But Cami *had* wanted Bruce at any cost.

Now she gets to be with him... *forever*.

A LETTER FROM THE AUTHOR

Thank you for reading *The Family Lies*. I hope you enjoyed Sabrina's story. If you'd like to hear about my new and upcoming releases, you can sign up for my author newsletter.

www.stormpublishing.co/angela-henry

If you enjoyed this book and could spare a few moments to leave a review that would be greatly appreciated. Even a short review can make all the difference in encouraging a reader to discover my books for the first time. Thank you so much!

Libraries have always held a special place in my heart, and books have been my gateway to explore worlds both real and imaginary, from the comfort of a chair. Even though I retired from a library career spanning over 30 years to pursue writing full-time, I still miss helping library patrons and being immersed in books. I found a remedy by blending my passion for writing mysteries and thrillers with my love of books and libraries.

In *The Family Lies*, I transferred that passion to librarian Sabrina Adams and gave her a perplexing mystery to unravel filled with secrets, deception, conflicting loyalties, and intricate family dynamics. This book allowed me to do what I love best, creating imperfect characters with twisted motives and backstories that lead to either their destruction or redemption. Finally, I wanted to show how the past can haunt us making it difficult to move on.

Thanks again for being part of this amazing journey with me and I hope you'll stay in touch – I have so many more stories and ideas to entertain you with!

Angela

facebook.com/authorangelahenry

instagram.com/angelahenry_author

tiktok.com/@angelahenryauthor

www.ingramcontent.com/pod-product-compliance
Lightning Source LLC
Chambersburg PA
CBHW011032190726
48290CB00011B/2805